Quite suddenly,
Mandy was ashamed

She felt not a trace of latent hunger for the tall sandy-haired man who had aroused her just minutes before with such a simple touch. She felt only sick to her stomach.

Joe Henderson might be a man, but he was still a former student of hers—a student she'd despised! And even now that he was a man, her older sister Ruth still considered him a bad apple. If she ever got wind of the crazy notion that Mandy was sexually attracted to Joe, Ruth would go berserk!

How on earth could I ever give in to my ludicrous desire for Joe Henderson? Mandy berated herself. *To even think of making love to him is . . . unthinkable!*

And she vowed never to think of it again.

ABOUT THE AUTHOR

Suzanne Ellison, a veteran Superromance author, always decorates her computer with postcards and objects that remind her of the setting of the book she's working on. While writing The Living West trilogy, Suzanne surrounded herself with postcards of Utah, Colorado and Arizona, and chunks of red rock! As she says, "Mindset is everything. If I'm not mentally on horseback when the hero is, how can the reader be?" Suzanne makes her home in California with her husband, Scott, and her daughter, Tara.

Books by Suzanne Ellison

HARLEQUIN SUPERROMANCE
165—WINGS OF GOLD
258—PINECONES AND ORCHIDS
283—FOR ALL THE RIGHT REASONS
308—WORDS UNSPOKEN
315—FAIR PLAY
369—CANDLE IN THE WINDOW
393—WITH OPEN ARMS

HARLEQUIN INTRIGUE
46—NOWHERE TO RUN

Don't miss any of our special offers. Write to us at the following address for information on our newest releases.

Harlequin Reader Service
901 Fuhrmann Blvd., P.O. Box 1397, Buffalo, NY 14240
Canadian address: P.O. Box 603,
Fort Erie, Ont. L2A 5X3

Heart of the West

SUZANNE ELLISON

Harlequin Books

TORONTO • NEW YORK • LONDON
AMSTERDAM • PARIS • SYDNEY • HAMBURG
STOCKHOLM • ATHENS • TOKYO • MILAN

For Jean LeCouteur,
eagle-eyed reader and patient friend,
through all the dark days
and all the sunny ones.
Words will never be enough.

Published September 1990

ISBN 0-373-70420-8

CHAPTER ONE

IT WAS ALMOST NOON when Mandy Larkin pulled into the parking lot of the nineteenth-century train station that had proudly served as home to Redpoint's famous steam locomotive for well over a century. The wooden siding on the main station house had been repaired and repainted over the years, but otherwise the cluster of ancient buildings had remained unchanged since 1865. The original engine, trailed by half a dozen cars, still valiantly carried passengers through red rock country—the crown jewel of the Four Corners area—though nowadays only tourists paid for a ride that took them out through the canyons and back again.

Mandy was not a tourist; she had dropped by the train station solely to surprise her niece, whom she'd been told worked at the snack bar in the train's caboose. Still, it was hard to ignore the sense of history that the old train exuded as it lumbered toward the station against a stunning distant backdrop of pink, orange and purple sandstone. The geological wonders of the rock cliffs that surrounded Redpoint had been continually sculpted by wind, sun and water since the dawn of time. The first time Mandy had ever seen that view, she'd been in awe of the original pioneer settlers, not to mention the generations of native tribes before them, who had managed to carve a life for themselves out of such a harsh, dry chunk of the continent. Even now, the cloud of black smoke, the chugachug of the iron wheels and the sustained treble note of the train's hoarse whistle made Mandy wonder for just a moment if she really had been transported back in time.

After all, nothing about the town's major tourist attraction had been changed except for its name. In yesteryear, she'd once taught her students, some awestruck passengers had called this train the Colorado Fireball. It had been, quite literally, the fastest thing in the West. Nowadays, in keeping with its altered role in a world of space shuttles, Concord jets and laser trains, the sign above the station house proudly heralded the Slow Joe Loco in chubby hand-painted letters. Karen, Mandy's niece, said it took a full four hours to run the twenty-mile loop through the hills.

In Mandy's memory, the trip seemed to take closer to four days. She'd been on the tourist train only once, over twenty years ago, when she'd shepherded a group of thirty-four rowdy sixth-graders during her first pathetic year as a teacher. Looking back on it—not just the field trip but the year itself—Mandy marveled that she'd remained in teaching long enough to discover that she liked her profession and was actually pretty good at it. Any way she looked at it, that first year in Redpoint had been a disaster.

To this day, she blamed a good deal of her failure on the rotten luck of having Joey Henderson in her class. Joey had been the sort of kid every teacher dreads. Every time an unscheduled "fire drill" occurred, the principal looked for Joey. Every time the overflowing sinks were stuffed with red crepe paper that gave the illusion of blood, the custodian searched for Joey. Every year when new class lists were passed out, each teacher saddled with his grade instantly scanned the names for Joey's. Mandy still remembered that odd, still moment in her first staff meeting after one old hand had tittered, "Who's got him this time?"

It was the teacher to her left who had slid an accusing finger through the names on Mandy's list before she'd pointed to Henderson, Joseph Paul, and declared triumphantly, "The new girl does!"

Idealistic Mandy, fresh out of college, had never heard of Joey Henderson. She loved small children and was determined to hold her own with the older ones until there was an opening in the lower grades. Cautiously she'd squeaked, "Is that good...or bad?"

The communal staff response had included chuckles, victory cries and a few sympathetic groans.

"I'll pray for you," said one good-hearted soul upon hearing Mandy's fate.

"They always say they just draw names out of a hat, but don't you believe it," said another. "They always give him to the low man on the totem pole. Baptism by fire, they call it. I stuck it out when I got him in kindergarten, but his first-grade teacher didn't hang around for a second year in Redpoint."

"Neither did the gal he had last year," somebody else recalled.

Mandy had chuckled, certain that the experienced teachers were just pulling her leg. But not one of them had cracked a smile...and not one of them had overstated the case. Just as they'd predicted, little Joey Henderson had swept into Mandy's class like a small hurricane, wreaking destruction wherever he went. Scrawny and unkempt, he had wild blond hair and dark, frantic eyes, and sometimes, when she wasn't furious with him, Mandy had felt great sympathy for the boy and wondered about the dark, explosive forces inside him that would not let Joey rest. He never held still long enough to concentrate on anything, and the only subject that held any interest for him was science—especially the mechanical operation of trains. For years he'd begged his well-meaning but ineffectual mother for a model train set for Christmas to no avail; the winter he was in Mandy's class, he'd tried to steal one instead.

Joey Henderson had treated school like a full-scale guerilla war. In his view, compliance with regulations was equivalent to laying down arms before the enemy; to turn in homework on time was to yield hard-won ground. Some of his pranks were just crude practical jokes—like filling the pockets of Mandy's coat with mud at recess—and some were downright malicious, like hiding her wallet in the ball box until after she'd replaced all of her credit cards, floated a loan from her punctilious sister Ruth and given up on the missing one hundred and thirty-eight dollars in cash left over from her first month's paycheck. Once Joey "accidentally" bumped into her new white blouse with an open black marking pen; another time he "inadvertently" tripped over her foot the day after she broke her toe. He was absent exactly five days all year, and Mandy had guiltily rejoiced each and every hour he'd been down with the stomach flu. On those few heaven-sent days she'd actually conducted reading groups uninterrupted, and the girls in the class had been able to finish their seat work without being poked with pencils, shot with rubber bands or surprised by wads of chewing gum in their hair that took hours to dig out. Not one fistfight had occurred on the playground during the week he was gone.

And for those five blissful days, and those five days only, Mandy had gone home every night without a migraine, believing that going into teaching might not have been the most catastrophic error of her life.

In desperation, she had decided to try to respond to Joey's interest in trains by taking the class to the Colorado Fireball when they were studying the settlement of the West. After all, she'd reasoned, what could she possibly lose?

Her reasoning had turned out to be wildly fallacious.

Even now, twenty-three years later, the mere sight of the old steam engine train brought back a rush of nausea as she recalled those panicky three hours she'd spent searching for a darling little girl Joey had locked in the station coaling shed forty-five minutes before reporting that she'd fallen off the train. The girl's father, a virile single parent whom Mandy had been eager to impress, had arrived with the police and the president of the school board before Joey had confessed what he'd done. If it weren't so hard to entice teachers to come to rural Redpoint, Mandy suspected that she would have been fired on the spot.

As she pushed away that haunting, fragmented memory, the Slow Joe Loco clattered into the station, tripling the already menacing cloud of smoke and dust. Mandy was casually dressed in a T-shirt and a pair of jeans, but she was still twenty minutes from her final destination and she had no desire to arrive at her sister's spotless house covered with soot as well as sweat; Ruth had no patience with untidiness. And judging by the mail she'd received recently from Redpoint, her sister's patience with the world was wearing exceptionally thin these days. In the past few letters, Ruth had found fault with every person she'd mentioned—including Mandy, whom she seemed to feel had neglected her by spending the month of July in Georgia visiting her married son instead of coming to

Redpoint so Ruth could "cheer her up." It was the first time in her life Mandy had ever taken such a long trip alone, and she was glad that she hadn't asked Ruth's opinion in time for her sister to talk her out of taking the trip.

Mandy had left her home in Denver before daylight and was hoping to surprise Karen and take her to lunch. Once she arrived at Ruth's for her scheduled vacation, Mandy knew that she and Karen would have precious little time alone. But though there were half a dozen young people in striped conductor's uniforms scattered among the tourists, none of them had the thick black hair and shining blue eyes she knew so well.

Although it had been over a year since Mandy had seen her niece, she had no doubt about how the girl would receive her. Karen had always called Mandy her favorite aunt, and as far as Mandy was concerned the feeling was entirely mutual. Mandy was fond of her late husband's nieces and nephews and Ruth's three other children, all in their twenties now, but Karen had always been like the daughter she'd never had. Her own two sons were out of the nest, doing well on their own, so it wasn't as though she'd ever felt deprived of motherhood. It was just that... well, Karen was special. And particularly dear to Mandy because she understood better than anyone how hard it could be for a young girl to live under Ruth's stern rule. She'd cowered in her big sister's shadow most of her life.

As the clouds of smoke threatened to overwhelm her, Mandy turned around and started back toward the relative safety of the enclosed station house, nearly colliding with a tall, sandy-haired man about her age. He wore a pair of engineer's overalls, an engineer's hat and a grin the size of Texas.

"Good afternoon," he greeted her cheerfully, tipping his squat striped hat. "Old Slow Joe's a bit much for you, I take it?"

"Well, I'm not wild about the smoke," Mandy confessed, his own wide grin eliciting a matching one on her face.

He laughed. "Where's your sense of adventure? Getting dirty's half the fun!" he pointed out, his bright teeth gleaming. His mahogany eyes met hers, then skimmed appreciatively over her figure. From Mandy's point of view, she was not an outrageously attractive woman—closer to pretty than plain, but a long way from beautiful with the frizzy red hair, fair skin and freckles that had been the bane of her teenage years. Still, there had been moments in her adult life when a man—her late husband Alan—had studied her with rapt adoration, so she knew how to recognize the look she now saw in this stranger's eyes. Still, it was a jolt, largely because it had been so long since Mandy had given any thought to the way she might strike a man. It had been a year and a half, in fact. A year and a half since Alan had died.

What was even stranger than the way this man was looking at Mandy was the way she now found herself looking at him. He was a good-looking fellow, though his features were not particularly distinctive. He had nice brown eyes—well, to be honest, they were *very* nice brown eyes—and sandy hair...make that thick, wavy sandy hair, maybe in need of a haircut to restore the attractive line that was still discernible. His nose was very straight; his complexion tanned and smooth. And despite his railroad engineer's outfit—which would have looked like a Halloween costume on anybody else Mandy knew—the man before her looked strong and robust, with a broad chest and rock-solid biceps that pulsed an inch or so below his rolled-up sleeves.

Suddenly his grin grew wider, and he laughed again. "I know you!" he suddenly declared. "I'll be damned if I can come up with a name, but I know your face. It's been a long time, but I think I used to know you very well."

Now it was Mandy's turn to chuckle. "Really now, I'm disappointed. Surely a man who's creative enough to find a job as a steam-locomotive conductor in the tail end of the twentieth century is creative enough to come up with a more original opening line." Her voice held no hint of rebuke or disappointment. She was flirting with this man and she liked it.

"You're right." Cheery confidence rang through his rich bass tone. "I am more creative. In fact, I've got half a dozen lines memorized for just such an occasion."

"What occasion is that?"

The laugh lines around his eyes dramatized his smile as his gaze came to rest more intimately on Mandy's mouth. "Oh, anytime I see a woman who can hold my attention for more than thirty seconds when there's a train around."

"Oh, you're one of those, are you?"

He nodded, mock shame in his eyes. "Alas. I am a railroader. A hopeless trainaholoic. My situation is incurable, I'm afraid."

"You've sought treatment, have you?"

He nodded again. "All my life. In and out of clinics. I think I'm over it. I tell myself I can walk away...and then there's the sound of that whistle or the smell of that burning coal! Hmmf!"

"It's tragic," Mandy agreed, helplessly giggling now.

"It surely is. It's cost me my job, my wife and my children."

"I'm glad to hear it. About the wife, I mean." The words were out of Mandy's mouth before she could stop them, and at first she hoped that he thought she was just playing along with his storyline. But as his expression took on the tiniest hint of solemnity, she found herself glad that her feelings were out in the open. Though she was not anxious to replace her beloved husband of two decades—had not, in fact, been seriously tempted to start dating again—she was forty-six years old and had no interest in playing hard to get when she accidentally tripped over a man she found this appealing.

When he quietly informed her, "I really am divorced," she felt a rush of pleasure, coupled with relief.

Mandy answered, "I'm a widow."

He lifted his hands in a helpless gesture. His expression grew genuinely solemn. "I'm not sure what to say to that. Part of me is glad, I've got to confess. But if your husband was quite dear to you—"

"He was." Suddenly Mandy felt that she'd been disloyal to Alan. "It really hasn't been very long."

The sandy-haired man licked his lips. Slowly his sympathetic gaze met hers before he said, "I'm sorry for your loss," as though he really meant it.

Mandy nodded, not quite certain what to say. An awkward silence stretched between them. She was grateful when he picked up the conversational ball again.

"Are you here to ride the train?" he asked. "Grandpa Howard—that's what the kids call the chief engineer—is officially on duty today, but he won't mind if I come along. I usually join the crew at least once a week just to keep a grip on things anyway. If you—"

Mandy shook her head. "No, I just dropped by to say hello to my niece. She works here."

He grinned. "Then you *are* a local! I *knew* I'd met you before. Honestly, that wasn't just a line."

Mandy held up one hand in disclaimer. "Sorry, but I'm not a local, just here to visit relatives for a couple of weeks. I lived here a long time ago, but only for a year."

And what a year that was! she might have added. *And not just because of Joey Henderson.*

Ruth had moved to Redpoint when she'd gotten married and had assumed that Mandy would come join her as soon as she finished college. As a sickly child in a home with a traveling salesman father and a quiet, docile mother who died young, Mandy had always revered and emulated strong-willed Ruth, eight years Mandy's senior, who'd bossed, badgered and protected her most of her life. But Mandy's unique personality had belatedly begun to flower when she'd gone away to school, and by the time she took the Redpoint teaching job that Ruth had arranged, and moved into the guest room Ruth had remodeled, she had ceased to fit well under Ruth's controlling thumb. And yet, in those days—and even now, when push came to shove—there were times when Mandy still longed for Ruth's bossy counsel as much as she resented it. The one unwavering pillar of her life had always been her sister's love.

"I've lived here all my life," the one-man welcoming committee informed her. "And I *know* that we've met before." This time he wasn't teasing. It was obvious to Mandy that he really did believe they were acquainted; he even seemed irritated that he could neither place her name nor get her to admit the possibility that their paths might have crossed in the distant past. Now he suggested, "I could scrounge up some character references to prove I'm a safe and decent follow, but I think it'd be easier if you just told me your name.''

He looked so expectant that Mandy laughed out loud. It hadn't even occurred to her to question his character; all of her instincts told her that he was a wonderful man. ''I'm sorry. I didn't mean to be rude. My name is Mandy Larkin.''

''Mandy Larkin?'' He closed his eyes for a moment, then shook his head in exasperation. ''Nothing. I don't know anybody in town by that name. You said you have a niece who works for me? What's her name?''

Mandy felt a tiny jolt of pleasure at his admission that he owned the Slow Joe Loco. Somehow it seemed more respectable to be flirting with the owner of the antique railroad than with an overgrown schoolboy playing trains in his spare time. ''My niece is Karen Hayward. Her mother is my sister.''

''Karen's a good kid,'' he said quickly, his tone surprisingly firm. It was almost as though he were defending the girl . . . as though, for some reason, he thought she was in need of defense.

''Yes, she is.'' Mandy could have added that, according to Ruth, she was going through a rebellious stage that was driving her mother up the wall, but that wasn't the sort of thing Mandy was going to reveal to a stranger. Besides, he was still studying her intently. Now he commented,

''Hayward is Ruth's married name. I knew her ex-husband before he left town. When you lived here did you go by Larkin or—''

''I was single when I lived here. It was over twenty years ago.'' Mandy felt a tremor of pleasure at the obvious anticipation on his face. He looked like a jigsaw puzzle champion who was about to fit in the last piece of a three-thousand-piece monster he'd been working on for weeks. By the time Mandy said, "My maiden name was Sawyer," she was almost ready to believe that she'd given him the missing clue he'd been looking for.

"Sawyer!" he burst out with an eager snap of his fingers. "I know that name! I mean, I knew it when I was a kid. Mandy Sawyer..." He licked his lips once as he pondered the name. "No, not Mandy Sawyer. Sawyer sounds familiar, but I don't think I called you Mandy. Amanda? No. I—"

"Maybe we should look at this the other way," Mandy suggested, certain now that he'd been right all along. Even though this intriguing hunk of manhood triggered no memory bells within her mind, he triggered a lot of other bells in various parts of her body that made her eager to make up for lost time. "What's *your* name?"

He looked surprised. "I thought you knew that. Hell, everybody does." He pointed to the sign above the still-spewing engine, then reached out for Mandy's hand as though they'd just been introduced by some third party. Despite the platonic nature of the gesture, his touch jolted Mandy with an unexpected quiver of desire. Her fingers gripped his more tightly than she'd intended. "My buddy, Brady, thought up the name Slow Joe—he wanted to name the place after me. It's sort of a joke—" his hand lingered warmly in hers "—because I was hyper as a kid. Lived for trains. I vowed to buy the Colorado Fireball one day and by golly, that's exactly what I did!" He grinned and pressed her hand with quiet intimacy, giving her a half bow without releasing it. "Joseph Paul Henderson at your service, ma'am."

Mandy rocked. She tried to quell the dizziness that gripped her, the creeping wave of nausea as the name staggered her memory. *My God, he's Joey Henderson!* she realized, amazed that she hadn't guessed it before. And yet, how could she have known? Joey had been a runt, a screwball, a blonde. The man before her—God, she couldn't think of this gorgeous hunk as scruffy little Joey!—was tall, muscular, successful...sexy! And his hair had darkened with age.

Slowly, through the dim smoke of the train and the cloud of disgust in her heart, Mandy realized that her hand was still in Joey's, her fingers now icy cold. She couldn't meet his eyes—not when he was stroking her palm so intimately—but somehow she couldn't quite pull away.

Suddenly his hand grew still. He released her gently, as though he knew he'd gone too far. But his smile was still warm and hopeful as he asked, "So does my name ring a bell?"

Mandy's gaze fluttered up to his accusingly. She could not hide the remembered anger from his knowing eyes.

Clearly stunned by her fury, Joey stepped back as though she'd hit him in the face. For a long, tense moment he stared at her; she could see him turning over the possibilities in his mind. At first he looked perplexed by her unspoken rejection. Then, quite suddenly, he blanched.

"Oh, my God!" Joey whispered in a tone that was less a prayer than a curse. "You're *String Bean Sawyer*."

It wasn't the sound of that hated nickname that surprised her; what made Mandy's scalp prickle was the loathing, the disgust, the pain—could it be?—that still filled those hoarse words after all these years. In the past when she'd run into former students, they'd often as not forgotten her.

But Joey Henderson had not. And his memories of their time together were clearly no happier than hers.

He took a quick backward step—as though he were hiking and had swerved to avoid a snake—and colored deeply. Mandy suspected that her own face was just as red; her fair skin always broadcast her most intimate feelings. She could not recall any time in her life that she'd ever been more embarrassed.

Quickly she took shelter in the only safe role she knew with Joey Henderson. He was the student, she the teacher. With most of her former students, a present-day conversation would have been tender and nostalgic, but in the old days most of her conversations with Joey had consisted of tense battles over his behavior. Now she scrounged desperately for something pleasant to say.

"Well, it looks as though you finally found a career that was compatible with your interests, Joey," was all she could come up with.

Dark, angry eyes flashed down at her, but his tone managed to convey a frigid sort of courtesy. "It wasn't *finally*, Miss Sawyer. Your class was the nadir in my pit of despair. I made the Honor Roll in seventh grade."

Mandy stared at him in disbelief. How could he have gone from champion troublemaker to Honor Roll in a single year? Granted, she'd always known he was a bright kid, but he'd battled the system tooth and toenail!

"What happened?" she asked, forgetting to congratulate him on his academic achievement. After all, what did his seventh-grade marks have to do with this sweltering summer afternoon and the man who was old enough to be a father to a twelve-year-old himself? "What turned you around?"

His eyes grew darker. "I could explain it to you if you were really interested, but frankly I suspect it would be a waste of time." Despite his hard words, his tone remained even. Civil, if not particularly friendly. Almost... forgiving.

But how could that be? What on earth had *she* done to require Joey Henderson's forgiveness? Surely it was the other way around!

"You don't strike me as a naturally malicious person," he continued coolly. "I'm certain that if you'd ever had the slightest idea what made me tick, you never would have put me through such hell."

"Hell?" The word was almost a shriek, ripping out of Mandy's mouth before she could mask her surprise. "*I* put *you* through *hell*?"

That strong, square jaw hardened before her eyes, and Mandy shivered as she remembered the stubborn mannerism that had always signaled some new disaster. But this time Joey Henderson didn't retaliate by soaping her pencils or dissolving her chalk in milk. His dark eyes glared daggers at her as he swallowed hard and struggled for control. For a moment she thought he might blow up, and she shuddered at the notion of wild Joey Henderson exploding with the muscular power of a full-grown man.

But there was no explosion; instead, there was a demonstration of inner strength in the man that had not been evident in the disgruntled boy Mandy had known. Slowly, the fury drained from Joey's face, so that he looked like a father who couldn't stay angry with a child too young to understand the impact of some great wrong she had done. There was no warmth in his voice when he finally spoke, but his tone remained even as he gave a convincing display of a man in control.

"If you'll take a seat by the ticket counter, Mrs. Larkin, I'll send one of my employees to go find your niece for you," he offered stiffly as he gestured toward a wooden seat by the wall. "I'm sure she'll be here in just a moment."

Dazed, Mandy stood perfectly still as he turned and marched away; she was too stunned by the whirlwind of sudden feelings to realize that she had been summarily dismissed. Never in her life could she recall feeling so silly and carefree one moment and so black with rage and hurt an instant later. Worse yet, she didn't really understand what had just happened. Oh, she understood her own reaction. She was embarrassed that she'd so blithely flirted with a former student—the most obnoxious youngster she'd ever known, no less! But why was Joey so angry? A shamefaced grin would have done nicely, or maybe an apology now that he had—hopefully—outgrown his difficult years. But he clearly harbored deep feelings regarding his former teacher, and they certainly were not affectionate ones.

As it turned out, Mandy didn't have very long to ponder their bizarre exchange before an attractive young blonde with "Sandra" embroidered on her uniform came to tell her that Karen had taken her lunch break the instant she'd gotten off the train and wouldn't be back until one o'clock.

"Mr. Henderson says you're welcome to wait here if you like. There's food in the caboose, and you might enjoy looking at the gift shop."

Mandy didn't need more than an instant to make up her mind; she could wait a few more hours to see her niece. At the moment Mandy wanted nothing more than to escape from the Slow Joe Loco.

She excused herself politely, jumped into her car and headed toward her sister's house a good ten miles from the town. Ruth had lived on the tiny spread since her three oldest children were toddlers. Twelve years later Karen had arrived unexpectedly, and shortly thereafter, Ruth's husband had moved out. Mandy had always wondered whether Karen blamed herself for the breakup of her family. Based on the reactions of so many of her students to their parents' divorces, it wouldn't have surprised her.

But knowing Ruth as she did, Mandy suspected that it was Ruth's hot temper and inflexibility that had driven Lowell out of the house. Ruth had been furious to find herself pregnant again at thirty-eight, and her subsequent excuse for declining social invitations, jobs and volunteer positions in the community from that point on had always been, "I'd love to if I didn't have to take care of this baby." Everyone in town knew how much she'd resented Karen's arrival. It was hard to imagine that poor Karen didn't know it, too.

As Mandy approached her sister's home on the squiggly gravel road engraved in her memory, she relished the distant view of the red rock hills. It was the only thing she missed about living in Redpoint. As much as she loved her sister, Mandy knew that she never would have grown up if she'd continued to live under Ruth's roof. On the few occasions she'd dated during her year in this end of Colorado, Ruth had ruthlessly grilled every man she'd brought home . . . and chased off more than one. Mandy cringed at the thought of her sister's reaction to the news that she'd actually been flirting with the grown-up version of little

Joey Henderson, whom Ruth had learned to hate on Mandy's behalf. The vision was more frightening than funny, and Mandy decided that her bizarre reaction to Joey was something she'd best keep to herself.

Mandy recalled her sister's house as bright and freshly painted yellow, but even at a distance it was obvious that the garage door was starting to peel—and the windows looked as though they hadn't been washed in months. The vegetable garden, once Ruth's pride and joy, was just a pile of dead weeds and dirt; the small lawn was largely crabgrass, as well. As Mandy approached the door, a quick glance through the living-room window told her that the interior of the house wasn't getting much care, either. Piles of unsorted clothes littered the sofa and the floor, and the remains of at least one fast-food dinner sat on the table. A handful of french fries lingered on the rug.

It was the french fries that caused Mandy to double-check the address. In her own home, such teenage transgressions had not been cause for the use of a cat-o'-nine-tails on her boys, but Ruth would have to be seriously ill to tolerate such disorderliness from Karen.

Yet Mandy had come to the right house. She rang the doorbell, but it made no sound. She knocked on the door...once, twice, three times, then turned the knob when nobody answered.

The silence in the house was eerie. Mandy visited Redpoint every few years, usually at Christmas, and Ruth's place had always been abuzz with nieces, nephews and Ruth herself hustling around in preparation for holiday suppers. Granted, this was midsummer in the middle of a stifling afternoon. But Ruth was expecting her; in fact, she'd insisted that Mandy come.

The silence, on top of the shabby condition of Ruth's formerly spic-and-span home, was truly unsettling. "Ruth?" she called out uncertainly. "It's Mandy."

A bed creaked. Some covers rustled.

"Mandy? Mandy, are you really here?" It was a pathetic croak from the back bedroom, the sound of a little girl in great pain. It did not, in fact, sound like the voice of anyone that Mandy had ever met before.

When she hurried into the room and found her straggly-haired sister lying under a mound of blankets—her dull eyes ringed with black circles of fatigue—she realized that this woman didn't look like anybody she'd ever known, either.

"Ruthie?" she whispered, suddenly feeling shaky with concern. "Are you okay?"

Her uneasiness flared into full-scale panic as her big sister—the rock of her childhood, the torment of her adolescence and model of her womanhood—took one look at Mandy and began to sob.

CHAPTER TWO

IT WAS NOT QUITE THREE O'CLOCK that afternoon when a light tap at the front door signaled the arrival of Brady Trent at Joe Henderson's restored conductor's house on the grounds of the Slow Joe Loco. Joe was quite pleased with the way he'd fixed up his small home. The outside was red with white trim and the interior was paneled with knotty pine and made homey with bright braided oval rugs. It looked just like the model engineer's cabin that crowned the layout in his living room.

"It's open!" Joe called from his favorite reclining chair in front of the TV. Bowlegged Brady had been his best friend since junior-high school; words were rarely needed between them. Certainly not mundane words like "hello" and "goodbye," especially when Brady lived only ten miles away and often dropped by in the afternoon. Brady's lifetime dream had been to run cattle on his own land, and for the briefest snatch of time, he'd achieved it. But nowadays he worked as a ranch hand for somebody else; most days he was riding fence by dawn and had put in a full day's work before the desert heat made outdoor work all but impossible. Since the bunkhouse he currently called home didn't have a television, he often joined Joe when the Dodgers played.

"It's the top of the third, 4-2 Dodgers," Joe announced by way of greeting as his old pal sauntered into the living room, tossed off his Stetson and plopped down on the couch. He took the bowl of popcorn Joe handed him without a word, then ripped off a can of soda from the chilly six-pack in his hand and tossed one to the recliner where Joe, still wearing his conductor's outfit, was already comfortably stretched out.

"Did you catch that double play in the second?" Brady asked. "I got part of it on the radio driving over."

"Yeah," Joe answered, his tone subdued. "Looks like that new shortstop Alfredo really blew it." He did not think that there was anything particularly unusual in either his voice or his comment, but Brady twisted sideways on the couch, eyed him warily, then asked, "What's wrong?"

For just a moment Joe met his friend's eyes, then swore silently under his breach. He had told himself that his encounter today with Miss Sawyer didn't matter, that she was only a relic of his dim and distant past. But despite the self-control he'd mustered in her presence, his insides were still churning with feelings that hadn't plagued him in years. Reluctantly he confessed, "Brady, I met a woman today that ... oh, hell, I *thought* I met a woman today who was ... well, interesting. Pretty. Fun. And she practically begged me to ask her out."

Brady lifted his eyebrows. "This is a problem?"

"It was when I found out who she was."

Serious now, Brady sat up, crossed one ankle over the opposing knee, and studied his unhappy friend. "Married? Best friend of your ex-wife? What?"

"Worse than all of the above. Worse than anything you can imagine."

"Give me a hint," Brady coaxed.

Joe exhaled slowly. "Tell me, Brady, in the years that you've known me, how many people have I really, truly disliked?"

Brady thought a minute, then answered, "None."

"Do I hold a grudge?"

"Nope."

"Do I even remember anything that happened more than a week ago?"

Brady grinned. "Not unless it's got something to do with your kids."

The tension in Joe's face relaxed for just a moment. He knew he talked about his kids too much. But he was damn proud of all three of them, and lucky enough to share joint custody with an ex-wife whom he still considered a fair-to-middling friend.

He wished he could think of Mandy Larkin that way. The trouble was, he couldn't think of the woman he'd met today as Mandy Larkin at all. The ghost of String Bean Sawyer colored every memory of those five rollicking minutes they'd enjoyed before she'd introduced herself.

Joe took a sip of soda, then met his friend's gaze. "When I first met you, there *was* somebody I hated. Somebody I felt had misjudged me, humiliated me, stolen a whole year of my life. Do you remember that?"

Brady, who knew every one of Joe's secrets, nodded slowly. "You were still pretty hot under the collar about your sixth-grade teacher—I remember that. 'String Bean' Sawyer, wasn't it? As I recall, you were sure that she hated you."

Joe's eyelids narrowed. "She still does," he admitted coldly. "I ran into her today at the station house."

"You're kidding!" Brady sounded stunned.

"I'm not. Believe me, I wish I were."

Brady's eyes grew wide. "I thought she left town about the time I moved here!"

"She did, but God help me, she's back. Just for the summer, but if Karen Hayward doesn't get her act to-gether—read that convince her mom to give her license back—I might have to face that—" he swallowed a harsh word and struggled for an innocuous one "—*person* every day."

In the five minutes he'd spent talking to Karen when the girl had returned from lunch, Joe had learned a great deal more about Mandy Larkin's scheduled visit to Redpoint than he'd wanted to know. Karen, whom he'd always thought of as a bright, sparkly sort of kid, had been so rattled by the news that her aunt had come looking for her that she'd begged Joe to recall every single word that had passed between them. While he'd fielded her questions and watched her bite her fingernails, he'd come to the conclusion that Karen was afraid the woman would uncover something about her work at the Slow Joe that Karen would just as soon keep under wraps. Since Joe ran a very wholesome family business and never hired kids that he suspected were involved with drugs or any other form of seedy behavior, his best guess was that Karen's secret had something to do with George Masters, an older boy who had picked her up for lunch on his motorcycle on more than one occasion . . . including today, unless he'd missed his guess. Joe had never been too impressed with George, who'd been on a softball team he had coached years ago, but he'd never had any reason to think the boy was involved in anything shady, either. More than likely poor Karen was simply paranoid about her family. An expert on juvenile trouble himself, Joe's sympathies lay with the girl. Ruth Hayward was a stickler for discipline, and Miss Sawyer, he knew to his sorrow, was even worse.

Brady slid one long arm along the patchwork-patterned couch and studied his friend across the room. "This one's for the books, Joey. How did you even recognize her after all this time? She must be an old lady by now."

"Ha!" Joe barked. "That's the killer. You'd think so! But she's only in her forties now and—damn, I hate to say it—she's gorgeous. Looks as young and fresh as a teenager. Natural red hair and cute little freckles. And *dimples*, no less! Hell, I figured it out. She was twice my age back then but now she's only a few years my senior. Ten, eleven, twelve years, maybe? Nothing at all to a man my age."

The barest hint of a grin tugged at the corner of Brady's mouth. "I take it that you . . . made these flattering observations before you discovered her true identity."

"You've got that right. I had plenty of time to put both feet in my mouth. I . . . oh, hell, Brady! I *came on* to the woman! And dammit, she was flirting with me, too. Openly! It was a mutual . . . well, attraction. That's the damnedest thing! You know I don't . . . well, get excited about every woman who crosses my path."

"True enough."

Actually, Joe had the mixed blessing of being one of the few unattached men in tiny Redpoint, and everybody from the mayor to the town's librarian seemed to feel obligated to steer him toward any single female over the age of twenty-one. While he took this communal matchmaking in good humor, he was actually quite particular about the sort of woman he wanted to spend a lot of time with, and though he had several platonic women friends he occasionally joined for a movie or a friendly meal at the local diner, he dated sporadically and only rarely grew sufficiently interested in a woman to recall that he'd gotten a vasectomy shortly after his divorce.

"When she suddenly froze on me when I told her my name, I thought maybe I'd just rushed her a little, so I didn't get the message right away," Joe continued. "I mean, one minute she was glowing, the next she was as stiff as a board. And then—as if that wasn't bad enough—she started talking teacher talk to me, as though I were still in her class! She even called me 'Joey!'"

Brady steepled his hands and studied his friend. "A lot of your friends call you that," he pointed out reasonably.

"Not like that. I mean there's Joey like 'Joey, old pal' and there's Joey like 'Joey, sweetheart' from a woman who wants me and then there's '*Joey!*' like 'Young Man I will not Tolerate that Kind of Behavior in My Classroom!'"

"And you're sure she meant it like that?" Brady asked. He tried, but failed, to hide his widening grin.

"What the hell are you snickering at?" Joe demanded. "You're supposed to be on my side!"

That was too much for Brady, who burst out laughing. "Oh, Joey, come on! Where's your sense of humor? I know you were embarrassed, but hell, it's funny! If somebody else were telling this story you'd bust a gut! Slow Joe Henderson coming on to the teacher he once hated more than anybody in the world? And String Bean Sawyer flirting with little Joey, the hellion of Redpoint Elementary?"

In spite of himself, a grin nudged itself onto Joe's face. A moment later he was chuckling with his friend. "All right. It does have its humorous side. But if you'd been there, believe me, there was nothing funny about the way she looked at me."

"Well, hell, Joe, do you blame her? Everybody says you were a holy terror back then. *You* even admit it!"

Joe winced. It was the truth, but hardly a legacy he was proud of, especially since his reputation had complicated school life for his oldest child. "Okay, I was rough on my teachers in grade school," he admitted. "Especially Sawyer. But that's only because she deserved it. She was so damned prissy—so determined to reform me. She didn't give a damn how I came out. She just didn't want me to mess up her evaluation as a first-year teacher.''

"Ah, Joe, are you sure that's fair? How often does Ira tell you a story like that and you end up siding with his teachers?"

Joe couldn't very well argue with that. But he also knew that Ira frequently got in trouble for things he hadn't done, or things that had been misinterpreted by an irate staff member. There was one particular teacher that poor Ira had greatly admired and had tried desperately to please. When she'd humiliated him in front of the whole class, he'd turned sour on her overnight. Joe had sympathized completely. The same thing had happened to him with Miss Sawyer.

"All I'm sure of, Brady, is that it's been twenty-some-odd years since I was in the woman's class and I still feel angry when I think about the sixth grade. Now that can't be right. *She* was the grown-up. *I* was just a kid. Maybe I did screw up, but I *was* redeemable. Mr. Wickers proved that."

Mr. Wickers had been in charge of the remedial summer program designed to shore up weak students before they plunged into junior high school, and in six weeks he did something for Joe that no other teacher had ever managed to do. The techniques he'd used—psychology, love, discipline and a mutual love of trains—didn't really matter. The bottom line was, he had taken a rebellious loser and transformed him into a bright, successful student. Joe had started the summer program certain that since Miss Sawyer had so obviously given up on him, it was only right that he give up on himself, too. Old Mr. Wickers, a veteran teacher ready to retire, had glimpsed some tiny spark of hope inside the troubled child and fanned it back to life. Joe would be forever grateful. He still sent the elderly man a card every year at Christmas.

"Joe," Brady pointed out, "Mr. Wickers couldn't have fixed you up if you hadn't wanted to be fixed. He had some good material to work with."

Joe ran a nervous hand through his sandy hair. "Same material Sawyer had." He shook his head. "It's like she's two different people, Brady. There's Miss Sawyer, this bitch I've hated all my life, and then there's this incredibly appealing female I met today. If Mandy Larkin were anybody else but String Bean Sawyer, I'd..." He let the sentence hang.

ONLY THE HEAVY SHADE of the Apache pines in Ruth's backyard made it bearable to sit out of doors in the Four Corners area on a summer afternoon. But after the dark despair that had permeated her older sister's bedroom, Mandy craved sunlight...of both the physical and emotional varieties.

For a good fifteen minutes after Mandy had arrived, Ruth had held on to her and wept. For the next fifteen, she'd apologized—for falling apart, for the condition of the house, and for having such terrible monthly cramps on the very day Mandy was scheduled to arrive.

"I've always gotten emotional during my periods, Mandy. You remember that," Ruth had insisted. "I'm always cranky at the wrong time of the month."

As far as Mandy was concerned, Ruth was cranky all the time. But she was never weepy. In fact, Mandy was hard-pressed to remember the last time she'd seen her sister cry. Even at Alan's funeral she'd remained dry-eyed. Mandy had sobbed almost continually for three whole days while Ruth had sat stoically by her side, rarely sleeping, insisting that Mandy eat, drink and rest. In Ruth's own stern way, she loved her sister dearly, but her typical greetings were never emotional. Right after hello, she generally launched a series of admonitions about Mandy's tardiness, suggestions about her appearance, or set-in-concrete plans for her visit. Ruth, after all, was always certain that she knew what Mandy would most enjoy. It was sort of like old-home week with one's former drill sergeant.

The Ruth of her memory bore only a vague resemblance to the bathrobe-clad woman who now huddled on the chaise longue. Ruth was taller than Mandy, and though she shared her green eyes and fair complexion, she had no freckles and insisted that her dark hair was "auburn" rather than red. Her carriage was statuesque, almost regal, and she always dressed with simple elegance. Even her aprons matched her Saturday-afternoon apparel. It had been years since Mandy had seen her sister without makeup. In fact, the last time had been when she'd visited Ruth in the hospital right after Karen's birth. It was a grimly apt comparison; Mandy suddenly realized that today Ruth could easily have passed for a hospital patient.

Even though Ruth was looking a bit brighter than she had when Mandy had first arrived, Mandy remained uneasy as they sipped lemonade and got caught up on the news. Ruth ordered her to report on her trip to Georgia, then asked if she'd brought something dressy enough to wear to the upcoming wedding of one of Ruth's dear friends. Although Mandy had no interest in attending a stranger's wedding, she took comfort from the realization that Ruth was starting to sound more like her old self and quickly promised to find something appropriate in her luggage.

Ruth wanted to know all the news about Mandy's boys. She found out that Kevin had just received a promotion and, after three years of marriage, was still delirious about his wife. Vince was looking forward to his first year of medical school. Then Mandy asked about Ruth's kids. The oldest three were long since grown and had families of their own, but Ruth still heard regularly from her two daughters, though she had a litany of complaints about grandkids not writing thank-you notes for gifts she had sent on their birthdays. Things were a bit strained with her son; apparently he'd been less than happy when his mother had advised him to leave his second wife who so clearly "wasn't good enough for him." The more Ruth talked about the incident, the greater grew her despair over what sounded to Mandy like a minor tiff with a young man whom she knew to be a very forgiving son.

After making several diplomatic efforts to help Ruth accept the situation—or take steps that might bring about a faster reconciliation—she decided that a change of subject was in order. Trying to lift Ruth out of the doldrums, Mandy asked brightly, "So how is my favorite niece doing?" certain that Karen was the one child about whom Ruth would have few complaints.

But to Mandy's surprise, her bossy big sister crumpled up like a rag doll and pressed both hands over her eyes. "She's my *baby*!" Ruth whispered with a depth of anguish that Mandy had never heard in her voice before. "I just can't believe that she lied to me!"

It only got worse after that.

IT WAS NEARLY FIVE O'CLOCK before Mandy broke away from her distraught sister and started the twenty-minute drive back to the Slow Joe Loco. One of the few coherent facts she'd unearthed in Ruth's blubbering recount of her recent troubles with Karen was that she had confiscated Karen's driver's license and was making the run into town twice a day so Karen could continue working. Since Ruth was clearly in no shape to drive, Mandy had offered to pick up Karen, despite the fact that returning to Joey Henderson's lair was not high on her list of personal preferences. However, she was delighted that she'd have a chance to talk to the girl alone. Not only did Mandy want to hear Karen's side of the story, but she wanted to know if Ruth's exceptionally emotional behavior was really just the result of a particularly bad case of monthly cramps.

As Mandy drove back to the Slow Joe—her back aching after a long day on the road—she mentally reviewed what her sister had told her about her troubles with Karen. According to Ruth, Karen had been forbidden to see her boyfriend, a young man who had offended Ruth on their first meeting by failing to stand when she'd entered the room. After days of tearful pleading for her mother to relent, Karen had apparently snuck off to see this fellow— George something or other—under the guise of spending the evening with a friend. In fact, she had surreptitiously met him a number of times before Ruth had inadvertently discovered her daughter's deceit. She'd been trying to relay a message to Karen from Wilma, the secretary at the Slow Joe, regarding a change in the following day's schedule. Ruth, who prided herself on her razor-sharp memory, had been amazed that she'd managed to confuse which night Karen had said she'd be with which friend. After four calls she'd begun to put the pieces together and had confronted Karen with her evidence when she'd come home. Mother and daughter had hardly been speaking since then. Except for work, Karen was "permanently" grounded.

It wasn't hard for Mandy to understand the sense of desperation that had probably driven Karen to deceive her mother. She also knew that Ruth was prone to exaggerate to make a point, so her revelation of the "countless times" that Karen had lied to her had to be taken with a grain of salt. Nonetheless, nobody could question that a major breach of mother-daughter faith had occurred, at least from Ruth's perspective. As a mother who had weathered adolescence—though mercifully her boys had given her a minimum of trouble—Mandy knew how very difficult living with a sixteen-year-old could be. She said a silent prayer of thanks that she hadn't had to teach Joey Henderson when he was in his teens—regardless of what he'd said about having straightened out in the seventh grade.

Karen was waiting on the curb when Mandy arrived. She was chewing on the fingernails of her right hand and watching the road like a hawk. She didn't recognize her aunt's white Toyota at once and did not wave until Mandy opened the door and called out a greeting.

"Aunt Mandy!" Karen gushed, quickly throwing her arms around Mandy's neck. She'd grown a few inches, had a new haircut—short and chic—and was clad in baggy engineer's coveralls, but otherwise she hadn't changed much. "I heard you dropped by at lunch. I hope you didn't waste a lot of time looking for me." She sounded genuinely concerned.

Mandy shook her head. "No, I was only here a few minutes before I heard that you'd already zipped off to lunch. I'm still not sure how I missed you, though. I was here when the train pulled in." She didn't mention that she'd been utterly beguiled by the owner of the Slow Joe Loco at the time. Instead she said, "Your boss certainly thinks a lot of you, Karen."

Karen blushed at the praise. "Isn't Mr. Henderson the greatest? He doesn't take any guff from any of us, you know, but he knows we call him Slow Joe behind his back—for fun, you know, because we like him—and he doesn't mind."

"Slow Joe," Mandy repeated, astounded that the hyperactive child she knew could ever have been saddled with such an ironic nickname. "He didn't strike me as a...well, laid-back sort of a person."

"Well, he's sure not lazy, if that's what you mean, Aunt Mandy," Karen informed her. "Wilma gets here at seven-thirty sometimes, and she says she's never once beat him to the office. He works seven days a week, he almost never goes on vacation and he's stayed home sick maybe half a dozen times in the ten years she's been with him. Isn't that incredible?"

Mandy found a rueful smile. "Actually, that's about the only thing that doesn't surprise me," she muttered to herself. "Damn kid was always as healthy as a horse."

"What did you say, Aunt Mandy?"

Remembering her audience, Mandy decided to thrust her thoughts of Joey Henderson out of her mind. Their encounter had staggered her solely because it had come as such a surprise. The fact that Karen's boss had struck her as handsome, virile, friendly and altogether charming had nothing to do with reality. The man was little Joey Henderson, still a hellion in disguise, and Mandy vowed to avoid him like the plague.

"Your mom is feeling kind of tired," she told Karen. "She suggested we go out to eat. Is that okay with you?"

"Sure, Aunt Mandy," Karen replied with a winning grin. "There's a great hamburger place right on the edge of town."

Mandy couldn't say that Hamburger Heaven was the sort of dining establishment she'd had in mind, but she decided the sparkling smile on her niece's face would make the sacrifice of her taste buds well worth the price.

"So tell me, Karen, what's been going on here?" she asked as Karen got into the car and they started toward the drive-in. "Your mom's having a rough time today. Do her periods always hit her this hard?"

"Don't ask *me* to explain my mother!" Karen burst out. "I think she's crazy. Why else would she take away my license when I've waited for it sixteen years and only got to drive for three months?"

Mandy quietly eyed her niece. Even allowing for a lot of exaggeration on Ruth's part, it wasn't likely that Karen was wholly innocent of lying to her mother and breaking a variety of rules. Quietly she asked, "Do you really think she had no reason whatsoever to take away your license, honey?"

Karen slouched and turned away, her eyes on the road. "Well, I know I shouldn't have lied to her, Aunt Mandy, but I honestly didn't know what else to do," she admitted. "I just *had* to see George. Mom's always pushed me around, but she's never acted this bad before! She's driving me out of my mind. I've actually considered running away from home."

Mandy shuddered at her niece's frightening confession, then realized that Karen never would have admitted her plans if she'd been serious about following through with them. Aloud she said calmly, "I certainly hope that if you ever found your mother's house intolerable, you'd make a call to Denver before you did anything rash. You know I've always got a spare room waiting for you."

Karen met her even gaze, then glanced away as her eyes filled with tears. "I'm so glad you're here, Aunt Mandy," she whispered. "Maybe you can make things right."

"I'm certainly going to try, honey," she promised. "But I'm going to need your help."

Karen nodded, then asked hesitantly, "What lies did Mom tell you about me?"

Mandy shook her head as she pulled the white compact into the Hamburger Heaven parking lot. "I doubt very much that your mother has ever told a lie, Karen. You know how strict she is when it comes to honesty."

"When it comes to *everything*!" Karen burst out. "Did she tell you why she forbid me to see George?"

Mandy hesitated, then answered, "I guess she just doesn't think he's right for you."

"She has no right to pick out a boyfriend for me! She has no right to ruin my life!" she thundered with typical teenage hyperbole. "How would you feel if you were madly in love with the greatest guy in the whole world and my mother told you he was a jerk and you ought to forget him?"

Mandy took a moment to answer that one, picking her words with care. "When I was twenty-four, your mother did exactly that."

"And?" Karen prodded breathlessly.

"I hated her for a while. I hurt over him for months." It had happened shortly after she'd left Redpoint, and she usually tucked the memory into the same dark corner of her mind. "But after she introduced me to Uncle Alan, I realized that she'd been right all along. My other boyfriend was a very nice guy, but he wasn't at all right for me, and Alan was just my cup of tea."

Karen stiffened, then glowered at Mandy. "I want to marry George," she declared flatly. "And he wants to marry me."

Mandy knew better than to give her a lecture on the statistical failure of teenage marriages; at the moment, she needed to keep the lines of communication open by holding on to Karen's trust.

"If it's meant to be," she said gently, "then I'm sure he'll wait for you until you're older or your mother has a change of heart."

"She doesn't *have* a heart!" Karen burst out. "And mine is broken!"

On that dramatic note, she flounced up the walk, leaving Mandy to follow in her wake. But the pout vanished from Karen's pretty face the instant she walked through the double glass doors with Mandy right behind her.

It would have been obvious to an imbecile that Karen's change of mood had something to do with the young man behind the counter. He was tall and slender, with dark wavy hair and earthy good looks. He looked a lot older than Karen—at least more sophisticated in the ways of women and men—and his gaze raked her youthful body with a lustful appreciation that he made no effort to conceal.

Karen tossed him a blazing smile that all but set the counter on fire, then gave him a warning look that silenced his suggestive greeting. "I'd like a double cheeseburger special with a Coke and fries," she blurted out quickly. "And my *aunt* would like something, too."

"Your aunt?" the boy repeated. Then, quite suddenly, he flattered Mandy with an obsequious grin. "And what would you like this evening, ma'am? Our salads are just the ticket for—"

"I'll have a hamburger," Mandy interrupted tersely, making a note of the embroidered George on the boy's uniform. She was a safe size twelve, but she'd spent too much of her life battling an incipient tendency toward hippiness to appreciate the slightest hint that a salad would be in her best interests. Besides, she was angry—with Karen more than with her boyfriend. She didn't like being played for a fool. She loved Karen, and it hurt her deeply that her niece had abused her trust so shamelessly.

After Mandy asked for a Coke, George asked if her order was, "for here or to go." She glanced at Karen, who was almost panting with eagerness and answered coolly, "To go, please."

Then, keeping her voice steady, Mandy told Karen, "I thought it might be nice to go eat on the picnic tables at the school since it's right around the corner. Now that the breeze has come up, it ought to be quite pleasant this time of night."

"Sure, Aunt Mandy," Karen replied in a monotone, her cheeks flaming. "If that's what you want."

"You don't have to wait in here, Karen," Mandy continued, making no effort to smile. "Go on out to the car and I'll be along as soon as our food is ready."

Karen glowered at Mandy, then briefly cast a longing gaze at George that was practically a caress. She slunk out the door—there was no other word for the way she moved—but she said nothing more until Mandy pulled up outside Redpoint Elementary a few minutes later.

It hadn't changed much. The playground still sported three tired old swing sets and one jungle gym. Four wings of classrooms led out from the office in straight, efficient lines. There was lots of grass on the giant playground, but now it was tough, uneven Bermuda grass, liberally seeded with brown patches and weeds.

Mandy had expected to feel a twinge of nostalgia. After all, this was the place where her beloved lifelong career had taken root. And she did feel . . . well, moved . . . to find herself standing on the blacktop again. How odd it seemed to see no children dancing all around her! How strange to feel no whistle in her hand!

"You didn't have to do that," Karen suddenly accused her after her long silent pout. She stood off to one side, clutching the hamburger bag as though it were a lifeline. "You sent me to the corner with a dunce cap on."

Mandy turned to face her niece squarely. She was still hurt, still angry. More important, she was getting a picture of how complicated this case of teenage rebellion had already become; maybe she'd sold her sister short. Mandy had expected her favorite niece to try to wheedle her into supporting her shenanigans, but she had not expected Karen to lie to her right off the bat.

"You used me, Karen," she said bluntly. "You deliberately deceived me. Your mother expressly forbade you to see that boy, and you had me take you to him the first minute I got into town."

"For just five minutes! What could it hurt? You were right there! What was he going to do to me right there in the restaurant?" Again her eyes filled with tears. "Besides, I thought if you could just meet George, you'd realize how wrong Mom is about him! I thought you'd be on my side!"

Mandy shook her head. "Under the circumstances, all you did was prove that your mother's right when she says you can't be trusted, Karen. I'm really disappointed in you."

Karen licked her lips and studied the ground.

Her misery was so apparent that Mandy's anger softened. She wasn't so old that she'd forgotten what it was like to be in love at sixteen. "Look, for all I know George is the world's nicest guy, Karen," she said gently. "He's certainly...good-looking." It was the only honest compliment Mandy could come up with, and it did cause Karen to glance up hopefully. But as Mandy reiterated that she had to back up Ruth's directives, Karen snapped at her again. When she tried to tell Karen that her mother's strict rules really were motivated by love, Karen did not reply.

It was only after she'd finished her cheeseburger a good ten minutes later that Karen said softly, "I didn't mean to lie to you, Aunt Mandy. I didn't ... I mean, I didn't lie to you straight out." It was more of a rationalization than an apology, but it sounded like a peace offering, and Mandy decided to take it as such.

"I'm willing to forget it if you promise me it won't happen again," she told her niece.

Karen shivered, although it was still very warm on the playground. "Okay," she finally consented, but her tone was ambivalent at best.

Mandy was disappointed; she'd hoped for a bit more warmth. After stuffing their trash into a can chained to a nearby tree, Mandy asked, "Would you like to see my old classroom?"

Karen shrugged. "If you want."

Taking the cool words for assent, Mandy started walking to Room Six-A, the last one on the east side of the playground. It was on the edge of the building, a position that provided Joey Henderson with a multitude of ways to escape her. One day, when he'd slipped out of the classroom, she'd gone down one hallway searching for him while he'd scampered back along the other at least a dozen times before the chuckling children had given away his game. Looking back on it, Mandy was amazed that she'd been naive enough to fall for so many of his tricks. Nowadays, she thought, if she got a child like Joey in her class, she would have a fighting chance of figuring out how to deal with him.

"Well, this is where I got my start," Mandy declared to her niece as she craned her neck to look in through the shaded glass of the windows. "What memories I have of this old room!'' When Karen did not reply, she went on talking, hoping to spark some interest in the girl that might lead her to forget about George for a moment. ''You know, there is nothing quite like the first year of teaching. It's a lot like having a baby, only you get to go home sometimes.'' Mandy laughed. ''I must have worked twelve hours a day that year. How hard I tried to be perfect! I had about a dozen reading groups, each child at precisely his own level. I tried six different kinds of math and all sorts of creative approaches to teaching social studies—that's always been my specialty, you know. I wonder, to this day, if any of the children ever appreciated how hard I worked.''

Karen said nothing.

''They're all grown-up now, you know. Professional people, good solid workers, homemakers with children of their own. I hope I taught them something worthwhile, something that helped each one get his or her start in life.'' She pointed to a chair near the front row. ''Kathy Reznick sat right there and cracked her knuckles all day long.''

For the first time, Karen responded. ''You mean you actually remember some of your first students? You've been teaching for over twenty years!''

Mandy chuckled softly. ''Once I was sure I'd never forget a single face. And I'm sure that if you gave me a few hints about somebody I've forgotten, one of them would eventually jog some chord in my memory. But the first year was so vital to me that I remember a lot of students. Especially the ones who were…well, unique. Extra sweet, extra smart, extra shy… or singularly obnoxious.''

Karen laughed. How good to hear that happy sound after the grim meal they'd shared, Mandy reflected. ''You love kids so much, Aunt Mandy! I've never heard you call one 'obnoxious' before.''

Mandy shook her head. "Well, I've had a few over the years that fall into that category, unfortunately. The funny thing is, the more difficult they are, the more I worry about them. It's those troubled kids that just break your heart."

Finally showing some interest, Karen peered into the window and looked at the room. "I thought they closed up these rooms for summer," she said. "There's a July calendar on the wall."

"Summer school, I guess," Mandy said. "When I taught here, I know they had a remedial class for sixth graders who needed some work to get ready for junior high."

"They had that when I went to school here, too," Karen concurred. "All the real losers had to go."

Mandy smiled. "We call them children with academic difficulties."

"Right," Karen said. "You telling me that none of them were goof-offs?"

"Well, as a matter of fact...there might have been a few."

This time Karen actually laughed, her problems with the love of her life temporarily forgotten. "Tell me who they were, Aunt Mandy! I bet some of them still live here. How old would they be by now?"

Just the right age. The words popped into her head unbidden, and Mandy struggled to thrust them aside. Here, with her face pressed up against Room Six-A's dusty window, she could almost see little Joey Henderson over there in the corner, scribbling something dirty on the wall. Her sensual response to him this morning before he told her his name proved that God had a sense of humor.

Suddenly Karen gave her a playful shove. "You should see your face, Aunt Mandy! Tell me who you're thinking of! It's somebody I know, isn't it?"

Mandy struggled desperately to keep a straight face and failed. "Oh, Karen, it doesn't matter anymore."

"Come on!" The girl was really excited now. In fact, she looked almost as animated as she had when she'd first spotted George. "Tell me, Aunt Mandy! I can keep a secret!"

Mirth overcame her, and Mandy laughed out loud. "Oh, it's hardly a secret. Little Joey Henderson was very proud of his exploits. I think he positively adored having the worst reputation in the whole school."

Karen's expression was almost bug-eyed as she leaned toward Mandy in dismay and delight. "*Mr. Henderson* was a goof-off? Slow Joe himself?"

"Mr. Henderson," said Mandy distinctly, "was a brat."

Karen howled. "I love it! He's always on somebody's case when they come in late or don't act nice to the tourists! And you're telling me that he was a class clown himself?"

"I'm not sure I'd call him a class clown, exactly. Nobody enjoyed the pranks he pulled—not even the other kids. I'd call him a human tornado. He wrecked everything in his path."

Karen was beside herself. "Mr. *Hen*derson! I don't believe it! He's such a swell guy now!" She slung a companionable arm around Mandy's waist. "Don't you think he's great, Aunt Mandy?"

Mandy struggled for a smile. "Well, I hardly know him as a man, Karen. He had to introduce himself to me. The Joey Henderson I knew—" she was reminding herself as much as she was informing her niece "—is somebody we secretly called Joey the Jerk, not Slow Joe."

"Joey the Jerk!" Karen hugged Mandy as she laughed. "Sandra won't believe it. He's just so cool! So straight and efficient, so nice to everybody! To think he used to be a troublemaker. . . . I guess there's hope for all of us, huh?''

Mandy wasn't concentrating too much on the last line; it was something else Karen had said that got her attention. ''I don't think you should tell your friends about this, Karen,'' she admonished her niece. ''Especially the ones who work at the Slow Joe. You remember you promised me you could keep a secret?''

''But Aunt Mandy! This is so great! Sandra would simply love it!''

Mandy shook her head. ''Maybe she would, but I have a feeling that your boss might not find it quite so hilarious.''

''You're wrong, Aunt Mandy,'' Karen insisted. ''Mr. Henderson has a terrific sense of humor, and he knows how to laugh at himself. If he were still a mess, I could see how it might offend him, but since everybody knows how great he turned out, I can't see how he'd mind me telling Sandra what you said. After all, didn't you say that everybody knew he was a screwup?''

''I said everybody knew it *then*. That's not the same as his ex-teacher coming back to town and spreading rumors about him twenty years after the fact. It's not appropriate, Karen. Professionally it might not even be ethical. I probably shouldn't even have told you.'' When Karen's jubilance faded from her eyes, Mandy hastened to add, ''But I'm glad I did. We both needed a good laugh.''

It was true. Ever since she'd first arrived at Ruth's and found the house in such a sorry condition, she'd felt uneasy about the state of her sister's health. Obviously Karen was also under strain; all in all, things were not going well for her loved ones in Redpoint. Was it possible that Ruth's ''directive'' for Mandy to come visit this summer had actually been a secret cry for help? It seemed unlikely that

Ruth would need help from anybody, let alone her little sister. Then again, she'd never thought it likely that Ruth would fall apart the moment she walked in the door.

Despite the brief moment of hilarity, Karen's mood blackened again. "Please, Aunt Mandy," she suddenly begged. "Talk to Mother for me. I wasn't kidding when I told you that sometimes I think I'm going to have to run away from home. I just can't stand it much longer. She won't let me do anything and she yells at me all the time!" Suddenly she broke into tears. "Aunt Mandy, I've just got to find a way to make her let me see George."

Instantly Mandy put her arm around the young girl's trembling shoulders. "I can't promise you I can change her overnight," she promised softly, "but I'll talk to her, Karen. I'll do what I can."

"Thank you, Aunt Mandy. I knew I could count on you." Karen leaned up to kiss her cheek, still weeping gratefully. "And you can count on me not to tell anybody what you think of Mr. Henderson."

She wanted to correct her niece, to tell her that whatever she'd felt about wild little Joey had nothing to do with her intense sensual response to the successful man who was now Karen's boss. But she realized even before the words could form that such an assertion would have been a lie. The owner of the Slow Joe Loco would live forever in her mind's eye as the angry child who had, despite her youthful idealism, turned her first year of teaching into a tortuous journey through hell. She could tell herself every day and every night for three thousand years that the adult Joseph Paul Henderson was somebody else who might well be worthy of her affection and respect, but deep inside, where the pain of that terrible year still lived within her, Mandy knew that she could never force herself to believe it.

CHAPTER THREE

JOE SAW MANDY LARKIN three or four times the first week after she arrived in town. He did his best to ignore her disturbing presence, but unfortunately, on several different occasions he was close enough to the parking lot to require an exchange of hellos when Mandy came to pick up Karen after work. Each time they met, the same scene was reenacted. Joe tried to pretend he didn't spot the white Toyota until the last possible second, and Mandy tried to pretend she didn't see him at all. Then they'd both wave almost simultaneously, exchanging artificial smiles. Joe would feel anew the sensation of desire for this appealing freckle-faced female, then recall, as he caught a glimpse of the stormy expression in her eyes, that she might *look* like a friendly, sexy woman, but at heart she was as hard as stone.

Prior to Mandy's arrival in Redpoint, Joe had not been in the habit of thinking much about the sixth grade . . . or any of his childhood, for that matter. As a hyperactive kid, he'd had a rough time. But his adult years had been quite rewarding, except for his divorce. And even that had not been nearly as painful as poor Brady's; despite his pal's never-ending stream of jokes, Joe knew that inside, Brady was still bleeding. In the past two years he'd lost his lifetime dream, his unborn baby and his wife, though the divorce paperwork was not yet final. Worst of all, Jake

Trent's role in the painful crush of events had left a permanent rift between father and son.

Joe was certain that, in time, his friend would recover from losing a woman who was so clearly ill suited to him; he was also hopeful that, in time, he would manage to forgive his dad. But there were times when he doubted that Brady would ever get over losing the ranch.

In comparison, Joe's divorce had been a snap. When Sarah had tired of him, she hadn't flown the coop with his kids or used a battery of lawyers to keep him out of their lives. In fact, the two of them still split up their parental time and obligations pretty much the way they had when they were married. Sarah took care of everything at school, since Joe was allergic to it, and Joe, who had a more flexible work schedule than Sarah's rigid nine-to-five, took the kids to piano lessons, medical appointments and softball practice. They stayed with him several nights each week and almost always moved in for the duration when they were sick.

It occurred to him that Mandy might have children also. Yet he found it difficult to imagine his straight-laced former teacher as a mother, let alone a wife. What man would have willingly embraced that hunk of ice? Yet now he sensed a softness in her that didn't jibe at all with his memories.

When he spotted her on Tuesday afternoon a little after five, Mandy was leaning against the hood of her car, chatting with an employee's mother who had once taught at Redpoint Elementary. Oblivious to Joe's presence, Mandy was chuckling in delight at one of her companion's comments. The dimples and ready laugh lines around her pretty mouth brightened her natural beauty and made Joe forget for just a second that he was looking at a woman he heartily disliked. If only he could forget their history, Joe knew he wouldn't let this freckle-faced wonder slip away from him.

He'd just turned to go inside when the woman with Mandy gestured for Joe to join her. She had a question about her son's weekend schedule that he couldn't very well answer by hollering across the parking lot. In fact, he couldn't answer it without Wilma, who generally supervised such things. In the end he found himself standing about three feet from his old nemesis, and when his exchange with the other woman had ended, courtesy required that he acknowledge Mandy.

"Good afternoon," was the best greeting he could come up with. "Lovely day, isn't it?"

Despite his trite comment, Mandy glanced at the distant canyons and sighed. "It certainly is. No matter how hot it gets here, the view always makes it worth it. I've traveled over half of this country and visited a couple of others, and I've never seen anything quite like this red rock."

Joe didn't doubt it. The Four Corners area was unique in all the world. The canyons were carved by a master hand that surely, with such incredible results, could not have left anything to chance. He'd seen chunks of the canyon rock for sale in a gem store once, each one as perfect as if it had been sculpted by hand. Most of the locals took the view for granted, but Joe never ceased to recognized his good fortune.

"I've never really understood how anybody could give this up to live somewhere else," he commented idly, thinking of Brady's ex-wife, who'd actually chosen to give up Colorado to return to New York City.

But Mandy stiffened visibly as she snapped, "Unfortunately scenery isn't the only factor a person has to consider when choosing a game plan for his or her life."

If her tone hadn't been so sharp, Joe would have asked her what she meant, but he sensed that they'd once again used up their two-minute limit on civility. The last time he'd tried to get past the weather-and-view stage, she'd asked him why the train so often brought Karen back late, and he'd explained somewhat defensively that unless they experienced sudden rain or a breakdown, the Slow Joe Loco nearly always ran on time. He'd considered mentioning the possibility that Karen's tardiness in meeting her might be tied to something other than her working hours, but he had no evidence to justify his suspicions and besides, Karen was a good kid and he didn't want to get her in trouble.

Since it was obvious that Mandy had no desire to continue their conversation, Joe excused himself quickly before fresh trouble could brew between them. "The train came in half an hour ago, so I'm sure your niece will be along shortly," he assured her, inexplicably disappointed that Mandy's cheerful mood had vanished so quickly. "Have a good evening."

"You, too," she replied stiffly, her mouth tightening as she looked away.

Well, at least I wasn't rude, Joe told himself as he marched into his office to wrap up the day's paperwork before he went home. Quickly he settled in at his huge oak desk, a relic of yesteryear that went well with the station.

Joe was an outdoor man, and he'd never enjoyed the bookkeeping end of his business very much. But in college, when he'd worked summers for Brady's dad at Trent Savings and Loan, Jake had taught him that the easiest way to cope with paperwork was to take care of the penny-ante details on a daily basis instead of letting them all pile up. He handled most of the Slow Joe Loco office work himself and he always checked anything he delegated to Wilma.

Boy, if Miss Sawyer could see my bookkeeping now! He chuckled to himself. How he'd battled against the deadlines she'd set for him! Yet now he welcomed deadlines—they helped keep his business strong. Well, maybe Mandy had been right about the value of self-discipline after all. But she'd also insisted that he'd never make a success of himself until he got over his "ludicrous obsession with trains" and she couldn't have been more wrong about that.

Joe had been working for maybe fifteen minutes when he was interrupted by a brisk knock on the door. He called out a hearty "Come in!" without asking who was in need of a word with him. If he'd given much thought to the possible identity of his caller, he would have expected Wilma or Grandpa Howard. Under no circumstances would he have mused on the likelihood of a private visit from Mandy Larkin. After all, she hadn't been in the mood for more than an exchange of obligatory hellos out in the parking lot.

But when the door flew open, String Bean Sawyer stomped into the room with a vigorous stride that Joe remembered only too well. She was angry. Streaks of red mottled her fair, freckled face. He remembered seeing that proof of her fury in the dark days of his sixth-grade year. He even remembered going out of his way to see if he could provoke her into a display of that very red-faced anger. What he did not recall was how pretty she looked when she was irate.

And, surprisingly, how vulnerable.

"Karen is missing!" she stated bluntly, without bothering to say hello. "I dropped her off here at eight o'clock this morning. 'I'm off at five,' she said. Well, it's long past five and here I am, and that nitwit woman who claims to be your secretary says that Karen went home sick around noon.'' Mandy advanced on him, her breasts heaving with exertion, her eyes darting, accusatory. "But Ruth and I have been home all day. There's been no phone call, no unexpected arrival, and there sure as hell as been no sign of my favorite niece!" She took one more step toward Joe, her jaw jutting out with fury. "You're supposed to be in charge here. Perhaps *you* can tell me how Karen could have disappeared? Do you allow sick kids to hitchhike home or take a ride with...with anyone? Just what kind of a place are you running here anyway, Joey?"

Joe took a deep breath. He would not, would *not*, allow Miss Sawyer to incite his ire. He was a grown-up now, and she couldn't send him to the principal's office, deprive him of recess or give him a three-day suspension. "Why don't you have a seat, Mrs. Larkin," he suggested calmly, "while I look into the matter?"

"Have a seat?" she bellowed. "This isn't a stray coat that might be in the lost and found! This is a human being, a precious child, a troubled teenager who might—" she stopped, gulping, before she finished hoarsely "—be anywhere!"

It was not until Joe saw the first glimmer of tears in her eyes that he realized that despite her raving, Mandy Larkin wasn't truly mad at him. She was scared. Scared that something terrible had happened to Karen. As terrified as Joe himself would have been if he'd shown up at school and discovered that Ira and Lynne or Sally had disappeared off the face of the earth.

It was a revelation to Joe. An hour ago, he would have sworn in a court of law that words like "fear," "love" and "family loyalty" had not been in the vocabulary of her heart. Yet now she stood before him, quivering, as all three of those powerful emotions danced across her face. She desperately needed help and reassurance, and Fate's cast of the die had forced her to turn to Joe.

There was a time when he would have gloated, but that time was long in the past. At the moment, there was only thirty-five-year-old Joe Henderson faced with a potential crisis involving a distraught woman and a sweet kid. His first goal was to calm the woman; his second was to find the child. He was an adult. He had no interest in revenge.

Quickly Joe stood and circled around his desk to steady Mandy, one strong hand gripping her quivering forearm. Her skin was warm and surprisingly silken, but he ignored the sensual response triggered by that physical contact. In a voice that was quiet but full of hope he said, "I understand why you're frightened, but I really am sure that Karen is all right. I have a hunch that I know where she is . . . or at least who she's with. Please give me a second to talk to some of my other girls. I'm sure I can get a lead on her."

Wild hope filled Mandy's frightened face. One hand reached out to clutch his shirt. "Are you sure, Joey? Are you sure she's okay?"

He nodded. "I'm positive," he lied. All he had was a hunch—based on his own observations of Karen and fifteen years of supervising other teenaged employees—but he saw no point in letting Mandy tremble any longer than she had to. He'd know the truth in a few minutes one way or another.

He slipped one arm around her shoulders and gave her a consoling squeeze. "I want you to sit down and take a deep breath. Give me five minutes. I'll have to radio the train to talk to Karen's best friend in the snack car, all right? If anybody knows what's going on here, it'll be Sandra. And if I ask her outright, she'll tell me the truth."

Mandy bit her lip, then closed her eyes as she sagged against him. "I'm sorry," she whispered. "I didn't mean to bark at you. I'm just so frightened, and I always yell at people when I'm scared." She gulped, then swallowed hard. "I guess you know that already, don't you?"

Joe gave her a warm smile because it seemed like the thing to do, but his head was swimming as he tried to sort out her words. He would have sworn that Miss Sawyer was not capable of apologizing to him for anything. It was equally incomprehensible that she might admit a weakness, let alone a weakness that referred to their other life together. But the strangest thing about her impromptu confession was that she expected him to *know* that she hollered at people when she was frightened. As a man, he'd figured that out just moments after she'd stormed into his office. But as a child—after nine months of regular verbal lashing—it had never once occurred to him.

"Sit down, Mandy," he repeated gently, dispensing with the "Mrs. Larkin" title he'd used to keep her at a distance. "I'll be right back."

She nodded while he patted her shoulder one more time. Then he marched out of the room. He was trying to focus on Sandra, who he was going to search out; once he found her he would insist that this was no time to cover for a friend who had undoubtedly snuck off to see her boyfriend. But in the deep recesses of his mind—or was it his heart?—Joe found himself wondering how many other surprises Mandy Larkin had in store for him.

And it *was* Mandy Larkin who was waiting for him in his office. It had to be, because String Bean Sawyer did not know how to cry.

DESPITE HER LINGERING PANIC, Mandy steadied herself as she waited for Joe. He seemed so confident that everything would turn out all right. it was as though he were determined to *make* Karen safely reappear. And one thing Mandy knew for certain was that determination was Joey Henderson's long suit.

Not Joey, she reminded herself tersely. *He's a man now. Everyone probably calls him Joe.*

The virile man who had just put his arm around her and promised to find her niece didn't seem to have much in common with the hell-raiser she'd once known. *This* Joe Henderson struck her as strong, efficient and ... well, exceptionally congenial. In fact, Mandy suspected that he might be *too* congenial, too respectable...and too damned appealing. Never in her wildest imagination had she conceived of a moment in which she might have gone to her class troublemaker for help. And now that she had, Mandy struggled to remind herself that she had no reason to go to him—ever—for anything else.

As she sat on the comfortable leather sofa, she glanced around the office, telling herself that she had no interest in what the room might tell her about Joe Henderson; she simply needed to keep from thinking about Ruth's reaction when she found out that Karen was missing. But Mandy could not stifle a moment's admiration for the Colorado State University diploma on the far wall and the Redpoint Softball League Coach of the Year trophy near the window. Other plaques and framed certificates revealed that Joe was a member of a men's service organization, past president of the local Friends of the Library, and a recipient of the Redpoint Church Valiant Volunteer award for restoring some brickwork on the centegenarian building. A cluster of pictures on his desk revealed the smiling faces of two young girls—fiveish and tenish—and a boy of eleven or twelve who looked so much like the Joey Henderson that Mandy remembered that she had to look twice to make sure it wasn't him. But the boy in the picture looked relaxed and happy. There was no haunted, wild look about him, no frantic desperation in his eyes. He looked like the sort of student that any teacher would be happy to have in class.

How, she wondered, had crazy Joey Henderson managed to raise such a son? How had he become, if his awards were anything to go by, a veritable pillar of the community?

She was still trying to figure that one out when the door opened and Joe himself stepped into the room.

There was something different about him, something Mandy noticed right away. He'd left the room looking sympathetic, sounding warm and concerned. Downright solicitous. Now his Adam's apple was pulsing and his jaw was rigid.

Caution told Mandy to wait until he spoke to her, but her own fear forced her to blurt out, "Have you found her, Joe?"

He met Mandy's gaze directly as he reported. "No. But I found out where she went, and I'm sure she's in no danger. At least...no more danger than any teenager faces when afflicted by an overdose of poor judgment and adolescent hormones."

"I beg your pardon?" Mandy asked, a little less frightened but no less confused.

"Wilma has just informed me that Karen has gone home sick three times in the past month. Always on Tuesday, right around noon. According to Sandra, George Masters only works half days on Tuesdays. He picks up Karen on his motorcycle in the parking lot after she signs out, then drops her off just before the time she's told you or her mother to pick her up."

Mandy blanched. How could she have been so stupid? How many times had she had trouble finding Karen when she'd come to the Slow Joe? How many times had she blamed Joe's "mismanagement" of the train because she thought he couldn't keep the old steam locomotive running on time?

She pushed from her mind her fear of an accident. She'd never let her sons ride motorcycles and she was certain that Ruth would never have sanctioned letting Karen zip around the countryside so unprotected even with a driver she liked and respected, let alone George.

"I got Sandra to confess all of this only because I pointed out that Karen is half an hour late and you were frantic," Joe continued. "She says that Karen asked her to call you this afternoon with a story about Karen having to work overtime for somebody who called in sick. Apparently she didn't want you to come get her until eight o'clock because George was taking her 'somewhere special.'" He rolled his eyes as though he had a good idea what George's idea of "special" was. "But during her break, somebody spilled catsup all over Sandra on her way to make the call and she was so busy cleaning up that she forgot all about it until now."

He paused while Mandy absorbed the girls' convoluted scheme, then added, "I really don't think Karen's in any trouble, Mandy...if you don't count the hot water she's in with you, with me, and with her mother."

Mandy felt a new wave of nausea as she realized that the worst would not be over when she found Karen, even if her niece were unharmed. Ruth would hit the roof when she heard what had happened. The thought made Mandy shudder. For some reason she felt as though *she* were the teenager in trouble, the family member about to pay for breaking Ruth's stringent rules. Her sister had been so edgy since her arrival, she was bound to yell at her, too.

"She's going to worry if you and Karen are late getting back," Joe pointed out, as though he could read Mandy's mind. "Why don't I have Wilma call her and tell her we're going out for dinner? By the time we get this straightened out, we may need a bite to eat, anyway."

Mandy had trouble imagining Joey eating anything but a Hostess Twinkie, and she couldn't imagine having a meal with him under any circumstances. Few things would arouse Ruth's curiosity—not to mention disapproval— more than the notion of Mandy deliberately seeking Joey's company. Without thinking, she blurted out, "It would never work, Joe. Ruth would smell a rat."

Joe's glance hardened, but he did not reply.

At once Mandy said, "I didn't mean that the way it came out. I just mean . . . she wouldn't expect us to go out together. Socially. I mean, you're the last person—"

"You've already got one foot in your mouth, Mandy. No point in stuffing in the other one, too. I'll have Wilma tell her that you and Karen are going out to eat. I don't think you can keep from getting Ruth upset if you try to talk on the phone."

It was just the sort of thing Alan would have said, the sort of decision Alan would have made. A sudden wash of loneliness swept over Mandy. She had loved her husband dearly, and she had never planned to spend her best years alone. Abruptly she burst into tears, tears she couldn't hide from Joe.

This time he didn't try to comfort her; he simply pulled his keys out of his pocket and opened the office door. Steadfastly he declared, "Time for tears later, Mandy. Right now we've got a job to do. You'll be okay as soon as we find her."

To her surprise, Mandy straightened with fresh courage. Joe Henderson hadn't babied her, but he'd managed to say just what she needed to hear.

As they hurried toward the parking lot, he said, "Let's take my car."

"Why?" Mandy asked, astonished, somehow, that Joey had learned to drive. She had no doubt that he would be a maniac driver, a menace to every car on the road.

Yet now he replied tersely, "You're nearly hysterical, Mandy. I don't think I'd feel safe with you at the wheel. Besides, you're more or less a newcomer to Redpoint and I know this area like the back of my hand."

Mandy couldn't argue with that logic, so she swallowed her discomfort as Joe ushered her toward a late-model blue station wagon that looked suspiciously like a family man's car, not a scrappy teen's hot rod. Joe unlocked the passenger door for Mandy, tossed two bats and a catcher's glove into the back seat, then waited until she was buckled in before he took his place behind the wheel.

He drove carefully but at a good clip, and Mandy could find no fault with his technique. In fact, she could find no fault with the way he was handling the search for Karen, period. They checked Hamburger Heaven and found out that George had indeed left work at noon; then they checked the boy's house and learned that he'd planned to spend the day "on a picnic," presumably with his friends. But they found his best friend washing his father's car and another pal packing for a summer vacation with his family. It was the third name they got that made Joey smile.

"Bingo," he declared.

"You know something?" Mandy pleaded.

"This kid used to work for me. He'll tell me the truth."

The boy in question, however, was not available for at least an hour, and during that time Joey insisted on checking every single hangout known to local lovers. As he drove to each site—checking for George's Suzuki—Joey started telling Mandy stories. At first his efforts were clumsy and poorly disguised attempts to calm her down, but she appreciated his efforts nonetheless. By the time they'd located the boy who'd once worked for Joe—who reported that George often took girls to the natural ramada in the mountains about half an hour to the south of town—she'd actually found herself enjoying the rich timbre of his voice.

While Mandy was still upset, her great panic had subsided during the course of their search. By now she was reasonably sure that while Karen had deceived her, there was no chance that George was sufficiently besotted with Karen to run off with her, let alone sneak off to Nevada for a quickie wedding. She was still afraid that the teenage lovers' afternoons together might result in an unplanned pregnancy, but she realized that this possibility was no more likely at the moment than it had been on any number of other days. Surely if Karen had the gumption to plan these sneaky assignations she'd also have had the foresight to plan birth control, if necessary, ahead of time.

"I'll never forget the time Sarah and I were camping and we stumbled over a sleeping bear," Joey declared as they headed out of town armed with a hastily drawn paper bag map of the gravel road the led toward the ramada.

"Sarah?" Mandy prompted, assuming he meant one of his daughters.

"My wife. Or rather, ex-wife."

"Ah, the one who left you because of your train addiction?" Her tone was teasing as she harkened back to their conversation on the day she'd first arrived at the Slow Joe Loco, but to her surprise, Joe answered her rather seriously.

"Actually that *is* why she left me. I wasn't kidding." He gave Mandy a sad smile. "She says she got tired of coming in second place to a caboose."

Instinctively Mandy asked, "Did she really...come in second place?"

Joey shrugged. "By the end, yes, to be perfectly frank. But that wasn't because the train came first. It was only because I got so much more satisfaction out of refurbishing the Slow Joe than I got out of my marriage to Sarah." He looked embarrassed now, as though he were revealing some kind of secret. He had an appealing grin that showed off his bright white teeth, and to Mandy's surprise, her answering smile came quite naturally.

"Don't get me wrong, Mandy," he insisted. "I'm not a bitter ex-spouse and I'm not saying that Sarah was entirely in the wrong. We just...well, we were childhood sweethearts who thought the same tastes in rock'n'roll and fast food were the sort of shared values that would take us through life. We got married when we were only twenty and we held on longer than we should have because of the kids. By the time they were all out of diapers, we both knew that we just didn't enjoy being together very much anymore. When Sarah realized she was on the brink of having an affair, she told me rather kindly that she thought maybe we should think about going our separate ways while we could still part as friends."

Mandy remembered the anguish Ruth had endured when she'd discovered that her husband had been meeting his floozy almost daily in their own home while Ruth had been off at work. Her bitterness toward her ex was still virulent after all these years. Joey's complacence was amazing.

"My pride was hurt, but not nearly as much as it would have been if she'd actually been unfaithful to me while we were still sharing the same bed," he continued. "We talked it out, and we talked to the kids. Sarah gave me a few months to refurbish the conductor's house and we amicably tried to balance out the money and the kids' time with each of us." He glanced at Mandy and managed a grin. "There were...well...some unhappy moments, but what's the point of dwelling on them? Life's too short to get hung up on misery. There's always some new adventure waiting around the bend."

Feeling the need to give credit where credit was due, Mandy commented, "I think that's the most mature response to a divorce I've every heard, Joey. I'm proud of you."

Joe's laugh was a harsh bark. "You're *proud* of me? That'll be the day." He glowered at her. "If you think I told you about my divorce to win your approval, Mandy, think again."

She stared at him, embarrassed and a little miffed that he'd taken her well-meaning compliment the wrong way. "Why did you tell me, Joey? Did you run out of other stories to take my mind off of Karen?"

"Something like that." Ruefully he shook his head, then muttered to himself, "I must be getting old. For a moment there, I almost forgot."

"Forgot what?" she prodded.

Joe snorted. "Who you are. Who you think I still am." He turned to face her squarely. "But you never forget, do you, Miss Sawyer?"

Before Mandy could reply, the road widened, revealing a motorcycle parked in a clearing right where Joe had expected it to be. Her stomach tightened as she realized that there were no helmets near the bike; the smallest accident could have been fatal.

Joe soberly pulled the station wagon over, killed the engine and climbed out just as Mandy did. For a moment they stood perfectly still, listening to the soft murmurs floating up to them from a shady tree near the riverbank. Joe's eyes met Mandy's, then he headed toward the half path in the bushes and hiked toward the stream with Mandy right behind them.

They hadn't gone more than twenty yards when they spotted two nubile young bodies, more or less intertwined. They were still dressed, but just barely. Karen's coverall straps were twisted around her slim young waist and the blue shirt Mandy had ironed just that morning was completely unbuttoned and hopelessly wrinkled. Her bra was askew. George—who wore a hamburger-stand uniform liberally stained with grease—was lying more or less on top of Karen; both of his hands were groping for her small, naked breasts. Her arms were wrapped around his shoulders and their mouths were merged in a rapturous, slobbery kiss.

"Excuse me, Karen," Joe declared in a remarkably businesslike manner. As the girl gasped—rolling away from the boy and trying to cover her breasts all in one hysterical, clumsy maneuver—he continued prosaically, "I thought you might like to know that it's customary, when one tires of a job, to give two weeks' notice to the boss instead of feigning illness until you get caught."

Karen's eyes grew huge, terrified, as she spied Mandy in back of Joe. She cringed like a wounded animal, unable to face either her aunt or her employer as she struggled desperately to button her blouse. Her fingers were shaking so much that she found the task nearly insurmountable; she finally gave up when she had only three buttons fastened, oblivious to the fact that she'd stuck them in the wrong holes.

George was slower to react, and he looked more angry than chagrined as he growled, "You had no right to follow us out here!"

Mandy took an instinctive step forward, but Joe grabbed her arm with such force that she couldn't move. As her eyes flashed up to meet his, she saw his lips form a whispered message that took her a moment to decipher and longer to understand: "Let her hate *me*."

Then he declared tightly to George, "I beg to differ with you, sport. In the first place, I don't pay this sixteen-year-old girl to roll around in the grass on Tuesday afternoons. Neither do I pay her to lie to my staff. And I sure as hell don't pay her to cost me two hours of valuable time soothing a hysterical aunt."

"That ain't my problem," the boy replied sullenly.

"No, it's not. That's *her* problem. Your problem is that you're nineteen years old, George, so you can be convicted of statutory rape if you have sex with this girl whether it's morning, noon or night. And you don't have to worry about whether or not she's got the guts to press charges. There's not doubt in my mind that her Aunt Mandy does." He leaned forward, glaring ever intently at the boy. Then, in a low, feral tone, he added, "And so do I."

George didn't even glance at Karen. He struggled to his feet, grabbing for his keys, which had fallen into the grass. "I didn't do *nothin'* like that!" he whined. "I just... touched her some. And I ain't gonna see her no more, so you just back off, okay?"

"No, George! No!" Karen cried out like a wound animal.

Joe let her anguished words hiss through the open air. George did not answer her; he never even glanced in her direction. A kittenish whimper broke from Karen's throat as she realized that her white knight was flagrantly abandoning her.

Joe said tensely, "I'll hold you to that promise, sport. Now get out of here."

George's lower lip puckered, but he stomped up the path without another word. Silence owned the glen as the three of them waited for the Suzuki's engine to roar to life. Joe's fingers still dug into Mandy's arm with a furious kind of intimacy that somehow gave her strength. She tried to concentrate on the dull pain instead of the sound of Karen's quiet sobbing.

Unable to bear anymore, Mandy hurried to Karen's side and put her arms around her. Karen's only response was to cover her face with her hands and sob even harder.

"Karen . . . honey . . . let's go home and get you cleaned up. Mr. Henderson has to get back to work and—"

"I *hate* you!" Karen suddenly cried out.

For a moment Mandy rocked with the shock, but found herself feeling both guilty and relieved to see that her niece was staring at Joe, hurling the terrible words in his direction. "You ruined my life!"

Joe stared at her, unmoving, but not, Mandy was certain, unmoved. He glanced at Mandy, his mahogany eyes full of sympathy, before he said softly, "I think I'll wait for you two in the car."

Mandy felt a warm rush of gratitude as she realized what Joe had just done for her. With compassionate foresight, he'd held her back, making sure that *he'd* knocked the crown off Karen's idol, that *he'd* rebuked the rebellious girl with the harsh words that had to be said. He had known that when he was done, when George was gone, when everything was over, Karen would have to hate somebody. Better Joe Henderson than the aunt whom she loved.

As Mandy watched Joe march up the path—his long legs striding, his strong jaw firmly set—she realized that it was the first time Joe Henderson had ever walked away from her that she'd been sorry to see him go.

CHAPTER FOUR

IT WAS NEARLY TEN when the phone rang, but Joe was a long way from sleep. He knew that his foul mood all evening was due to that terrible scene with young Karen Hayward by the Redpoint River. Even with twenty-twenty hindsight, he wasn't sure that he would have done things any differently, but he still felt lousy about everything he'd said to the girl. He suspected that when she remembered this day—which she probably would for the rest of her life—it would be her mortification and her abandonment by her first love that would linger most painfully. The fact that she'd lied to her family and her boss would probably get lost in the shuffle.

And then there was Mandy. Joe didn't have the slightest idea what had happened with *her*. She'd stormed into his office as huffy Miss Sawyer, then promptly collapsed into a vulnerable female he couldn't possibly hate. For two solid hours he'd devoted himself to soothing a stranger in distress—a delectable, immensely feminine stranger in distress—ignoring Mandy's past and thinking only about her present. He'd been astounded that he'd actually managed to let his guard down enough to talk about Sarah…and furious when she'd patronizingly praised him for turning out all right!

Joe got to the phone on the fourth ring, and he knew he didn't sound too friendly when he barked, "Hello."

"Joe?" It was a woman's voice, a lot like Mandy Larkin's.

Ridiculous, he told himself. *I'm just as likely to get a personal call from George Bush.*

He was stunned to hear her say, "This is Mandy Larkin. I'm sorry to bother you at home, but I . . . I guess I just—"

"It's okay, Mandy," Joe assured her when he recovered from his shock enough to speak. It was inconceivable for Mandy to call him at the office, let alone at home. Instantly his mind started racing for explanations. Had she left her purse in his car? Or some article of Karen's clothing? No, he decided, she probably needed to clarify Karen's job situation. Assuming the teenager still had any job to clarify. Joe hadn't quite decided what to do about that. "I've been thinking about Karen all evening," he confessed. "How is she?"

Mandy's voice was strained. "Humiliated, angry, full of self-loathing. Right now she's sure she's the scum of the earth."

Joe couldn't say he was surprised. He took a moment to assimilate her words before he answered, "I'm sorry, Mandy. Maybe I overdid it. But I know she's better off without that jerk. I expected him to squirm, but I didn't think he'd turn tail and run so fast."

"Neither did Karen. That's what's hurting her so badly right now. I don't think she's really come to grips with the fact that she'd lost her job and just about destroyed what was left of her mother's faith in her. I think she caved into George because he called her a baby and pretty much threatened to drop her if she didn't . . . well, come across. I don't think she's slept with him yet, but it was just a matter of time."

"Damn that boy!" Joe muttered. "It's the oldest ploy in the book. Karen's such a bright girl. I would have expected her to know better."

"Women in love tend to lose their perspective," Mandy replied. "It doesn't seem to matter how old or young they happen to be."

They were strange words from the woman who'd once been so rigid in her attitude toward almost everything. Now, confused and feeling more than a little guilty himself, Joe said, "If you really think it would be in Karen's best interest for me to give back her job, Mandy, I'll consider it. But I think it's imperative that she go through the process here. Accept the responsibility for what she's done, apologize not just to me but to you and her mother and Wilma, and make a verbal contract with me that she'll never lie to me or try to see George on my time again."

Again, awkward silence greeted him. Just when he was about to speak, Mandy asked in a wounded tone, "Is that why you think I called you, Joey? To plead for Karen's job?"

"I . . . I don't know," he replied, frustrated that she'd suddenly reverted to calling him "Joey" again. If she'd been anybody else, he might have believed that he'd hurt her feelings. "Frankly I was too surprised that you called to give much thought to your reasoning, Mandy. I mean, you and I have never been exactly—" he searched for a word "—chummy."

At once her voice chopped through the silence, high, sharp, shrill. It was Miss Sawyer's voice, the one she'd always used when he'd lost his homework on the way to school.

"Please forgive me for troubling you, Joey. And thanks again for your assistance this afternoon. I'll have Karen return her uniforms in the morning."

The turnaround of the conversation was too quick for Joe; he almost let her hang up before he blurted out, "Mandy? Hold on a minute. I didn't mean—oh, hell, I didn't mean you shouldn't have called. I'm glad you did. I'm just—" he was too rattled to give much thought to his confession "—I'm always surprised when you treat me like an adult. I never know whether I'm talking to Mandy Larkin or that old witch Miss Sawyer." That sounded even worse, but he couldn't seem to organize his scrambled thoughts. "I don't mean—"

"I know what you mean, Joe," she answered stiffly. "You've made it perfectly clear that the sixth grade wasn't exactly the highlight of your academic career."

Joe sighed; his knuckles whitened as he gripped the phone. "Mandy, I don't know how to talk to you. I don't know what you want from me. When I was a kid, I never had the slightest idea what it would take to please you. And now that I'm a man, I still—" he gulped, afraid she'd misinterpret whatever he said "—I still don't have the slightest idea how to make you happy."

This time her voice was quiet, confused. "Do you ... have any interest in my happiness, Joe? There was a time when you did everything in your power to bring me grief." Now her tone grew harsh. "And you succeeded in your mission, I might add. My first year of teaching was without question the worst year of my life."

"I find that hard to believe," he snapped back without thinking. "I would have thought the year your husband died took that dubious honor."

This time the silence was frigid; Joe knew he'd gone too far. Desperately he scrabbled to undo the damage, though he had no idea why hurting Mandy should trouble him. "Mandy... for God's sake, forget I said that," he begged her. "I just ... hell, there's so much anger left. Can you understand that? I know you're a different person now. So am I. But you left me with so many scars." He gave her a moment to answer, but when she remained silent he rushed on. "Look at poor Karen, how vulnerable she is, how terribly sensitive to criticism, even as a near-adult. It was a hell of a lot worse for me when I was twelve. Everything I did was wrong. I never got through a single day without somebody reminding me that I was a loser. Half of the time it was you! It doesn't matter whether or not I deserved your fury. I mean, it makes no difference to my memory. There was a time when I tried desperately to please you, and no matter how deliberately I sabotaged your teaching later, in my heart all I really wanted was to make you notice me."

Again the silence made him edgy. But this time, when Mandy spoke, it was with wonder and confusion of her own. "I find it hard to believe that the Joey Henderson I knew wanted anything from me but the joy of combat," she admitted slowly. "But if you insist—I mean, now that you're a man—that maybe there was more to it than that ... well, I guess I'll have to take you at your word."

A curious stirring welled up within him, a stirring that had nothing to do with Karen Hayward or the Old Miss Sawyer of his preteen memory. For no reason that Joe could fathom, he suddenly wished that Mandy were there in person, beside him on the couch, so he could ... so he could what?

"Mandy," he said slowly, "I think we have a lot of old business to straighten out. Maybe if we talked things over we could put some of these old hurts to rest. Could we ... meet somewhere for coffee?"

She took a moment to process his words before she replied, but she still couldn't conceal her surprise. "Oh ... I don't know, Joe. Maybe ... sometime—"

"I meant now, Mandy. Tonight." For some reason it suddenly seemed very important to him.

"Oh, no." This time there was no doubt in her voice. "I can't leave Karen tonight, and I think she'd go crazy if you came over here. And it would get Ruth upset all over again."

Joe knew he couldn't argue with her logic; at the moment Karen was probably sticking pins into a Slow Joe voodoo doll. "Tomorrow, then," he suggested evenly. "Are you free for dinner?"

"No." Again the word came too quickly. "I mean, things are going to be pretty tense here for a while. I think I should stick close to home."

The force of his disappointment astounded Joe. It had been a bizarre day, but what on earth was the matter with him? Was he actually trying to make a *date* with his nemesis? And feeling wounded because she was turning him down?

"Mandy," he asked suddenly, "why exactly did you call me tonight?"

"I . . . I don't know, Joe." There was a long pause before she admitted, "I guess I . . . needed to talk to somebody who understood what I've been through today." She sounded surprised by her own confession.

"Thank you," he said quietly. Than, after a moment, he tacked on, "I take it Ruth doesn't . . . understand?"

Mandy sighed. "Ruth is hysterical. I'm afraid she had trouble getting past the sexual angle. She asked Karen about three times if she might be pregnant. Each time Karen started to cry again and insisted she hadn't done anything that could get her pregnant, but if her mother was going to accuse her of it anyway, she might as well have."

"Typical teenage logic."

"I'm afraid Karen's not on speaking terms with logic at the moment."

"We all have that problem now and then."

Awkward silence crippled the moment once again. Joe found himself wondering what might have happened if he'd been able to look into Mandy's wide green eyes, or touch her trembling jaw. He was all in a tangle and Karen wasn't even his kin; he could imagine all the things that Mandy must be feeling.

Until this afternoon, Joe had considered Mandy Larkin impervious to hurt. Now he wondered how many ways had he caused her pain? Did the fact that he had been a bull-in-a-china-shop kid while she had been an adult really free him from all the guilt in their stormy, mutually destructive relationship? Did it make it impossible for either of them to ever mend the wounds of the past?

"I'm glad you called me, Mandy," he said softly. "I needed to share this with somebody, too."

"Thank you for listening, Joe," she answered, her voice trembling with some nameless ache. "I think I'd better say good-night."

He wanted to press her for dinner again—breakfast, lunch, midafternoon dessert—but he knew that she needed time to sort out her confusion. Would she be embarrassed when she realized that she'd turned to "little Joey Henderson" for comfort tonight—and worse yet, admitted it? Would she pull back and turn cold on him again? Or might they have paved the way to a new relationship based on mutual respect? And if so, where would it lead?

Joe had no answers to his questions. He had no idea what Mandy wanted from him, and he wasn't much clearer on what he wanted from her. The only thing he was sure of was that if they were ever going to get to know each other better, they'd both have to start looking toward the future instead of back into the past.

JOE WAS MAKING his daily check on the Slow Joe's engine when he spied Mandy's white Toyota pulling up outside the gate the next morning. Karen, dressed in shabby jeans and a heavy sweatshirt despite the summer heat, crawled out of the passenger side and literally slunk toward the station house, clutching a pile of striped conductor's clothes in her trembling hands.

Slowly he straightened, waiting for her to meet his steady gaze. Her eyelids were red and swollen, as though she'd cried all night. Joe hurt for her so much it was hard to remember that he was supposed to be angry.

At first she strode right past him, staring at the ground. Then, abruptly, she about-faced and headed in his direction. When she gave him a shaky greeting, he responded gently. After a few awkward exchanges about the weather and the return of all her uniforms, Karen shakily apologized for screaming at Joe in the ramada. She said that her aunt had convinced her that it wasn't Joe's fault George had turned tail and run; any man worth his salt would have stood up for Karen and owned up to their love in the light of day. She didn't sound convinced, but at least she was trying to accept the fact that she'd lost her first love.

Her poorly disguised pain touched Joe so deeply that he ended up offering to reinstate her at the Slow Joe . . . with certain mutual understandings. No lies, no false illnesses, and no George. He also made her promise to apologize to Wilma for her lies, which caused Karen to start crying all over again. Still, she looked a little brighter when she started back toward the main station house than she had when she'd arrived.

Joe decided to go tell Mandy not to wait for Karen since she'd be working all day. But the sudden increase in his pulse rate as her eyes met his warned him that he had more than business on his mind. There was something about Mandy that . . . well, dammit, that moved him. Maybe it was the unexpected sweetness he'd found buried underneath all those layers of defenses; maybe it was her vulnerability or her tender compassion for her kin. Maybe— it was a possibility he had to consider—maybe it was the challenge of proving himself to the woman who'd once ground him beneath her heel. Whatever it was, he knew that he was excited about spending time with Mandy Larkin again.

Her voice was tense with concern as Joe approached her car. "What was all that about?" she asked.

"A little contract renegotiation. I've given Karen a second chance at her job, like we discussed."

Mandy's eyebrows raised. "I'm still surprised."

He studied her soft lips, her cherubic dimples, the worry that still darkened her lovely eyes. Without hesitation he told her the truth. "She was bleeding inside. I've felt that way more than once in my life. When I screwed up as a kid, I would have given anything if somebody had given me a second chance."

He'd meant the words straightforwardly, but at once he saw Mandy's hands tense on the steering wheel. "Can you honestly stand there and tell me that *nobody* ever gave you a second chance?"

Joe glanced away. "All I meant was, I think she's hurt enough. I laid some pretty stiff ground rules, but at least she's not afraid that she has nothing left to live for."

Just then Wilma poked her head out of the station house and called, "Joe! Phone call! Brady!"

Joe's first response was to tell Wilma to take a message; he wasn't at all ready to let Mandy go. Brady, who had promised to call this morning with details about the tuxedos the two of them were going to wear as ushers in his widowed dad's upcoming wedding, would certainly understand. But then an idea came to Joe, and he quickly rushed toward the station house.

"Sorry, Mandy, this is a call I've been expecting," he called back over his shoulder. "Why don't we get together for lunch and I'll give you all the details?"

"Lunch?" she echoed. "But Joe, Ruth will want to know what—"

"Peggy's diner. Twelve o'clock." He didn't give her a second to argue. "See you then."

Before Mandy could answer, he ducked inside the station house, grinning with relief. He would have preferred it if Mandy had agreed to meet him on her own terms, but she was only going to be in town for another week or so and Joe had a feeling it was going to take a lot of time to convince her that... that what?

All of the possible answers to that question made sense when he thought of the woman he'd arranged to meet for lunch as Mandy Larkin, but they were incomprehensible when he pictured her as String Bean Sawyer. For that reason, if none other, he vowed to put his sixth-grade year to rest by the time their noonday meal had ended.

As he stifled a cheery whistle and answered the phone, it occurred to him that burying the hatchet might be easier said than done.

Especially for Mandy.

MANDY PASSIONATELY WISHED that she could have avoided meeting Joey Henderson for lunch. It was so awkward...so embarrassing. Although she'd gained a lot of comfort from their phone conversation the night before, now she wondered if she'd inadvertently opened the door for all kinds of future problems. Mandy knew—and she was sure Joe did, too—that it wouldn't have taken him more than two minutes in person or on the phone to debrief her on his "contract" with Karen. Oh, they'd discuss her niece over lunch, of that she was certain. But that would be only the beginning of the conversation. She suspected that Joe wanted to talk about a lot of other subjects Mandy would have preferred to avoid.

She also realized, as she arrived at Peggy's diner at ten to twelve, that she would rather not be seen in public with her most infamous ex-student. In a town this size, everybody was bound to know Joe's life story, and it was even possible that somebody might remember Mandy. How could she possibly explain what they were doing together?

Mandy had dressed with care. In a studied effort at nonchalance, she'd tugged on an old lavender sundress that was not yet shabby but certainly too worn for a date. It was the sort of thing she might wear to meet an old friend for lunch at a hot dog stand.

She wasn't at all sure what Joe would wear. His conductor's coverall's, perhaps? As a boy he'd always worn blue jeans—the same dirty pair every day—and one of three T-shirts, each with a negative slogan such as Here Comes Trouble or When I'm Elected President the First Thing I'm Going to Do is Outlaw School. They were always some garish shade of orange or red that overpowered his fair coloring.

Many seated herself in an obscure corner of the restaurant away from the street, hoping that no one would notice her. Not even Joe! But unfortunately, a middle-aged waitress arrived with a pitcher of water almost immediately.

"Special of the day is chicken fried steak," she cheerfully informed Mandy. Her beehive hairdo, decades out of style, made her look like a caricature of a waitress in an old fifties movie. "You want a menu?"

"Yes, please," Mandy told her. At least it would help keep her busy. But when the waitress returned to take her order, there was still no sign of Joe, and the next time she arrived, Mandy had to confess, "I'm waiting for someone. I think I'll wait to order until after he arrives."

"No problem. Who is he? I'll keep an eye out for you. He's going to have some trouble finding you back here in the dark."

"Oh...I doubt if you know him," Mandy said quickly. "I'm sure he'll spot me soon enough."

The woman laughed. "Honey, if he lives in Redpoint you can bet your bottom dollar that I know him, and if he's a stranger, I'll pick him out because he'll be the only one."

Mandy didn't doubt the truth of her assertion. Afraid that she would only make things worse by stalling, she said, "I suppose you know Joe Henderson? He owns the—"

"'Course I know Joey Henderson. I used to change his diapers. Besides, his boy is my grandson's best friend." She grinned, as if to show her approval, then gave Mandy a once-over. "You're a bit long in the tooth for Joey, aren't you? I reckon me and you are about the same age."

Mandy colored. The waitress was probably a few years her senior—and looked considerably older due to her lack of grooming—but her teasing remark struck far too near the mark. "This is a luncheon appointment, not a date," she said crisply. "If you'll just tell me when Mr. Henderson arrives, I'll be able to place my order promptly."

The older woman stiffened, clearly stung by Mandy's tone. "I'll be sure to tell him where to find you, ma'am. And I'll also warn him that you're not in a very good mood."

Mandy grimaced as the insulting waitress flounced off. Was this what she could expect whenever her name was linked with Joe's? Somehow he'd conned her into this public meeting, but Mandy knew she couldn't allow a second rendezvous even though the mere thought of him was enough to trigger a wild thump of confused anticipation within her.

A moment later, when a man shadowed her table, Mandy glanced up expecting to greet Joe. But her visitor lacked Joe's height and sleek silhouette; his broad girth was as wide as his merry smile. With his balding dome and facial wrinkles, he looked about sixty. Mandy was certain that they'd met before, but she couldn't place his name. Clearly he remembered her.

"Mandy Sawyer? Is that really you after all these years?"

Mandy offered him a tentative smile. "Mandy Larkin, actually. I got married shortly after I left Redpoint."

"I'll be damned! You're the last person I expected to see at Peggy's today. I've been interviewing all morning and I just ducked out to get a sandwich before starting the afternoon rounds. Are you still teaching?"

"Uh...yes. In Denver."

"Cold up there in the winter?"

"You bet. Even colder than it is here." By this time she was reasonably sure she'd taught with the man, but she still couldn't remember his name.

Suddenly he seemed to realize that she was just faking it. He winked as he asked, "You don't remember me, do you?"

Mandy gave him a sheepish grin. "I'm sorry. I know we taught together, but it's been so long that I just can't recall your name."

"Gerry," he prompted generously. "Gerry Cottonwood. I was in the room next door to you the year you taught here and got stuck with Joey Henderson. I'd had him in fourth grade—you cried on my shoulder a lot."

"Oh, yes!" Now it all came back to her. Gerry had been in his late thirties then, married with three darling kids, and supportive of all the new teachers on the staff. "Please sit down, Gerry. And forgive me. It's just been so long that I can't remember anybody in this town."

He chuckled as he slid into the booth across from Mandy. "I bet you remember Joey."

Mandy tried to chuckle, but the sound that came out of her throat was sort of a strangled rasp. "I will till the day I die."

Gerry's smile was as friendly as ever. "You took it too hard, you know. Joey was a hellion in my room, too, but I'd had enough good years under my belt to know that it wasn't really my fault. I mean, you can't win 'em all. When you skedaddled after the first year, I was afraid you might give up teaching."

"I almost did. Fortunately I couldn't afford to quit working and I wasn't trained for anything else. The next year I got a terrific group of second-graders and rediscovered the joy of teaching. I've had a few difficult students over the years, but I never had another year that came close to the hell I went through at Redpoint."

"I know what you mean," Gerry agreed. "Now that I'm a principal I have to watch so many talented young folks slog their way through that terrible first year. They don't believe me when I tell them it can only get better. I wish you'd believed me when I told it to you."

"Well, you weren't my boss, Gerry. And Mr. Erskin didn't look at it that way. He seemed to feel that if I couldn't handle Joey, I was a failure as a teacher."

"Mr. Erskin was embarrassed that *he* couldn't handle Joey, so he tried to dump it all on you. One of the reasons you couldn't make any headway with that kid was that Joey knew you had no administrative backup. He's a very intelligent fellow, you know. He straightened himself out in junior high and even got a scholarship to Colorado State. He owns Redpoint's historic train now and is considered a leader in this community. Would you believe it? He was a rotten kid, I've got to admit, but nowadays he's a terrific guy."

Before Mandy could summon up a response, she heard a familiar voice drawl, "Thanks for the testimonial, Gerry. I'd like to hire you to make small talk with all the pretty ladies I meet for lunch."

Mandy could not stifle the pink tide that flushed her fair skin. She couldn't think of anything to say; it was hard enough just to make herself face Joe. True to her memory, he was wearing a T-shirt and blue jeans, but he couldn't have looked less like the straggly-haired, hostile child she remembered wearing the same garb.

The jeans were new, spanking clean, and clung to every long, lean inch of Joe's enticingly masculine legs. The T-shirt was a heavenly shade of baby blue that was perfect for a sandy blonde. There was an appealing picture of the Slow Joe Loco on the front and the train's name was spelled out in an old-fashioned script. Joe's bronze belt buckle—also with a rendering of a steam engine—added to the crisp, casual look.

"My goodness, Mandy, why didn't you tell me you'd already looked up Joe?" Gerry asked companionably, oblivious to her distress. "It's always rewarding to see how well one of your students turns out."

As he waited for an answer, Mandy forced herself to say, "You're right, Gerry. Joey has done very well."

Gerry took in Mandy's discomfort, then glanced at Joe as he slid into the booth beside her—so close that their legs all but touched—and picked up the conversational ball as though the three of them often met for lunch. "So how's your summer going, Gerry? Are you about ready to go back to school? I know Ira's counting the minutes."

Gerry chuckled on the last ironic note, then answered Joe's question seriously. "Actually I've been scrambling around all week trying to find another teacher. Yvonne Calloway went down to the Navajo reservation for some kind of summer work and fell madly in love with an archaeologist who's based back east. Called me the tenth of August—the *tenth* of *August*!—to tell me she's getting married and won't be back. So here I am using my vacation to interview the castoffs nobody else wants! I'm beginning to think we'll have to start the year with a long-term sub." Suddenly he turned to Mandy and narrowed his eyes. "Hey, you're not free to hang around here, are you?"

Mandy shook her head at once. "Sorry. I've got a wonderful job in Denver. My fellow staff members are just like family. Besides, my home is there."

Gerry nodded, unsurprised. "That's right. I forgot that you're married."

To Mandy's surprise, Joe said, "She's a widow, Gerry. Actually I suspect she has no reason to stay in Denver now."

Mandy reeled at his words. Anybody listening would think that Joe Henderson was a close friend who knew her whole life story. A person might even get the impression that he *wanted* her to stay in town!

Clearly that was Gerry Cottonwood's impression. "Well, now, that does put a different light on things." There was a chuckle in his voice that revealed his amusement at the unexpected alliance of Joe Henderson and Mandy Sawyer Larkin.

Mandy tugged a paper napkin out of the container on the table and started to twist it between tense hands. She swallowed hard, overcome with embarrassment as Joe stretched out his arm along the back of the booth behind her head. He didn't touch her, but with a jolt Mandy realized that she secretly *wanted* him to.

Gerry's gaze narrowed somewhat as he studied the two of them. "Seriously, Mandy, if you have—well, any personal reason for staying in Redpoint this fall—I'd be grateful if you'd consider coming to work for me. The other sixth-grade teacher I just hired is straight out of school—long on energy and short on experience. I need an old hand in the other sixth to keep her on an even keel."

"Sorry, Gerry, you're barking up the wrong tree," Mandy insisted. "I have no reason to stay in Redpoint and every reason to go." The words were too crisp, but Mandy couldn't seem to soften them, not with Joe sitting beside her, his body heat subtly inflaming her.

It can't be, she told herself fiercely. *I cannot, I will not, respond sensually to this young man!*

For the first time, Gerry Cottonwood looked embarrassed. Pointedly he glanced at his watch. "Well, I guess I ought to be heading back. I've got another interview in half an hour."

"It was good to see you, Gerry," Mandy offered belatedly.

"Good to see you, too." Suddenly Gerry's eyes met Joe's. "Catch you later, Joey."

"At the wedding," was Joe's quick reply.

Mandy felt a moment of panic as she wondered if this was Joey's idea of a joke. He'd done everything in his power to give Gerry the impression that they were romantically involved, and now he was talking about a wedding? But before she could jab Joe in the rib cage, Gerry answered, "Wouldn't miss it for the world. Jake's been alone way too long. Is Brady going to be best man?"

"You bet," Joe replied, apparently having forgotten Mandy. "He's actually pretty excited about the whole thing, all things considered."

Gerry nodded with such sympathy that Mandy wanted to ask Joe what he was talking about—who was Jake and what "things" called for Gerry's sympathy in the midst of this happy occasion? But suddenly Gerry was saying goodbye, and Mandy was left sitting alone with Joe... entirely too close to Joe, who was still on her side of the booth. She could feel his thigh barely grazing hers—or did she just wish it were close enough to touch?—and her resulting arousal was impossible for Mandy to deny. The best she could hope for was to conceal it from Joe.

"I'm not sure what you hoped to gain by that little demonstration," she snapped, "but now that Gerry's gone you go sit on the other side of the table where you belong."

Joe stiffened, but he did not move. When he spoke, his voice was very low, and his warm breath played with her nearby ear. "I don't recall telling Gerry anything that wasn't true."

Mandy turned to face him hotly, desperately hoping that her thin cotton sundress concealed her stiffening nipples; desperately hoping that nothing in her eyes or voice would reveal her ludicrous longing for his touch. "I thought you were done with your old games, Joey. You told me you had no further interest in humiliating me."

To her surprise, Joe colored. He still didn't remove his arm from the booth behind her. "Forgive me, Mandy, if I said anything you found insulting. I thought you'd take my... vote of confidence in you as a Redpoint teacher as a compliment. After all, my children go to that school."

Looking at it that way, Mandy felt small. Still, she knew that Joe had deliberately led Gerry to believe that their luncheon appointment was a date; he'd never even mentioned that she'd agreed to meet with him to discuss her niece. And that was the only reason she'd come. Wasn't it?

"Joe, you went out of your way to give him the impression that you and I are... well, linked in some way. Romantically. If he spreads it around, it could only serve to embarrass both of us. And Ruth would have a fit."

Joe's eyes hardened as he turned ever so slightly in the booth to face her squarely. The motion caused his shoulder and arm to all but embrace her, and his knee, now bent, pressed provocatively against her tense thigh. The touch of their bodies made Mandy feel shaky, restless, out of control.

"I wouldn't be at all embarrassed to have people think you were interested in me," he declared firmly, his lips just inches from hers as he spoke. "You're an appealing woman very near my age."

"Joe, I'm twice as old as—"

"You *used* to be twice as old as I am," he corrected her. "You seem to have trouble remembering that I'm thirty-five now, Mandy. I've been married, divorced, raised three kids, run my own successful business for over a decade and served my country overseas. Any woman between twenty-one and fifty could be the right age for me."

Mandy tried to look away, but Joe's gaze was too compelling. There was defiance there—a brand of defiance she remembered well—but that was all that remained of the boy she'd known. There was a sensual power that pulsed beneath the stark declaration, a warning, perhaps, that he could reach out and claim any woman—even Mandy—anytime he wanted.

But he wouldn't want to, she reminded herself sternly. *Joey Henderson hated you with a passion. Even if he's triumphed over the bitterness as a man, the dregs of that anger will always remain.*

"Let's order, Joe," she said shakily. "I'm really rather hungry."

But Joe's hunger seemed to be for something other than food. For a moment he remained twisted in the booth, half holding her as his sultry gaze swallowed her helpless feelings. She knew that it would take only the slightest movement for her to slip into his arms; she knew that if she offered him the slightest invitation, Joe would make the first move.

Mandy knew the last thing she wanted was a romantic liaison with Joey Henderson; the very notion was absurd. But suddenly she couldn't remember why she wanted him to retreat to the other side of the table, or why she'd agreed to meet him for lunch, or even why she'd once hated him. She was suffused by the manly smell of clean soap, the sight of his square, freshly shaven jaw, and the unquenchable longing to feel Joe Henderson's masculine hands on the most sensitive areas of her feminine skin.

"Mandy," he whispered intimately, "I'm hungry, too."

Mandy didn't know if he was responding to her suggestion that they order lunch . . . or reading the rising urgency he surely read in her eyes. All she knew was that she was aroused, she was in trouble and she was going to need every scrap of willpower she possessed to turn the conversation back to Karen and survive this lunch with her pride and dignity intact.

She also knew that somewhere in the tangle of hard feelings from days gone by and the unexpected warmth of their time together yesterday, Joey had forgotten the teacher he'd hated as a child. Now, inexplicably, this virile stranger—this new, compelling Joe Henderson—was reaching out to the person he called Mandy Larkin, a new woman in his life, a woman whom he could conquer with the simplest smile.

And, for no reason that Mandy could fathom, something inside of her was reaching out to him, too.

CHAPTER FIVE

"LOOK AT YOU, JOEY!" Brady burst out when he spotted Joe in his tux preening before a mirror at the church half an hour before the wedding. "You're almost prettier than the bride."

Joe finished adjusting the royal-blue cummerbund and studied his friend, who wore an identical outfit. Brady had gotten a haircut recently and wore a hint of after-shave, but even in a tuxedo, he looked as if he'd just ridden in off the open range. "You don't look too shabby yourself, old pal," Joe assured him. "Are you hoping to impress that sweet little blonde your step-mama-to-be teamed you up with?"

Brady chuckled as he explained that the maid of honor he'd be escorting out of the church was Arleen's beloved granddaughter, but there was something sad in his laughter. "I've given up impressing women," he admitted tiredly. "Besides, that girl must be ten years younger than I am."

"Better ten years too young than ten years too old, I always say." The words were out of Joe's mouth before he could stop to ponder them.

"You do? Since when?"

"Since lunch last Wednesday."

Brady lifted his eyebrows. "I take it there's a story to be told here?"

Joe shrugged, not certain he wanted to go into the abysmal tale of his last encounter with Mandy. But since he was eager to keep Brady from dwelling on the last wedding in which the two of them had participated—Brady's wedding to Claudia, at which Joe had been the best man— he decided that talking about his own problems might be a good way of keeping Brady's mind off of his.

To say that Joe had been dissatisfied with the way his lunch date with Mandy had turned out would be an understatement. For half an hour she'd sat beside him, as fresh as a morning glory still kissed by dew at dawn, so close he could have touched her...while her eyes had ordered him to keep his distance.

And yet...there had been moments when it seemed to Joe that she'd been too quick to look away, too slow to come up with glib answers to his questions. When another old friend had dropped by to chat, Joe had turned back to Mandy abruptly at one point in the conversation and caught her staring at him with...well, with an expression that was definitely intense but most assuredly not hostile. If she'd been any other woman, he would have been sure that all the clues added up to proof that Mandy Larkin wanted him.

"Hell, Brady, it wasn't much. After the day we went looking for Karen—" he'd told Brady a whitewashed version of the incident on the phone "—I thought she'd softened in her hatred of me just a little, or at least figured out that I was a full-grown man."

"And you, I take it, have softened in your hatred of *her*?" Brady asked pointedly.

Joe slipped both hands into his pockets as he faced his friend. "I have never hated Mandy Larkin."

"You know what I mean. There was never any love lost between you and Miss Sawyer."

Joe shook his head. "I'd like to forget Miss Sawyer and just concentrate on Mandy. When I see that woman smile—rarely at me, unfortunately—I have a hell of a hard time remembering any good reason to dislike her."

Brady leaned back against the door frame and pondered Joe's words. "Has it occurred to you that she can probably recall plenty of good reasons to hate *you*, Joe?"

He frowned. "Yes, that's occurred to me."

Brady shrugged sympathetically, then winked as he suggested, "Or maybe she's got good taste in men."

Joe shook his head. "I'm telling you, Brady, I don't think I'm imagining her interest in me. It's just that obnoxious twelve-year-old kid she wants to keep her distance from." He studied his friend thoughtfully before he added, "Too bad you didn't move to town a year sooner, Brady. If I'd shaped up before sixth grade, I wouldn't be in this mess."

"If you'd shaped up before sixth grade, you would have had other friends and I'd still be the new kid on the block with nobody but Dad to keep me company."

Their eyes met. Brady looked away first.

Into the tense silence, Joe said, "In the loyal friend department, Brady, you couldn't have done much better than your dad."

"Then." The single word was bitter, hard.

"You've got to forgive him sometime, Brady. You know he only did what he thought was best."

"Best? For whom?"

"For you. And for the baby. You know he never cared much for Claudia, but any fool could see that she couldn't afford to be half a day from civilization in the dead of winter with a difficult pregnancy. If Jake hadn't offered to let her stay with him, I would have asked her to stay with *me.* Hell, Brady, if she'd lost the baby while she was still on the Rocking T you'd have guilt to add to—''

"I know what would have happened! You don't have to remind me. But you seem to have forgotten that after we lost the baby, Claudia didn't come home. Dad *told* her to stay in town. For all I know, he even told her to go back to New York! I still can't believe that I followed her.''

There were times when Joe couldn't believe it, either. He knew that Brady had been hopelessly smitten with his beautiful wife—and she, in her way, had loved him, too— but he couldn't believe that anything meant more to Brady than the Rocking T. After a winter with Jake—who had encouraged her to fight Brady's passion for the ranch at every turn—Claudia had gotten up the courage to go back to "the real world" as she called it. In Joe's opinion, part of the problem was that she'd just lost a baby and needed to spend some time with her mother and father back home. Brady, snowlocked on the ranch, hadn't been around to comfort her. When he'd finally been able to get into town, Claudia was already gone and Brady figured out that if he wanted his wife back, he'd have to go to New York to get her.

Brady did—only to have Claudia tell him that she loved him, but she just couldn't go back to the tiny hand-built cabin he called home. She wanted their marriage, but she wanted civilization more.

Brady had conferred with Joe on the phone; he'd conferred with his dad. For the duration, he'd gotten a job and an apartment in New York—he didn't want Claudia living with her folks another minute—on the assumption that his father's promise to "do anything to help" included a standard-percentage bank loan. Without it, there was no way he could continue to pay the mortgage on the ranch. And despite Claudia's proclamations, Brady still believed that if he gave her time to get over losing the baby and proof of how much he really loved her, someday she'd come back to Redpoint when Brady could afford to build her a decent home.

But Jake had turned him down. The ranch, he'd insisted, was the root of all Brady's problems. He reiterated his offer of a bank partnership; he said Brady could move back home. He would even loan him money to pay for expenses in New York or buy a new place in Redpoint proper, but not one penny would he contribute toward Brady's "insanity," Brady's beloved ranch—Brady's lifelong dream, which was just beginning to pay off.

On the surface, Brady and Jake were still close. Neither one ever said a bad word about the other in public. But Joe, who was close to both men, felt the gaping maw that now filled the emotional space where they had once stood side by side. Once they'd shared an easy camaraderie, a blend of quiet understanding and unspoken humor. Now Brady clowned incessantly when he was around his dad, and Jake never laughed at all.

"You've got to forgive him sometime, Brady," Joe suggested softly.

"No, I don't." The words were not as angry as they once had been.

"This is his wedding day. Arleen makes him happy. It's what you've always wanted for him. Don't rob him of the moment by leaving this unresolved, Brady. You've got a few minutes before the ceremony starts to make things okay."

Before Brady could reply, the groom himself slipped into the room. Jake was combing what was left of his hair with touching intensity; the expression on his face reminded Joe of how he'd felt on his first date.

"If you're looking for a place to hide, Dad, you better try somewhere else," Brady suggested with artificial cheer. "Arleen is sure to look in here."

Jake gazed helplessly at his son. "I don't want to hide, Brady. I just want all of this to be over." He frowned at Joe. "You understand? You know how much I want Arleen to be my wife—I just wish there was some way I could marry her without having to go through a church ceremony!"

Joe clapped an arm around Jake's slightly stooped shoulders. "It's okay, Jake. Brady and I won't let you do anything stupid. He's got the ring and I'll help you out if you forget the bride's name." Too late he remembered that Brady had gone blank on Claudia's name during his own ceremony—a failure, he'd wryly reported later, for which Claudia had made him pay dearly on their wedding night. Now, eager to keep his friend's attention on the joyful event at hand, Joe said, "Everything's going to be fine, Jake. But I think we need to get out there and start seating the guests. Isn't that what you're paying us for?"

Jake swallowed hard, and Joe shook his hand. Brady did likewise, but his hand lingered in his father's, as though he had something more to say. Joe quickly slipped out of the room to give the two a moment's privacy, but Brady followed on his heels so quickly that he knew no last-minute hatchet-burying had taken place.

When they reached the sweltering sanctuary, soft organ music was filling the air, and half a dozen guests were already sitting in the back pews of the quaint church that had been built by the first settlers in Redpoint well over a hundred years ago. For the next ten minutes, Joe greeted old friends and welcomed one or two out-of-town strangers as he ushered people down the aisle. He wasn't at his happiest wearing a tux, but neither was he as miserable in fancy clothes as poor Brady, who wore jeans and boots about ninety-eight percent of the time. Joe was almost enjoying himself when he turned around, heading for the narthex, and spotted a radiant redhead in a stunning mint-green dress.

The sudden lurch of his heart told him that he was in bad trouble; the speed with which he hurried to beat Brady to Mandy's side warned him that he was about to throw caution to the wind. With his luck, he'd get there just in time to help Ruth totter down the aisle.

She looked positively gray-faced; in fact, he'd never seen Ruth look so sour before. Vaguely he remembered that Ruth and Arleen were friends, which would account for Ruth's and Karen's—and Mandy's—presence here. But he couldn't think of any reason why Ruth would look so unhappy. He didn't know a soul in town who wasn't thrilled with this match.

Out of the corner of his eye, Joe saw Karen slip off to sit with Sandra. Dead ahead he saw only Brady's back as his best friend greeted the two sisters, then turned around with a woman on his arm.

Mercifully it was Ruth. She nodded crisply at Joe as the two of them went by, but Brady winked and stifled a knowing grin as he cleared Joe's way to Mandy.

In an instant Joe was standing directly in front of her, his warm gaze taking in the gentle lines of her youthfully freckled face. She looked stunned at the sight of him, as though she'd just spotted a movie star or a tuxedoed stranger. But there was no doubt whatsoever that this time he'd caught her off guard. Her lips opened in a tiny sigh, and sensual appreciation tinged her fair skin as she stared at him. Her awed expression filled Joe with hope for something he hadn't really allowed himself to dream of before.

"Hello, Mandy," he said softly.

"Hello, Joe," she whispered back. It was a church, after all, with a wedding about to begin; low voices were expected. But still her hushed tone moved him, spoke to some quiet part of his soul that she had never touched before.

Joe tried to think of something else to say, but the situation didn't call for conversation. In fifteen minutes, when the ceremony would be over, they could agree that it was a beautiful wedding, enjoy the cake and ask questions about the honeymoon. But right now he had no excuse to stare at her elfin beauty, no justification for telling her that she looked like a beautiful young girl.

Swallowing hard, he offered her his arm. It was his job as an usher, after all. But Mandy stared at his elbow as though the gesture were frighteningly personal until Joe whispered, "I should seat you before the ceremony begins."

She blushed even more. With that fair white skin there was no hiding it; her cheeks turned a gorgeous rose hue. Belatedly she drew her gaze away from his and slipped one small hand through the crook of his arm. Her fingers burned him right through to the skin.

It seemed to Joe that the walk down the aisle took a hundred years. Mandy, who had once towered over him, now seemed remarkably petite. She also seemed unsteady on her feet in those strappy white heels; he kept having to push her slightly upright. At some point Joe's free hand slipped over her fingers where they pressed against his arm, and she tightened her grip accordingly. Not once during that long walk did Joe look at Mandy, and not once did she look at him. But twice his thigh brushed against her hip, and his awareness of her feminine curves all but undid him.

He found Ruth sitting in a pew near the front, and he stopped to let Mandy join her. By then he felt the faint beginnings of a tremble in the delectable female who pressed so close to him, and he squeezed her hand just before he let her go.

Mandy met his eyes, just once, and her expression was a mixture of hazy desire and embarrassment. He had no idea what image his own countenance conveyed to Mandy. He tried to smile as he left her, but he wasn't sure if his stiff lips had moved, whether he'd offered her an invitation on his face as well as in his mind.

Nor was he sure, as Jake and Arleen exchanged solemn vows, that Mandy was watching the bride and groom. A dozen times during the ceremony Joe braved a glance in her direction, and every time he had the distinct impression that her attention was largely focused on him.

MANDY WASN'T SURE how she survived the wedding. At first she told herself that she kept staring at Joe because he was the only person in the wedding party that she knew personally; the fact that he looked absolutely irresistible in that slick tuxedo could not possibly have a thing to do with it!

It was a charming ceremony. When it was over, the middle-aged bride and groom exchanged a chaste but tender kiss and walked down the aisle holding hands. The ushers followed suit; Joe left with the beautiful brunette bridesmaid on his arm. The girl was in her early twenties, and she was too young for Joe. Mandy didn't know why she was so certain of that fact, but she knew that the two of them were worlds apart in life experiences. Joe was a father, a businessman, a man who knew how to deal with a troubled teenager. The pretty girl on his arm still had one foot in adolescence herself.

"I want you to keep an eye on Karen," Ruth declared as they left the sanctuary. "Make sure she doesn't have a chance to slip away. That boy could be anywhere."

Mandy made no comment. Since that terrible incident at the ramada, Karen had stopped talking about George, stopped demanding to see him, which could either mean she'd given him up or—it was not impossible—had found a secret way to meet him. She'd been quiet and courteous to both her mother and her aunt. Still, Ruth grilled her daily, as though she were certain that with enough pressure, Karen would confess to yet other heinous crimes she had committed. Things were so tense between mother and daughter that Mandy hated to think of the two of them living alone together after she returned to Denver. In fact, she'd already decided to postpone her trip for another week or two, hoping to smooth things out a bit. After all these years in the classroom, she could get ready for school in just a few days if she had to.

Mandy tried not to think about September as she followed Ruth across the street to the wood-and-brick hotel—surely a hundred years old or older—where the reception was to be held. Even now, in the early evening, the small historic building, devoid of air conditioning, was unbearable for more than half an hour at a time. Ruth had complained about the heat all afternoon and looked fatigued—which she claimed was the result of sleeplessness since Karen had "betrayed" her—so Mandy suggested that they skip the receiving line and offer congratulations to the bride and groom later. It was, she assured herself, strictly coincidental that once the formal receiving line was dissolved, she'd be able to approach Jake and Arleen without having to shake hands with Joe Henderson in his tuxedo-clad splendor.

Flowers of every description filled the large wicker baskets on the grass outside of the hotel. The three-tiered wedding cake, which adorned a long table in the lobby, was flanked with napkins embroidered with the words "Arleen and Jake, From Now Until Forever." The parking lot that the hotel shared with the Slow Joe Loco had been cleared and marked off as a dance floor.

Mandy had been to many weddings in her lifetime, and they always made her think of her own. But this was the first one she'd attended since Alan's death, and it somehow seemed...incomplete...without him. Almost since the day Ruth had first introduced them with a knowing look in her eyes, Alan had been Mandy's backbone, her conscience...quite literally, her better half. When they'd promised to love each other "till death do us part," Mandy had assumed that somehow they'd die together. And it was true that a part of Mandy had died right along with Alan. At least, she'd assumed that the romantic part of her had died until Joe Henderson had inexplicably reawakened the seeds of romantic need within her.

Mandy found a nice padded chair for her sister, and kept her company as dozens of wedding guests began to fill the yard. From her position, she could see the backs of the wedding party.

It was Joe's backside she focused on.

He stood between one elderly usher and the skinny, bowlegged best man who had led Ruth down the aisle. Mandy had never been able to study Joe so freely, never been able to appreciate that ever-so-enticing trim bottom and those long, well-muscled legs. Nor had she ever gotten to watch Joe in action as he hugged loved ones and warmly greeted strangers, showering each person with the same generous attention in spite of age, sex or beauty.

Mandy was surprised when the sudden thought occurred to her: *Joe Henderson really is a nice guy.*

"Do you know everybody in the wedding party, Mandy?" Ruth asked as she studied the group right along with Mandy...though probably with very different thoughts. Her eyes were circled with rings of fatigue; she looked on the edge of collapse.

"No," Mandy replied. "The only one I know is Joe Henderson." Her tone softened just a hair as she tacked on, "I didn't realize that he was going to be here today."

"Oh, my, yes," Ruth replied briskly. "He and Jake's boy have always been close. Joey never had a father, you know, and Jake more or less took him in. Sometimes I wonder if he didn't make a mistake, letting Joe and Brady stay best friends."

Unable to stop herself, Mandy asked, "Why do you say that?"

"You ought to know better than anybody how unpredictable that boy is," Ruth scoffed, still unforgiving of Joe's treatment of Mandy despite the passage of so many years. "Jake took him under his wing after Joey's mother died. It was less than a year after she remarried, poor thing. Joey was still in high school, though it's a wonder he didn't drop out. Jake always maintained that the little beast was misunderstood and could make something of himself if somebody just had a little faith in him."

"And?" Mandy prompted. "It looks to me as though he's turned out all right."

"Well, of course he's turned out *adequately* or I wouldn't let my daughter work for him," Ruth proclaimed, "though he could certainly do a better job of supervising his staff! But I sometimes think his wildness rubbed off on Brady."

Mandy felt a sudden sinking in her chest. To her surprise she realized that she didn't want to hear anything bad about Joe. She certainly didn't want to hear that he'd contributed to another man's downfall.

"Just look at Brady now," Ruth continued haughtily. "That boy just about broke his father's heart."

Ruth pointed bluntly toward the bowlegged man. He was good-looking, though not as handsome as Joe, and his smile seemed honest, though a bit strained.

"What's wrong with him?" Mandy asked, certain that her opinionated sister would tell her anyway.

"Well, after all the money Jake spent getting him through school so he'd join him at Trent Savings and Loan, he went off and turned into a cowboy after college. Used his mother's trust fund to buy a ranch in the middle of nowhere and brought home an eastern city slicker for a bride. He lost the ranch, of course. Lost the bride, too... and a baby, as I recall. Still won't help Jake run the bank. He actually works as a *cowboy* nowadays." She sniffed. "Can you imagine?"

After that Ruth proceeded to gossip about various other acquaintances who were unlucky enough to come into view. It amazed Mandy that her sister knew so much about people she didn't like and rarely saw. It was an uncomfortable reminder of how fast news could sweep from one end of a small town to the other. No big city newspaper could ever compete with the efficiency of the small town rumor mill.

After Ruth had demeaned several locals and started railing about one of Karen's friends, Mandy decided that she'd better go check on Karen and make sure that her niece was toeing the line. Happily, Mandy found Karen in a cheerful mood. Her niece oohed and ahhed over the bridesmaids' dresses, the flowers and the darling little flower girl who'd trailed the women down the aisle. She was still gushing when Mandy glanced up to see Joe and Brady Trent heading in her direction—or at least in the general direction of the fruit punch nearby—as the last guest greeted the bride and groom.

"Hi, Mr. Henderson," Karen greeted him awkwardly, as though she hadn't yet forgiven his role in her fiasco with George. "You look...funny. I mean, different. In a good sort of way." She blushed, then turned to Mandy, her eyes begging for help. "Doesn't he look great, Aunt Mandy? I mean, don't you just love tuxedos?"

Mandy glanced at Karen, then looked up at Joe. His mahogany eyes met hers with hope and some embarrassment.

"Not every man looks good in a tuxedo," Mandy heard herself proclaim. "But I must confess that all the ushers today look...striking."

"Why, thank you kindly, ma'am," said Brady with an exaggerated drawl. He elbowed Joe. "The little lady done gived us a compliment, Joseph. The least you can do is tell her you 'preciate her fine opinion."

Joe glowered at his friend, but there was no malice in his expression. "Mandy, let me apologize for this buffoon. My friend, Brady Trent."

Brady tipped a make-believe Stetson. "Pleasure, ma'am."

Mandy grinned. "The pleasure's all mine." She offered the cowboy-clown her hand, which he took gingerly and pretended to kiss. "I'm Mandy Larkin."

"Aw, shucks, ma'am, you didn't need to tell me that. What with your pretty red hair and snow-white complexion, I knowed you had to be that sweet li'l thing my buddy here's been jawin' about ever since you comed to town."

Joe rolled his eyes; he looked truly embarrassed now. "I really think that's enough, Brady," he said quietly. "This is a wedding, not a rodeo."

The incorrigible prankster grinned at Mandy, then surprised her with a wink. "I can take a hint. Come along, Miss Karen. Doc and Miss Kitty want some time alone."

On that note he offered Karen his arm and led her toward a second table where fruit and luncheon meats were set out.

"Forgive him if you can," Joe said as soon as they were gone. "Brady just likes to clown. He doesn't mean any harm." For a moment he seemed to hover on the edge of revealing something more, but as his gaze followed his friend, then swiveled back to Mandy, she realized that he felt obligated to keep whatever secret he wished he could share with her.

Mandy smiled uneasily. "I kind of like him, Joe. Does he always pretend he's a cowboy or does he do other acts?"

"Strictly cowboy," Joe replied, looking a bit more relaxed. "And it's not all an act. He's been roping and riding and dreaming of a cattle herd since he was a little tyke. He works on a ranch and owns a few horses of his own."

"Ruth told me that . . . he used to own a cattle ranch," Mandy mentioned. "I didn't get all the details, but I . . . I got the impression that he's had a hard time."

For a moment Joe shut his eyes, and he looked sadder than Mandy had ever seen him. "Brady's been through hell," he finally revealed.

Mandy felt humbled by the depth of Joe's feelings for his friend. "I'm sorry, Joe," was all she could mutter. "I don't know what to say."

Joe took a paper cup and filled it with punch. He handed it to Mandy—his eyebrows asking if she wanted it—then filled a second one for himself.

"You don't have to say anything. I guess I'm just asking you to... well, to cut Brady a little slack if you're offended by the way he clowns around. There's a lot more to him than you can see on the surface."

Like you. The realization jammed into Mandy's mind with such sudden force that for a moment she thought she'd said the words out loud. instead she blurted out, "I think a lot of people use jokes to protect themselves from exposing their true feelings."

Joe's eyes widened, but he held his peace.

"What did I say?" Mandy asked. "Why do you look so... so startled?"

He shook his head. "It doesn't matter. Do you want something to eat?"

"No." The word was too clipped. "I want you to answer my question."

"Or you'll do what? Send me to the principal's office?"

The words struck Mandy like a blow to the solar plexus. Had she really forgotten to whom she was speaking? Why had she pressed him in the first place? It was obvious that he didn't want to talk about jokes and feelings anymore.

She glanced at the bride and groom, who had started dancing; she looked across the yard for Ruth. Her sister was nowhere in sight. Neither was Karen.

"I think I should be getting back to my family," she said quietly, swallowing hard as she turned her back to Joe's piercing gaze.

At once he reached for her elbow. Her summer dress was sleeveless, so there wasn't a hint of fabric between his skin and hers. Mandy was stunned by the way her stomach tightened at that firm but gentle touch. She couldn't pull away from him, couldn't even tell herself to go. Suddenly she wanted to press back against him, disappear into his arms. Instead she held perfectly still, trying to find a way to breathe.

"I'm sorry," he whispered, his breath just barely grazing her sensitive ear as his lower half all but cupped her tingling buttocks. "I'm not at liberty to tell you any more about Brady, and I . . . I don't take well to orders."

"I know." Slowly Mandy turned around. He was close, too close, but he didn't step back and neither did Mandy. Their body heat seemed to sizzle in the air between them. "And I didn't mean to sound . . . teachery," she confessed huskily. "I just felt . . . slapped in the face by the way you cut off the conversation."

Joe took a step closer. She was almost in his arms. "You asked a question I couldn't answer without talking about . . . then. About the way I behaved to cover up what a miserably lonely kid I was. I didn't want to spoil the moment. The times are few and far between when you treat me like an adult."

His lips, so close to her own, were full and sensually curved; his eyes, such a rich shade of brown, bored into hers. In the tux he looked like a king. Not one thing about him reminded Mandy of the hyperactive child she'd once taught.

"Oh, Joe," she heard herself confess with a throb in her voice. "Believe me, I know you're a full-grown man."

A magnetic surge of longing charged the air between them. Joe's grip on her arm changed into an erotic caress. As his masculine aura seemed to surround her, Mandy struggled for breath.

"Let's dance," Joe ordered thickly. Then he took her hand.

Mandy could have fought him; she could have said no. But blindly she followed him away from the table, away from the crowd . . . toward the sheltering darkness of the far side of the parking lot. When his arm slipped around her waist, she knew that anyone watching would have recognized the moment for what it was.

A confession. A beginning. A whisper of longing that cried out for the merging of their hearts.

Mandy had no idea what had happened in the past few moments, no idea how to undo the damage that had been done. All she knew was that her body was pulsing to the music, pulsing to Joe's touch, and she could not think of any reason in the world that was good enough to turn her back on anything that felt so good. But as she began to tighten her fingers around Joe's, the music came to an end. Reluctantly, he let her go.

They stood there, not quite touching, a silent duo in the sea of celebrating bodies, transported to a world that only had room for the two of them. When Mandy raised her eyes to meet Joe's, her chin also lifted in an age-old invitation. Although their lips dared not meet, the erotic pulse of that almost-kiss vibrated between them with such force that Mandy squeezed her upper thighs together as she fought the rush of desire. When Joe reached for her as the music mercifully began once more, he was shaking.

Mandy went into his arms as though she'd spent a thousand nights in his bed. This time he crushed her against his chest, and her nipples grew instantly taut. His legs seemed to wrap around hers as they moved, and he brought his lower body just close enough to hint, to tantalize, to promise, but no more than that. They were in a dark corner of the parking lot, but propriety forbid them to get any closer. However, propriety didn't keep Joe's ever so subtly moving fingers from tracing circles around the most erogenous parts of her spine, and propriety didn't keep him from resting his stubbled cheek against her temple. No did it keep her from sliding her hand beneath his collar, teasing his neck with the edge of her nails as they danced.

By the time the second dance was over, Mandy was more aroused than she'd ever been in her life. With Alan, sex had been very pleasant, but it had never been *electric*. And somehow she felt electrified right now. She wanted to say, *Take me somewhere, Joe. Anywhere! Ten minutes in which we can be alone.* She knew it was irrational; she knew she wouldn't have followed him to bed right then even if she'd had the chance. Yet some part of her brain kept begging for a miracle, a way to ease this sudden wild hunger for the man who last week had unexpectedly filled her with respect . . . and tonight, just as suddenly, had filled her with desire.

"May I cut in?" A voice from far away intruded on the moment. There was just an edge of impatience in the voice, as though the speaker might have repeated the same words already more than once. "I promise you can have her back later, Joe, but Mandy and I have some business to discuss. I want to wear her down while she'd feeling friendly toward our dear little town."

Lost in the desert of shimmering desire, Mandy struggled to focus on the man who was tapping on Joe's shoulder. It was Gerry Cottonwood, the Redpoint Elementary principal. He looked complacent and jovial, part of the real world. Like a man who expected professional behavior from his staff.

It was Joe who got a grip on the situation and managed to untangle Mandy's fingers from his collar without bringing her sensual massage to the other man's attention. He looked remarkably cool, in control of the situation. Only his eyes burned with desire as he released her.

"I promise to return the lady in a few minutes, Joe. Why don't you get something to eat while she and I talk?" Gerry suggested cheerfully.

"Good idea," Joe answered. With one more searing glance of promised intimacy to Mandy, he turned around and disappeared in the direction of the wedding cake.

Mandy struggled desperately to get a grip on her feelings, and tried to smile at her new dance partner; she wondered if he could read the strange glittering in her eyes.

If he could, he didn't mention it. After a few preliminary comments about the wedding, Gerry got right to the point. "I've been interviewing all week, Mandy, and I haven't talked to one candidate I think is acceptable. I'm going to have to hire a long-term substitute unless a miracle occurs." He gave her a winning grin. "I'm hoping that my miracle might be you."

Mandy laughed and shook her head. "I'm flattered, Gerry, especially since you've only seen me at my worst. I mean, I'm a considerably stronger teacher now than I was twenty years ago."

"I don't doubt it," he agreed. "And you weren't too bad even then." Suddenly he grew very serious. "I need a good teacher, Mandy. I think maybe you need...a good reason to postpone your return to Denver. Maybe we can help each other out."

Mandy glanced across the yard at the chair where she'd left Ruth sitting and wondered if her sister's personality changes were obvious to anyone else but her. Karen was in no condition to objectively appraise her mother's behavior, and Mandy didn't know any of Ruth's friends well enough to ask for their opinions. Yet there were troubling questions in her mind about Ruth's condition. There were times when she acted almost...like somebody else. The fact that she'd let Mandy handle Karen's situation at work by herself was proof enough of that! Between Ruth's extraordinary fatigue, horrendous cramps and jagged disposition, Mandy was almost tempted to suggest that Ruth get a checkup...or consider some form of counseling. But she knew that Ruth would only take umbrage at any hint from her "little sister" that she might be in need of help, and besides, Ruth had always been allergic to doctors.

It wasn't until Gerry spoke again that Mandy realized that he'd taken her thoughtful silence for possible assent. She also realized that he had the wrong idea altogether about the reason she'd extended her stay in Redpoint.

"Well, I hope that whatever magic Joe's weaving on you will help convince you to spend the next year with us," he suggested companionably as the dance came to an end. "You know, his son is going to be in the sixth grade. With any luck at all he might end up in your class. Just like old times." He winked, oblivious to the impact of his teasing words. "How does that sound to you, Mandy?"

Quite suddenly, Mandy felt not a trace of latent hunger for the tall sandy-haired man who had aroused her just minutes before with such a simple touch. She felt only sick to her stomach...and full of shame.

Joe Henderson might be a man, but he was still a former student of hers. A student she'd despised! And even now that he was a man, Ruth still considered him a bad apple. If she ever got wind of the crazy notion that her little sister was sexually attracted to Joe, she'd go berserk! And Karen's behavior was already pushing her close to the edge.

How on earth could I ever give in to my ludicrous desire for Joe Henderson? Mandy berated herself. *To even think of making love to him is...unthinkable!*

And she vowed never to think of it again.

IT HADN'T BEEN EASY, but Mandy had managed to slip away from the wedding without speaking to Joe. When Gerry Cottonwood had finished making his pitch, she'd found Ruth, now putty-faced with fatigue, and insisted that they all go home.

Mandy was relieved when Joe didn't hurry after her, or call her after she returned to Ruth's. She tried to tell herself that she'd only imagined that erotic near-kiss on the dance floor; she tried to tell herself that she hadn't been aroused at all and neither had he. But her self-deception counted for nothing the next morning when she took Karen to work and found Joe waiting for her in the parking lot.

He was wearing his engineer's outfit, which made him look like an overgrown child. Yet there was nothing childish in his firm shoulders and solid hands or the brushy chest hair that peeked out of his V-necked shirt. A sudden vision of what else might be hidden from her view jarred Mandy, and she had to take a quick breath to steady herself.

Joe greeted Karen with a wink as she bolted out of the car, then knelt down to face Mandy, eye to eye, through her open car window.

"Good morning," he said gently. His tone was warm, but tinged with wariness. "You sort of slipped away last night."

Mandy swallowed hard. "Ruth was exhausted. I thought she was going to pass out."

He nodded. He did not refute her. Instead he asked, "Is she feeling better today?"

"Much. We all...I mean, everybody gets overtired sometimes. Sometimes we try to do too much."

Joe nodded, then said, "And sometimes we...don't try to do enough." His index finger touched her wrist; it was the simplest of gestures. To Mandy's amazement, the skin-to-skin contact filled her with fire. His voice dropped to a husky tone as he asked, "How about lunch today?"

Mandy pulled her arm away. "I can't."

"Because?"

"Because... because I—" reluctantly she met his eyes "—because I don't think it's a good idea, Joe."

"Why not? It sure as hell seemed like a good idea yesterday."

Mandy shook her head. "It was never a good idea. It was just an accident. Weddings are so romantic—you know. Everybody needs to feel sentimental, I guess."

Joe's lips tightened. "It's not exactly 'Auld Lang Syne' between us, Mandy. The only fireworks we're likely to generate is in the present."

Mandy took a deep breath and focused on the steering wheel. Even though she still had no intention of taking Gerry up on his offer, she stonewalled. "Joe, if things don't improve between Karen and Ruth, I might end up teaching here. Surely you can see how... awkward this would be."

"I think it would be *convenient* if you ended up teaching here. We'd have more time to get to know each other."

Now her eyes opened wide as she stared at him. "Dammit, Joe, we *do* know each other. We know each other only too well! That's the problem. Don't you see?"

"The only problem I can see is that you're so hung up on the past they you can't see the present that's staring you in the face! Something's happening between us, Mandy—between you, a woman and me, a man. Not some fragile first-year teacher and a pain in the neck, snot-nosed kid!"

She slammed her palms down on the steering wheel. "Do you have any idea how embarrassed I was when Gerry Cottonwood started making jokes about you and me?" she demanded. "The waitress at the diner did the same thing! Can you imagine what this town would think if word ever got out that 'String Bean Sawyer,' as you so bitterly refer to me, and little Joey Hend—"

"Dammit, Mandy, don't you 'Joey' me!" He took hold of her chin and forced her to face him. His grip was firm, uncompromising, but there was still an underlying gentleness in his touch. "I want you, Mandy, and I'm pretty damn sure that you want me. Now I'm asking you straight out—what do you plan to do about it?"

At no time in Mandy's life could she imagine a man being more forthright with her. It was admirable. It was impressive. It was scary.

It also made her ashamed of her cowardice. She clutched the steering wheel until her knuckles whitened. Then she whispered, "I don't plan to do anything about it, Joe. I thought I'd made that very clear."

For a moment he was silent. In fact, he was silent for so long that Mandy finally turned to look at him, desperately hoping that she could cope with whatever he had to say.

His eyes were dark, puzzled, wounded. "What you've made very clear—" he opened his hand and laid it ever so softly against her cheek "—is that your feelings for me are just as tangled up as my feelings for you." His thumb dipped down to caress her jaw. Warm fingertips grazed the shell of her ear, then slipped into her frizzy red hair and stroked her scalp. "Can you deny that, Mandy? Can you deny that you feel something special for me?"

Against her will, Mandy closed her eyes and swayed toward him. Never in her life had any man's hand felt quite so right against her skin. Never had it been harder to remind herself why she needed to pull away.

"Joe," she whispered. "I . . . I don't pretend to be indifferent where you're concerned. And maybe if we'd just met, I . . ." She couldn't say it.

"I've known you for twenty-three years. Are you telling me I'd have had better luck as a one-night stand?"

Mandy tossed her head and tried to pull back, but suddenly Joe's free hand cradled her neck and he stepped yet closer to her, squatting down to press himself against the car door. The warmth of his sweet breath fanned her senses. She thrust a hand against his chest to push him away, but her fingers seemed compelled to examine his shirt, tracing the stripes that ran up and down his muscular chest.

"Joe—" she could barely choke out the word "—please don't do this. You know why this can't ever be."

"No, I don't know. I know we've got some things to talk out, some things to lay to rest. But they're all in the past, Mandy. I'm a free man and you're a single woman. That's all that matters now."

Helplessly she shook her head, aching to be free of the strong fingers that were bracing her neck and tracing erotic patterns against the soft quivering flesh of her white throat. "Joe, that's not all that matters. I'm eleven years older than you are and—"

"That means nothing to me. It shouldn't mean anything to you."

"Joe, it's more than that! You'd be hysterical if one of your son's teachers led him into an affair!"

"Mandy, my son is twelve years old!"

"Well, *so are you*!" she burst out. "In my mind, Joe. In my memory." Each word was clear and crisp now. Of this she was quite sure. "I am still your teacher, and you are still a young boy in my class."

His gentle fingers ceased their ministrations, but lingered hotly on her skin. "The most obnoxious student you ever had."

She swallowed painfully, then admitted, "Yes."

"You've hated me all these years."

She stared at his chest; it was just too hard to face him. "I've had . . . unfriendly thoughts," she confessed.

"So have I, but I'm willing to work on healing the wounds, Mandy."

"Well maybe I'm not!" she burst out, finally meeting his eyes. "Maybe I just think the whole thing is too complicated. Maybe I just don't think it's worth the trouble. Maybe—" she took a deep breath before she voiced a fear she hadn't even known she'd harbored until now "—maybe I'm afraid that getting involved with you might mean falling for the cruelest practical joke that Joey Henderson ever pulled on me. The ultimate revenge."

Once the idea came to her, it was so frightening that it suffused all other possibilities. *Oh, God,* she moaned to herself. *How could I have been so stupid?* Everything she knew about Joey Henderson pointed toward exactly that sort of trick. He'd do it just for fun; he'd do it for revenge. Why else was he so eager to forget all the bad blood between them and push things so fast? In desperate self-defense she finished coolly, "Or then again, maybe I'm just not interested."

Joe blanched. There was no way he could fake the surprise—and the hurt—that suddenly shadowed his virile features. His hands fell off her throat as though her quivering skin had burned him, and to her amazement, she felt instantly bereft.

For a long, terrible moment, Joe stared at her with more anguish than she had ever read in those dark, wild eyes. It was a new emotion, one she did not recall from his reckless preteen days. But it reminded her of one thing she remembered well about all the times that hostile child believed that she had crossed him. Joe Henderson might be a calm and rational man, but the Joey she remembered was long on memory and short on forgiveness.

Desperately she tried to think of some way to ease the hurt she'd caused him. Secretly she prayed for the feel of his fingertips once more on her face. But as she struggled to come to grips with the whirlwind of emotions that was tossing her Joe hurled out his parting shot.

"I think you're right about this whole scenario being the ultimate revenge, Mandy," he declared in a dark, feral tone as he turned his back and sharply marched away. "But I think String Bean Sawyer is the one who finally got the last laugh."

CHAPTER SIX

FOR THE NEXT LONG WEEK, Mandy tried not to think about Joe...about the look on his face when she'd told him she couldn't even think about a relationship with him, about the way her body had tingled when he'd touched her. She trained her sights on Denver, where life was peaceful and secure. The only trouble was she couldn't go back to Denver until things settled down between Ruth and Karen, and things were getting worse.

Even though Karen never left the house except when Mandy took her to work—the only exception to her total grounding until school started up again—Ruth quizzed her whenever the phone rang asked questions when she took late evening walks. Sometimes Mandy went with her, and sometimes she went alone. "I've just got to get away from her for a few minutes, Aunt Mandy," she'd beg. "You understand, don't you?"

Mandy understood only too well. Ruth's constant harping, interspersed with bouts of weeping, made it difficult to have rational conversations with her...or with anybody else in earshot. When Mandy's older son, Kevin, called from Atlanta to share the marvelous news that his wife was expecting a baby shortly after Christmas—Mandy's very first grandchild!—Ruth interrupted with advice about pregnancy, labor and rearing ungrateful teenagers so many times that Mandy finally told him she'd have to call him back.

Sharing Karen's mounting frustration with her mother, Mandy slipped out the back door with her niece for a walk in the desert's healing quiet. For several moments, they didn't talk, just ambled along in companionable silence.

At last, Karen said, "I know you think I'm exaggerating, Aunt Mandy, but I really think Mom is losing her mind. I mean, she's always been hard on me, you know, and never made any bones about the fact that I was a mistake to begin with—"

"Karen, honey—"

"But she was never *weird*. I mean, when she yelled at me before at least I knew why. Either I really had done something lousy or at least I could figure out what she *thought* I'd done. But sometimes now I just say 'Good morning,' and she starts to rail at me." She turned to face Mandy, and the moonlight illuminated her incipient tears. "Honestly, Aunt Mandy, I'm afraid there's something terribly wrong with my mother. I don't want you to leave me all alone with her. What if she goes completely nuts?"

Mandy put her arm around the girl and gave her a consoling hug. "Honey, your mom is just feeling impatient right now. I think she's just especially irritated because she's been so tired lately. And she is, well, a bit disappointed with you because you lied to her about George."

"George!" she wailed. "But that was *ages* ago! I haven't heard from him since the day you and Slow Joe found us in the ramada!" Her tone turned bitter. "He never even sent me a message through Sandra or anybody. Not even goodbye!"

Mandy didn't know quite what to say to that. Cautiously she suggested, "I guess that means it wasn't meant to be, Karen. Chalk it up to experience."

"Experience? What have I learned except how lousy it is to have your heart stomped on and all torn up?"

"Maybe," Mandy suggested, "you've learned that you deserve a young man who respects you enough not to try to get you to lie to the people you care about to see him on the sly."

Karen hung her head. "Aunt Mandy, you can't blame all that on George. Or even on me. The truth is that Mom would hate anybody I tried to date. She doesn't like any of my friends, either." She straightened. "And they're nice kids, you know. Slow Joe even said so."

"He did?" Mandy hadn't expected Joe to continue playing a parental role with Karen after the way they'd parted that day in the ramada, but she was grateful for his obvious compassion. "What exactly did he say?"

Karen thought a moment. "Once he told me—I mean, a few days after George left and I was still feeling down— that just because I'd misread George didn't mean I should doubt my own judgment because I had really good taste in friends. He told me how pleased he is with Sandra's work, and Jill's and David's, too."

"I know Sandra," Mandy said. "But I don't think I've met David or Jill."

Karen grinned. "Oh, Jilly's that real tiny blonde who's got so much spunk and heads the hospitality crew. And David tends the firebox—you know, the part of the boiler that makes the steam for the engine—which is almost as important as actually running the train like Slow Joe and Grandpa Howard do. David just graduated and he's going to college in Grand Junction part-time in the fall, but Mr. Henderson says he's willing to rearrange David's hours so he can stay on at the Slow Joe whatever days he's not in class."

Mandy was pleased by Karen's description of her nice friends and even more pleased that Joe was trying to steer her in the right direction. They talked a while more, about

Karen's father and her dreams, then strolled back toward the house.

It was an exquisite desert night; the fierce summer rays had begun to ebb into a cooling quiet, which would not have been the same if it had been chilly during the day. In the distance Mandy could see the red rock buttes that jutted up into the sky, and she realized, with keen longing, that she'd never quite forgotten this staggering beauty, unique in all the world. It was one of the things about Redpoint she would miss greatly when she returned to Denver. Almost as much as she'd miss Joe.

Even though she'd done her best to avoid him the past few days Mandy had been acutely aware of his presence at the Slow Joe, and once or twice they'd had to exchange obligatory waves and terse hellos. And—though she was reluctant to admit it—she still harbored furtive hopes that maybe, in some other time and place, she could allow Joe to cultivate the seeds of longing he'd planted within her, which had taken root and refused to die. If only she could purge that hateful memory of Joey the boy from her mind...and from Ruth's.

The nights were the worst. Right after Alan's death, Mandy had often had trouble falling asleep. Nowadays she dozed off all right, but after an hour or two in bed, she'd wake up suffused with the carnal rush of a half-finished erotic dream. Her X-rated visions astonished Mandy. Not only did the Joe Henderson of her hot dreams touch her as intimately as Alan had, he also touched her in ways that Alan had not. In fact, he touched her in ways she'd never even *wanted* Alan to touch her when she was his wife.

Some nights Mandy woke up with Joe's imaginary hand between her knees, his imaginary lips tugging achingly on the peak of her breast. Once she woke up with him on top of her; another time she boldly climbed on top of him.

And one morning around five o'clock she bolted upright, shuddering with desire, from a dream that had climaxed when Joe's incredibly sensual tongue began working its way up the inside of her thigh. In the dream, she hadn't done a thing to stop him.

So why, she asked herself as Karen opened the front door to the house, *do I have to stop him in real life?* She had had her tubes tied when the boys were small, so she couldn't even use fear of pregnancy as a shield between them.

Just then she spotted Ruth pacing the living room, clutching the front of her ragged terry-cloth robe. Her sister was hunched over and her face was contorted almost grotesquely. "You've been out to see *him*, haven't you?" she screamed at Karen. "You think I don't know what you're doing when you go out at night?" She turned to Mandy as if for support. "'A walk,' she says. 'I need air,' she says. But she sneaks off to see that horrible boy and she thinks I don't know it!" She turned back to Karen, advancing on her slowly. "Well, let me tell you, young lady—"

"Ruth!" Mandy broke in, unable to quell a rush of alarm. "Don't you remember? Karen left the house with *me.*"

"And took off on her own with some excuse or other, I'll wager. She's so sly! Just like her father. But I've got her number now and—"

"Mom, I was with Aunt Mandy the whole time!" Karen yelped. "And I haven't seen George since the day Mr. Henderson and Aunt Mandy caught me with him! I swear it!" Suddenly she burst into tears. "I don't even *want* to see him anymore!"

"Oh, don't you give me that!" Ruth hollered. "And don't you raise your voice to me!"

Mandy took Ruth's arm, gently but firmly. "Ruthie, honey, listen to me. Karen was with *me* tonight. And I'm sure she hasn't seen George any other time."

Ruth's eyes rolled a bit wildly. "So now you're on her side, too, are you? Well, it won't do any good. She's still my daughter and I know what's best for her!" She turned back to Karen. "You, young lady, get on up to your room!"

Karen's eyes widened, then she shouted, "What good does it do me to be good if I get treated the same as if I were still breaking all the rules?"

Mandy thought she had a point, but she knew that this wasn't the time to say so. Nor was it the time to fly in the face of Ruth's lifelong fear of doctors and suggest that she seek medical advice.

And it most assuredly wasn't the right time for Mandy to return to Denver.

"HAND ME THAT FLUE ROLLER, will you, Ira?" Joe asked from the corner of the firebox in which he'd managed to wedge his lanky frame. "There's water leaking between this pipe and the crown sheet. I'm going to have to flatten the flue to stop it."

Ira, who could have handed him the roller and kept his distance, chose to crawl over the grate and wriggle closer to his father. "Is this the right one, Dad?" he asked proudly.

"That's the one." Joe took the roller, winked at his boy, then went on to explain the procedure as though Ira might be ready to carry out the maneuver by himself any day. "This is pretty tricky, son. You've got to wedge this spindle up into the flue and crank it until the metal is pressed flat against the side sheet."

"'Cause the boiler will explode if there's any problem in the firebox, right?"

Joe nodded, or at least tried to convey that impression without banging into the crown sheet that hovered precariously close to his head. "It's rare for a crew to survive a boiler explosion, Ira, and it's terribly dangerous for the passengers as well. Nothing's more important than safety, son. Nothing. Don't ever forget that."

Ira grinned. "When I take over the Sow Joe, you mean? When you're too old?"

Joe gave him a mock glare. "I've got a few years of life in me yet, kiddo. Grandpa Howard must be three times my age and he's still kicking around."

Ira giggled.

Joe loved the sound. A happy boy at the tail end of a joyful summer. A boy who loved his dad.

Joe had had his worries, as would any parent enduring a divorce, when he and Sarah had first split the sheets. But he'd been determined not to lose his kids, and mercifully, Sarah had been determined for them not to lose him, either. The funny thing was, he and Sara still had a lot of respect and affection for each other. They just lacked that magical oneness that lay at the heart of a good marriage, and had the sense to admit it instead of tearing their lives to pieces.

He wondered what kind of marriage Mandy and Alan had had...and what kind of man Mandy would look for when she married again. Since their last painful goodbye, he'd done his best not to think about her, not to run into her in the parking lot, not to ask Karen for any scrap of news. Of course, he'd bumped into her a few times anyway, but he'd kept the civilities to a minimum and promptly disappeared. He was still angry with the way Mandy had pushed him out of her life, hurt by the way she'd dismissed his frankness and his longing. He didn't want her to win another round by getting under his skin, and he vowed almost daily to erase all memory of her from his mind. But there she was anyway, lingering, lingering in the—

"Damn!" Joe burst out as the spindle slipped, pinching his finger between the foller and the flue. Abruptly he remembered that Ira was by his side, and he tried never to swear in front of his kids.

"Are you okay, Dad?" Ira asked.

Joe sucked his purpling finger. "Yeah, just let my mind wander for a moment there." *Damn you, Mandy,* a voice within him railed. *You're still hounding me, lady. Still lurking around the edges of my life, my memory, my hopes. Why the hell don't you go back to Denver where you belong?*

He tried to pound away the memories as he hammered the flue, but Mandy's ghost continued to haunt him. He's never had this much trouble forgetting a woman, and he was counting his lucky stars that Mandy's summer vacation would be over soon.

At least, he clung to that hopeful thought until Karen skipped out of Wilma's office with a message right about the time he finished flattening the flue. She looked so happy that he couldn't help but grin. "Good to see you so merry, Karen. Are you sitting on some wonderful secret news?"

"Oh, nothing secret, Mr. Henderson, but it's good news, all right," she trilled. "My aunt's decided not to go back to Denver!"

Joe jerked upright so quickly that he banged his head on the mud-burned edge of the firebox and had to swallow another curse. "What do you mean she's not going to go?" he demanded. "You mean not yet?"

"I mean, she's taken a leave of absence from her job for a whole year, or at least a semester. She's going to be teaching a class at the elementary school."

"Teaching a class?" Joe repeated, too stunned to make much sense of her words. "You mean she's going to be right here for... for a long while?"

Karen nodded cheerfully. In fact, it was the most cheerful he'd seen her for weeks. "You bet. Isn't that wonderful?"

Somewhere, deep in his pocket of heart's gifts for kids, Joe found a smile and gave it to Karen. But his lips stiffened as soon as she turned away.

MANDY SPENT THE ENTIRE WEEK before school started preparing for her new class. She'd made a quick trip to Denver to retrieve books and materials from her former school, arranged for her leave and closed up her house for the duration.

It hadn't been easy. Wrapping things up had been more than an exercise in prudent home ownership. It had been an emotionally draining period during which she'd found herself talking to Alan almost as much as she had right after his death. She'd felt a compelling need to justify her abandonment of their marital home, and had focused on Karen's misery and Ruth's unstable condition. Not once— to Alan's "ghost" or to herself—had she admitted that a tiny part of her was excited at the prospect of spending a few more months in Joe Henderson's part of the world. And the one night she'd had an erotic dream of Joe in the bed she'd shared for so many years with Alan, she'd awakened with more guilt than desire.

She knew that Alan had been gone long enough that she had no reason to feel disloyal about wanting to date again. But Alan would not have approved of Joe Henderson. He would have picked out someone older and more urbane. He also would have chuckled in dismay at the thought of Mandy hungering after one of her former students, and he would have told her sternly that there was something downright strange about being drawn to the only child she'd ever admitted outright that she'd actually hated.

He might have gotten a chuckle out of the irony of Joe's son being placed in Mandy's class, but Mandy found no humor in it. She'd spotted the name on her class list at once—looked for it right off, in spite of herself—and felt a tug of old remembered hurts as she gazed at that terrible name: "Henderson." She tried to remember the appealing picture of Ira she'd seen in Joe's office and took comfort from the fact that this time around nobody at school had gleefully pointed out that she'd gotten the bottom of the barrel.

Fervently Mandy vowed to give the boy a terrific year in her class. Not just to show Joe and herself that she could do it, but for the sake of young Ira Henderson himself.

If Joe's memory of sixth grade was anything to go by, she had a lot to atone for.

THE FRIDAY NIGHT before school started Joe picked up his kids for the weekend. He wished he could have taken them off on some glorious vacation, but summer was his busiest time and he couldn't leave town for even a day. However, he had promised to take the kids to a movie this weekend—a sci-fi adventure that would be exciting for all of them—and he'd already squirreled away all the ingredients for exotic banana splits in his fridge. His youngsters were heading into prison—school—and he wanted them to have one last fling before the bars clanged behind them.

"Hi, Daddy!" Sally, his five-year-old, greeted him ex-uberantly as she catapulted herself into his arms and wrapped her chubby legs around his waist. "Did you get the ice cream?"

He gave her a hearty hug. "You bet."

"What kind?"

"What kind did you want?"

"Chocolate!"

"I got it."

"And strawberry, too?" asked Lynne—attempting so-phisticated restraint now that she was nearly ten—as she sidled into the room.

Joe plopped his youngest on her feet and bent over to noisily kiss Lynne's cheek. "Not only strawberry but that orange sherbet that you like and Rocky Road for Ira."

Lynne grinned. "I bet you forgot the cherries and nuts," she said teasingly.

Joe started to tickle her, remembered that she'd out-grown that a few months ago, and casually patted her arm instead. "Old Dad never forgets a thing. Haven't you learned that yet?"

The girls giggled, and Sarah, coming into the room, of-fered Joe a friendly smile.

"Ira's almost done cleaning up his room, Joe. Can you wait five minutes?"

He nodded. He had friends whose ex-spouses created such delays as powerplays, but he knew that wasn't the case with Sarah. They had agreed long ago that they wouldn't let the fact that they were married interfere with the fact that they were coparents to these three wonderful kids and had to continue to raise them in an intelligent, mutually supportive way.

"He's not giving you any trouble, is he, Sarah?" Joe asked. He always felt a little guilty when he checked up on

Ira this way, half expecting him to go wrong the way he himself had. But he also knew that some firm but loving handling early in the game might have saved him years of grief, and he was willing to do anything at all, no matter how awkward or painful, to save his son from a similar fate.

"No, Joe, not really. He's just not terribly interested in hanging up his clothes, but that hardly makes him unique." She ruffled Sally's hair, then told Lynne to go put on a clean shirt. "By the way, the kids' classes were posted at the school today. Sally's with John Hanover and Lynne's going to stay with Meredith Carver because they decided to make that a combination third and fourth grade after all. Ira's teacher is new this year and I haven't met her yet."

A sudden lurch of forboding rocked Joe. "I think both of the sixth-grade teachers are new this year," he told Sarah, earning a surprised glance from his ex-wife, who knew that he rarely acquainted himself with happenings at school. "Do you know her name?"

Sarah nodded. "Larson, I think. I heard she was a middle-aged woman who's been teaching a long time. We're lucky Ira got her because the other teacher is a greenhorn just starting out this year."

Joe was struck dumb for a moment, curiously blindsided by the news. *Why the hell didn't I see this coming?* he silently raged. By the law of averages Ira always had a fifty-fifty chance of ending up in Mandy's class . . . better than that if Gerry still thought he and Mandy were exceptionally chummy.

"Her name is Larkin, not Larson," he corrected Sarah bitterly, overcome with a fierce paternal urge to protect his son. "You're telling me that my boy is in Mandy Larkin's class?"

The surprise on Sally's face turned into open curiosity. "How do you know so much about it?"

He fought the blackness that surged within him, glanced down at his beautiful blond daughter and managed to remember that he never swore in front of her. "Honey, I need to talk to your mom in private," he told her. "Please go to your room for a few minutes."

Sally's eyes widened. "I won't say anything! Can't I just—"

"No." He didn't raise his voice, but uttered the word in a tone that brooked no opposition. It was the same voice he used a moment later when Bill, Sarah's husband, walked in the door and offered him a hearty handshake and a grin.

"Hello, Bill," Joe said coldly, though he normally had no problems with the man. "I don't mean to be brusque, but Sarah and I need to talk alone."

Bill, a large, round-faced man who was accustomed to getting along with his wife's ex-husband, looked startled and a bit hurt. "Well, sure, Joe. I didn't mean to interrupt anything. Do you mind if I put down my briefcase?"

Joe knew he wasn't being fair, but he was too angry to care. "Put down anything you like. Sarah, would you come outside with me?" And he took a deep breath and glared at Bill. "And would you keep the kids in the house?"

Bill flushed. "Yes, sir!" he snapped, his typical good humor beginning to fade.

Sarah, mercifully, said nothing in front of her husband. She just kissed Bill hello before she followed Joe out to the street. Then she lambasted him. "I trust you have some good reason for being rude to all of us, Joe. If you did this very often, I'd—"

"Mandy Larkin is *Miss Sawyer*," he interrupted, his tone iron hard and glacially cold. "You've got to get Ira moved out of her class!"

Sarah stopped, stared at him and pondered his words. "Miss Sawyer? You mean, *the* Miss Sawyer? The one you used to hate so much?"

Angrily he exhaled. "String Bean herself. There's only one, God help us. You've got to get Ira out of there!"

Sarah laid a hand on his arm, the gesture she'd always used when she wanted to calm him down. It hadn't worked when they were married and it wasn't working now.

"Joe, are you sure it's the same woman? Sawyer's not that uncommon a name. Besides, you said she left town after the year you were in her class. She might even have left teaching."

"Don't I wish!" he burst out. "Sarah, I've talked to her several times since she came back." When her eyes widened, he tacked on defensively, "She's Ruth Hayward's sister. She comes to the Slow Joe to pick up Karen." That was the condensed version, and he hoped Sarah couldn't read between the lines. Intuition had never been her long suit.

"Well, Joe, maybe she's changed. After all, it's been a long time."

"Not nearly long enough!" he roared. "Now, I'm telling you, Sarah, you've got to get him away from her!"

"But Joe, it would be so...well, so rude! Besides, we don't know if the other teacher would be any better. In fact, you always say that a teacher with some experience is a safer bet."

"Sure, when the odds are even. But *anybody* is better than Sawyer! If she were the only sixth-grade teacher at Redpoint Elementary, I'd move him to a private school!"

"But Joe, the nearest private school is in Grand Junction! One of us would have to move!"

"Then I'd move!" he bellowed.

"That's absurd!"

He stopped, struggled for breath and tried to listen to how he must sound to Sarah. He wondered, for a moment, if he was being fair to Mandy—who wasn't really Miss Sawyer at all anymore—and to his ex-wife. There were other factors influencing his feelings, factors he wasn't about to share with her. But he pondered the situation, and—rage aside—he still knew that having Ira with Mandy could only spell trouble for all three of them.

He thrust his hands into the pockets of his jeans and tried to keep his voice calm. "Sarah, you know I don't usually mess with things at school. I trust you. But this is different. I *can't* let this woman get her hands on my son." His eyes met hers. "She shamed me, Sarah. Broke me as a boy. I can't let that happen to Ira. Especially when he...well, he's going to be starting sixth grade with a bit of a reputation for trouble. A reputation the poor kid didn't earn in the first place."

Sarah studied him for a moment, then acquiesced. "Okay, Joey, if you really think it's that important."

"I do."

She nodded uneasily. "I'll go talk to Gerry and explain the situation. Since there is another teacher now, maybe there's something he can do."

Joe took a deep breath. When he was at Redpoint Elementary, there had been no safety valve, no other choice. Sixth grade that year had meant Miss Sawyer.

Sixth grade had meant hell.

MANDY RUSHED INTO THE OFFICE on the first day of school, quickly grabbed the notes in her box and greeted the green teacher who'd taken over her old room. Young Patty Richardson, it seemed to Mandy, was practically trembling with all the joy and terror of starting her first year of teaching. Mandy, who would never forget her own hellish first year in Six-A, offered to walk with Patty to the upper grade wing while she answered her questions and offered consoling tidbits of advice.

It was already hot outside, but the sunlight was clean and fresh and invigorating. Despite her concern for Ruth, Mandy felt hopeful, eager, the way she always did at the start of a new school year. After twenty-three years of teaching, she still couldn't sleep the night before the first day in September, still started the day with all the excitement of a girl on her first date.

She wished Patty good luck and zipped inside her own room next door. Dropping her things on her desk, Mandy smiled with satisfaction at the American Revolution bulletin board she'd worked so hard to prepare. Briskly she glanced at the notes she'd collected from her box. The parents' organization had sent her a note welcoming her to the school. Two kids had had a change of address since last year. Another had been moved to Patty Richardson's room.

His name was Ira Henderson.

Mandy read the small note three times before the full impact of the message set in. Over the course of the years, she, like any teacher, had had students moved out of her class after the class lists were drawn up for a dozen reasons—some of them reasonable, some absurd. Sometimes she'd been disappointed, sometime relieved. Once or twice she'd actually believed that the switch was important for the youngster, even when she knew she'd miss the child very much.

But this transfer was different. Although no explanation was offered—and none required by custom or law— she felt Joe's hand slap her in the face, knew that there was nothing random or coincidental about the fact that she would not be teaching his son. Despite her apprehension about dealing with Ira, the bottom line was that she'd been prepared to give the boy her best, and she'd secretly hoped to prove to Joe that she'd learned from her mistakes. She really *was* a good teacher now.

But Joe had tried and convicted her without waiting for the evidence to come in. Joe had exiled her to a permanent bad-teacher hell.

And only Joe could revoke her sentence.

THE DAY AFTER SCHOOL STARTED, Joe dropped by the public library—a turn-of-the-century building made of old brick—to pick up a book he'd ordered on the changes in Soviet transportation since Gorbachev had taken over. He'd also selected an early Richard Martin Stern novel he'd somehow missed and snatched up Carl Sagan's latest epistle on space before he headed to the checkout desk where Joyce Williamson, going on her thirty-third year as Redpoint librarian, greeted him with sheer delight.

"Joey! I didn't see you come in. I'm so glad you're here because there's a new gal over in the children's section looking for books about Redpoint. I showed her everything we had, of course, and told her to read the old copies of the *Redpoint Register*. I handed her our book on the Slow Joe, but of course nobody can tell its history like you can. Do you have a minute to go chat with her?" She dropped her voice and whispered conspiratorially, "She's very pretty, Joey, and I don't see a ring on her finger, if you know what I mean."

Normally Joe would have done his duty just out of deference to the dear old librarian, but now he simply welcomed the idea of meeting an attractive woman. Any decent female who could help him forget Mandy Larkin would be a much appreciated addition to his life. He had thought that by moving Ira he'd be able to solve his problems where Mandy was concerned and lay the old sixth-grade ghosts to rest. But he couldn't seem to forget the way she could make him swell with passion...or drown him with regret.

"Sure, Joyce," he told his elderly friend. "I'll go say hello and see if I can be of any help." It occurred to him, as he dipped into the children's alcove, that he should have asked Joyce what the woman's name was, but he realized, a moment later, that he already knew.

Of course it's Mandy! he groaned inwardly as he spotted that fluffy red hair blocking the face of an avid reader buried in a book. *Who better than a teacher to be researching local history?*

For a moment he stood there silently, inhaling the musty smell of old books. He fought the unbidden surge of need always triggered by the sight of this compelling woman, reminding himself of how cruelly she'd rejected him. He didn't want to face her, didn't want to explain why he'd moved Ira from her class. But he wasn't about to turn tail and run, either, so he girded his loins and strode across the room.

Joe took a chair beside her, struggling to ignore her sweet, feminine scent. He tried to blind himself to the vision in front of him; he filled his mind with memories of her scowling face when she'd told him that she had no interest in him. He tried to forget that she had adorable dimples when she smiled.

When Mandy didn't look up right away, Joe found himself moved by the excitement that flashed across her vibrant green eyes while she read... and he wondered if she'd always been this eager to learn about new things. Before he had a chance to weaken, he said brusquely, "Good afternoon, Mandy. Joyce asked me to speak to you."

Her head jerked upright as surprise and—was it fury?— zigzagged across her pretty face. "Joyce?" she repeated. "I don't have a Joyce in my class."

Joe colored at the terse reference to her class, but he stoutly held his ground. It had occurred to him that Mandy might take Ira's removal from her class as some sort of personal revenge, but his son's well-being was not something he could afford to barter with. If she couldn't understand why Ira needed to be placed with a disinterested third party, it couldn't be helped.

"Joyce Williamson," he explained. "The librarian. She said you were interested in learning all you could about the history of Redpoint."

Mandy eyed him coldly. More coldly, it seemed to Joe, than she had ever looked at him before. "So why would she refer me to you? You're hardly an authority when it comes to research."

He stiffened at the unexpected jab, surprised, somehow, that Mandy had once more taken up arms against him. Their last few encounters had hardly been warm, but they had all been civil.

Suddenly she glanced at the books in his hand, even picked up the one about Gorbachev and read the title out loud. "The railroad must be the backbone of Soviet transportation," she declared coolly. "I can't see what other subject would hold your interest for four hundred pages."

Without thinking, he shot back, "Almost any subject would hold me for four hundred pages. *After* sixth grade I was lucky enough to find a terrific teacher who had no trouble teaching me to read."

Mandy's fair skin flamed. Her lips tightened as she glanced away from him. He knew he'd hit her below the belt, and his first instinct was to apologize. But she'd zapped him, too, more ways than he could count, and he wasn't going to grovel to the woman who'd so brutally shut him out of her life.

"Is there anything you want to know about the Slow Joe, Mandy?" he asked, forcing himself to maintain an even tone.

"Is there anything you want to tell me?" she tossed back.

I want to tell you that I'm sorry it's come to this, he ached to confess. *I want to tell you that I could have forgotten the past. I want to tell you that I didn't move Ira to hurt you. I just had to protect my son.*

Out loud he said in his most professional voice, "The Slow Joe is over a hundred and thirty years old. We sell books with more details in the gift shop. Call the office for prices and reservations."

"Thank you," Mandy answered rigidly. "Is that all?"

"Looks that way, doesn't it?"

They weren't talking about the Slow Joe anymore. They weren't talking about local history. But there hadn't been enough between them to hash over; after all, nothing much had ever happened. Yet what had happened was hard to forget.

Glad to be done with the awkward task—glad to be done with *her*—Joe stood to go. He'd taken maybe five steps before Mandy's voice reached him...a gentle, almost pleading voice he had not heard before.

"Joey?"

He stopped, turned around and wrapped the scraps of his anger more tightly around him. *Don't you be sweet to me,* his dark eyes warned her. *Don't try to kiss and make up.*

Mandy's eyes met his, eyes that curiously looked not enraged but wounded. He was reminded of the day they'd searched for Karen, when Mandy had been so hurt and frightened. When she'd needed him so much.

But it hadn't made any difference. In the end she'd cast him aside, blasted his pride, made him feel like horrid little Joey. If he let her break down the barrier he'd erected now, she'd only verbally slap him in the face again.

"What?" he snapped in self-protection.

Mandy drew back as though he'd struck her.

Shame gripped his insides, and he wanted to tell her, *How did it end up like this, Mandy? I wanted you so much.*

But then Mandy pointed out, "You didn't say goodbye."

He steamed at the reprimand and glared at her again. "It's a little late to be teaching me manners, don't you think?"

She colored even more. Her freckles made her look young and helpless, and for a moment, he almost imagined that she might cry.

"Joey, I didn't mean—" She broke off, sucking her lower lip in frustration.

Suddenly it all seemed crazy to Joe. A few weeks ago, he had ached for this woman. She'd hurt him, no doubt about it. And then he'd hurt her back—but not for revenge. Just because fate had forced him to move Ira from her room.

That's got to be the end of it, he counseled himself sternly. *Bury the hatchet. Say goodbye nicely and tell her you have to go.*

He took a step back toward her, but restrained himself from taking her hand. It would have been so easy. She might have taken it as a peace offering...might have taken it as a gesture of love. Either way it would get him into trouble. Indifference just wasn't possible for Joe where Mandy was concerned.

"Sorry if I was a bit short with you, Mandy," he declared rather formally. "I'm kind of in a hurry. Good luck with your research." When she stared at him, her aching eyes struggling with a question she did not seem able to put into words, Joe concluded more gently, "I've got to get back to the station. Have a good day."

"You, too, Joe," he heard her murmur as he marched briskly from the room. But there was no heart in her husky words, and Joe knew just how she felt. With things so strained between them, the day's glum fate was already sealed.

CHAPTER SEVEN

IT WAS FRIDAY AFTERNOON, after an exhausting but productive first week of school, when Patty Richardson arrived in Mandy's room and flopped down unceremoniously on the rug in the book corner.

"Whew! Am I bushed. They never warned me I was going to die of exhaustion before the first week was out."

Mandy gave her a sympathetic grin. She'd almost gotten over her unreasonable jealousy of petite, blond Patty when she'd learned that Joe had chosen her as a teacher for his son. Their encounter at the library had confirmed her suspicion that the younger woman had nothing to do with his decision. He would have preferred any teacher on the face of the earth to String Bean Sawyer.

"It gets better, Patty. Trust me," she consoled the young woman. "In fact, the worst is already over. You survived the first week."

Patty grinned. "Don't get me wrong. I love it! I just didn't think I'd be so tired." She sat up, sitting Indian style, and tugged on the hems of her designer jeans. "You know, Mandy, I've been talking to the kids about the science experiments I want to do. Bio-chem was my major, you know."

Mandy, busy correcting math papers, nodded. "I think you mentioned that."

"Well, I've got a great science program planned. The only thing getting me down is that so many kids think science is boring. I mean, some of them actually groaned when I started talking about chemistry. Can you imagine?"

Mandy, who had never had the slightest interest in chemistry, could imagine only too well. But she managed to say gently, "Well, some of my children aren't too excited about role-playing the Continental Congress, either, but I figure I've got enough enthusiasm to make up for it." Actually most of them were already fighting over who got to be Ben Franklin, Betsy Ross or George Washington leading troop across the Delaware.

Patty stood, approached Mandy's desk, and said forthrightly, "I'm not good at social studies, Mandy. It's so...fuzzy. I like hard facts to work with."

Mandy wasn't sure how to answer that. The very thing she loved about social studies was the give and take, the free flow of ideas. "Surely you encourage the children to formulate their own opinions when you teach science, Patty," she said.

"I encourage them to formulate theories and hypotheses!" she gushed. "Opinions are so...unscientific. So vague."

Mandy laughed. Science had never been her long suit, though she felt she'd learned to teach it competently over the years.

In sixth grade, Joe had loved the subject. Even within the dry confines of the old six-grade science text—which in those days was all Mandy had known how to use—his eyes had lit up when she'd started the fall with the chapter about machines. But later in the year when they'd gotten to electronics—after he'd declared war—he'd told Mandy flatly that there was nothing about the subject that *she* could teach him, and during science lessons she'd ignored him completely after that.

And you got back at him in the library, didn't you, when you told him he had nothing to teach you now, Mandy realized in painful hindsight. Her zing had been cruel and unintentional, but her feelings had been too raw for tact. She'd wanted to tell him outright that she was sorry she had denied her romantic interest in him after the wedding, sorrier still that he'd pulled Ira out of her class. But Joe had clearly been in no mood to smoke a peace pipe, and her tentative efforts at diplomacy had failed.

Forcibly tugging her mind away from memories of Joe, Mandy said, "I have a feeling that we look at some things a bit differently, Patty."

"Exactly!" Patty replied with such zest that Mandy knew she'd been had. "I teach science, well, because I love it! And you've got all these great ideas about social studies because that's your special field. Don't you think our kids would benefit from our... respective fields of expertise?"

Mandy studied her carefully. "What exactly do you have in mind?"

"Teaming. You take half of my kids; I take half of yours. They can choose which subject they want the first semester. The second semester they switch. Or we can switch at quarters. But *you* and *I*—" she grinned "—never switch. You teach what you're best at, and I teach science all year."

Mandy had teamed with other teachers before for various reasons. Sometimes it had been disastrous; other times it had worked out very well. But she barely knew Patty, and she wasn't at all sure how she felt about forming an alliance so early in the game. "Patty, I'm really not sure I can handle teaming right now," she hedged. "I've got a lot of other things to worry about."

That was an understatement. Ruth was disintegrating before her eyes. Yet she'd turned livid when Mandy had tentatively suggested during one of her calmer moments that she might be suffering from more than occasional menstrual pain and tension exacerbated by her troubles with her youngest child, and some medical attention might be in order. In the meantime, poor Karen was spending most of her time at home hiding in her room and Mandy was tempted to do the same.

But Ruth, who had bought Mandy's lie about the reasons she'd decided to stay in Redpoint—"I'm so lonely without Alan and the boys . . . why don't I make my home with you and Karen?"—seemed to feel obligated to keep Mandy company whenever she was home. This new priority of hers did little to sweeten her increasingly nasty temperament, and her annual checkup with her aging general practitioner—who had prescribed tranquilizers and patted her on the back as he'd told her how he'd lived through his own daughter's turbulent adolescence—had done nothing to ameliorate her wild mood swings, either.

While Mandy stewed over her troubles at home, Patty hung her head in a way that reminded Mandy of how very young she was.

Mandy finally relented in the face of those big, pleading eyes. "Maybe we could try it for a couple of months. Just long enough for you to get your feet wet and get a feel for what I do."

"Great!" Relief sweetly colored her young face. "You won't be sorry, Mandy! I promise!"

On that note Patty galloped off to her own classroom, while Mandy tried to decide if helping out Patty was worth the extra chaos that teaming might bring to her own class. Then she realized that her students might genuinely benefit from Patty's state-of-the-art science teaching techniques and enthusiasm with which she regarded the subject. That was a plus.

Then she thought of a minus. For half an hour a day, Joe's son would be forced to return to Mandy's class, and there was nothing that either one of them could do about it.

IT WAS STILL SUMMER-HOT in the desert, but after sundown, when both Brady and Joe had the most free time, it was comfortable outside, and every now and then Brady talked Joe into taking an evening ride through the red and purple sandstone buttes outside of town. Joe was a competent horseman, but to him riding was a hobby, not a way of life. He never tried to compete with Brady in the saddle.

One night, about a month after school started, they rode together toward the south, in the general direction of Brady's former acreage. It was a long, long way, of course, and not a trip a sensible person would undertake by horseback unless he had a week or more to spare. But Brady always rode south, never north, and tonight he seemed especially haunted by his former life on the Rocking T because the new owner had just put it up for sale and seemed open to carving it into parcels.

After several slowly loping miles, Joe pulled up his horse, took a drink from his old canteen and asked, "How far are you planning to go tonight, Brady? All the way back to the Rocking T?"

Brady pulled up his gelding, locked one knee around the saddle horn, and studied Joe in silence. After a moment he admitted quietly. "Yeah, Joey. That's exactly where I plan to go."

Joe felt a somersault of alarm. "Brady, when a dream dies you've got to bury it and move on," he cautioned softly. "I did it with my marriage. So did you. I know you love the Rocking T as much as you—"

"No, Joe." His friend's voice was confident, firm. "I *won't* bury the Rocking T. It—" he flushed "—it *calls* to me, Joey. Like a big magnet stuck in the ground. I belong there. I've got to go back."

Joe sighed. Who was he to argue against a feeling that strong? Here he was one hundred percent convinced that he had no future whatsoever with Mandy Larkin and he still found himself aching to find a way to gain her respect. Not even his urgent need to spare his son from the teacher who'd poisoned his childhood could alter his longing for the compelling woman who'd spurned him as a man.

Mercifully he hadn't tripped over her in town since that day in the library, but the hard words between them on that occasion had left a bad taste in his mouth. There had been a moment there—maybe more than one—in which Mandy had held out an olive branch. He could have taken it, but instead he'd snapped it in half.

It's better this way, he told himself. *We can both forget about it and move on.* The only trouble was, he hadn't forgotten about Mandy. And he still half hoped that she hadn't forgotten him.

"Brady," he said gently, determined to push her from his mind, "I wish you could go back to the Rocking T. I'd give my right arm to help you do it. But there just isn't any way."

Brady's jaw jutted out. "There's a way. I just haven't figured it out yet."

"Brady, you're dead broke. After paying alimony on that chicken-feed salary you bring in—"

"My lawyer says I might not have to pay alimony when everything is settled because Claudia's got more than I do. She might even have to pay some of it back."

Joe shook his head. "That'll be the day."

Brady lovingly slapped his buckskin gelding on the neck. "Look, Joe, the point is, I'm starting fresh," he rationalized. "I didn't have any money the first time I bought the Rocking T, and I made it work. At least until Claudia bailed out on me."

"But Brady, you had a trust fund. Enough for a down payment."

"So, I get another nest egg. What do you think banks are for?"

"No bank is going to loan you a down payment. The first law of banking is you don't loan money to anybody who really needs it."

Brady couldn't deny that, but still he pressed on. "Maybe a regular bank won't. But don't you think my dad..." He let the sentence drift off.

Joe didn't know what to tell him. Jake Trent was Brady's father and loved his son dearly. But he didn't think the Rocking T was the answer to any of Brady's problems—it hadn't been before Claudia had left him and it certainly wasn't after. "If you want me to lie to you, Brady, I'll say you're right. If you want me to tell you the truth, then I'll tell you flat out that I think your dad would loan you money for almost anything *but* the Rocking T."

Brady grimaced. "What if I promised him a year as a fair exchange?"

"A year of what?"

"A year at the bank. A year to hoard every penny with his guarantee that he'll give me a loan for my services."

"Brady, are you nuts? You'd go crazy working there! Besides, in order to save anything you'd have to live with him!"

Brady's eyes darkened. He did not move. He waited in silence until Joe said, "Or you could bunk with me."

Streaks of pink gratitude colored Brady's face. "Joey, if there was any other way..."

Joe gripped his friend's elbow. "Dammit, Brady, I'm not your problem. You know I'll do anything I can to help. But I think you'll hate yourself if you cave in like that. You'll hate him for winning, and he'll get his hopes up that you're coming back for good and then he'll be crushed when you don't."

Brady pulled back and slipped his foot back in the stirrup. "I don't know what else to do, Joe. How else can I get the cash?"

"Brady, I don't think that's the question. I think what you ought to be thinking about is the most *logical* compromise you can come up with between what you wish you could have and what you're going to have to settle with."

Brady stared at him, lips tight, as he declared, "No, Joe. If I do that I'll kick myself for the rest of my life. I've got to find a way to get the Rocking T back. All I want to know is, can I count on your support? In spirit if nothing else?"

Joe studied the peach-and-mauve horizon, grappling with the hot potato Brady had tossed in his lap. Brady wasn't talking about moral support. He was asking if Joe would put his friendship on the line with cold, hard cash. Cash that Joe knew he didn't really have to spare.

But when he saw the desperate hope in his best friend's eyes, he did the only thing he could. He pulled out his wallet, plucked out a five-dollar bill, and symbolically handed it to Brady.

"What the hell is this?" Brady demanded.

"A beginning. With all the blood, sweat and tears you're going to be putting into this venture, the least I can do is put up some cash if we're going to be partners."

"Partners?" He sounded stunned.

"Well, hell," Joe told him, "if I'm going to cosign your loan and chip in on the down payment, the least you can give me is a share of the Rocking T. I've always been partial to that old ghost town on the far side of your house. They used to talk about running a train down there."

Brady stared at him a moment, his eyes almost watering with emotion. He tucked the five into his pocket, then offered Joe his hand.

Joe shook it, clenched hard for a moment, then said solemnly, "We've got time to ride a few more miles, Brady. Shall we keep heading south?"

Brady touched his heels to the gelding's flanks, and the old horse seemed to know which way to go.

THE FIRST DAY that Patty's rowdy sixth-graders bounced into Mandy's room for social studies, Ira Henderson didn't say a word. He didn't look like the sunshiny boy she'd seen in the picture in Joe's office. He didn't raise a ruckus as his father had in the sixth grade, but he didn't contribute to the class discussion, either. He sat in the back, stiff-lipped and rigid, watching Mandy as though he expected her to catch on fire or swoop down on him like an enormous vulture. She didn't know what Joe had told him about her, but she knew it wasn't likely to be good.

Still, she couldn't say that Ira Henderson was a trouble-maker. Recipient of that honor was Frank Raskin, a belligerent, dark-haired boy who had poor Patty crying on Mandy's shoulder every other day. Mandy, who had learned over the years how to nip trouble in the bud, chose

Frank for the coveted role of George Washington and kept his body active and his ego fed as he charged from the field of battle to Philadelphia with his daily reports, pretending they were letters delivered from a commander in the field.

She gave Joe's son a minor role as a little-known delegate from South Carolina in which he could assert himself or not as he chose. The first week she left him alone, to sulk or watch or worry. The second week she called on Ira as often as she called on any of the other children, and he answered accurately without enthusiasm or elaboration. The third week, when they finished the Continental Congress unit, she threw out some bait, hoping that Ira—and the other six boys who still hadn't thawed—would take the hook.

"Where I teach in Denver, I usually start a unit on local history in October," she told the class. "But I don't know much about Redpoint. Some of you who have lived here a long time probably know a lot more about the history of this area than I do. Can anybody suggest events or themes we might focus on?"

Actually Mandy had carefully studied the history of the area the first time she'd taught here—and had used the last month to give herself a refresher course. She had three solid concepts that she thought would translate well into activity-based units: the coming of the railroad, the settlement of the pioneers whose wagons had broken down on the Santa Fe Trail, and the unique political structure of the local Ute Indian tribe. It was possible that one of the children would come up with something else, and if the group was in favor, she was more than willing to consider another option. But she never launched this sort of free-for-all discussion without having a fallback position.

"Well, we've got the Slow Joe here. It used to be called the Colorado Fireball. That's sort of history, isn't it?" asked Susie Boswell, one of the girls from Patty's class.

Please, God, not the Slow Joe, Mandy prayed. In recent weeks she'd almost managed to push Joe from her mind... at least during her waking hours. Of course, just three nights ago he'd slipped into her subconscious in the middle of the night, dressed in a tuxedo as they danced in the dark and empty hotel parking lot. Or at least, he'd started the dream dressed in part of the tux. He'd worn the long-tailed coat and the bow tie, but no shirt; the bright blue cummerbund, but below that...

Mandy had realized that once the class started discussing Redpoint history, sooner or later some child would suggest that they take a trip to the Slow Joe or have "Ira's dad" come to talk about it. But she vowed to steer the conversation in some other direction unless the subject seemed to be the only way to draw Ira out.

"It's history, but I know all about it," Ira surprised Mandy by declaring without even raising his hand. "I mean—it's real neat and my dad could tell you all about it, Mrs. Larkin, but it's nothing new for me or any of my friends. I was hoping we could do something different. You know—" he shrugged almost apologetically "—kind of like the Continental Congress. That was sort of...well, different, I guess. Getting to *be* some person in history instead of just reading about how it was back then or seeing it in films."

From silent Ira those cautious words were high praise. It was a great deal more than Mandy had hoped for, and she responded instinctively with a beaming smile. "I'm glad you enjoyed the role-playing, Ira. I thought it was a lot of fun, too. Can you think of something else that would be different—" she deliberately used his word "—from something you've studied before?"

She waited hopefully, but Ira shrugged again. Clearly his speech was over. But another boy said, "Ira's dad's not the only one in his family who knows history stuff. He's got an uncle with a covered wagon."

"A covered wagon!" Mandy burst out, truly delighted. "You mean a *real* one?"

"Oh, yeah," Ira said, smiling shyly now. "Actually I think he's got two or three that he left on Dad's back lot when he had to sell his ranch. He's sort of nutsy for all that wagon train stuff—pots and pans, wooden wheels, yokes and beat-up harnesses for horses and oxes."

He looked so pleased that Mandy restrained the urge to say, "oxen, not oxes," and encouraged him to go on. "You mean he collects historical artifacts, Ira?"

"Well, yeah, I guess you could call them that. Mom always says it's just junk. And it *is* awful old and rusty. But it's neat stuff," he tacked on enthusiastically. "He's got barbed wire, too. About a hundred kinds. Little pieces. And he can tell you why they used each kind and why it didn't work out."

"I only thought there was one kind of barbed wire," said Frank Raskin, reluctantly revealing his interest. "How come there's other ones?"

Again, Ira shrugged, but this time he smiled as though he didn't mind being the center of attention. "I don't know, really. Uncle Brady does, though."

Just as Mandy was trying to figure out if Ira's "Uncle Brady" was the dear friend of Joe's she'd met at the wedding, little Susie Boswell said, "Hey, Ira, could you get him to bring his wagon train here? That would be so neat!" Before Ira could answer, she turned to Mandy. "Would that be all right, Mrs. Larkin?"

It's more than all right, my dear, she wanted to crow. *It's precisely that sort of family involvement I always hope for.* The only kind of family involvement that worried her was the possibility that for some reason, Joe would not want Brady Trent to come.

MANDY WENT HOME THAT NIGHT to another row between Ruth and Karen. The details didn't matter, at least not to Ruth. She'd decided that Karen was probably meeting George or some other indecent boy during her lunch hour and wanted to arrange for Karen to check in with the school secretary during her free time to prove her whereabouts. Karen, mortified and alarmed, had flatly refused.

It frustrated Mandy that every time Ruth seemed to be mellowing out a tad, something would happen and she'd blow up again, or fold up, quite literally, with the pain in her abdomen. On this particular occasion, Mandy realized that barely a week had passed since the last time Ruth had gone to bed with terrible cramps. In fact—she sat down with a calendar and tried to remember the dates of Ruth's worst "attacks"—it seemed to Mandy that her sister fell apart on a fairly regular basis during alternating weeks.

"Ruthie," she asked cautiously after Karen had gone to bed. "Have your periods been coming awfully close together lately?"

"No," Ruth declared. "They've always been right on schedule. Twenty-seven or twenty-eight days."

"And you have this terrible pain—" she decided to leave out the accompanying mood swings "—the week before each period and about halfway in between?"

Ruth shrugged. "I'm not sure, exactly. I think it gets worse during the middle of the month." Her voice dropped a little, and she sounded very young. "When something hurts all the time, you can't tell when it's better and when it's worse."

Mandy studied her sister closely. "And your abdomen never really stops hurting altogether?"

Soberly Ruth nodded. "More or less."

"How long has it been this bad?"

Ruth made a flailing gesture with her hands. "I don't know. I've always had bad cramps. I think it just seems worse lately because I've been so upset with Karen."

Mandy took a deep breath and said what had to be said. "Ruthie, I think it's more than Karen. I've never seen you this emotional with any of your kids. You weren't even this edgy when Lowell walked out on you."

"I'm older now," Ruth grumbled. "I'm raising a teenager alone."

Mandy shook her head. "The pain in your abdomen just isn't right, Ruth. Cramps start and stop in two- or three-day intervals. They don't go on all the time. And no cramps should be this bad." She waited for a moment, but Ruth did not reply. So she bravely said, "I think you need to see a doctor, Ruth. And not dear old Dr. Hawthorne. A gynecologist who specializes in—"

"A gynecologist would just tell me it was P.M.S. or menopause or something. And I'm not *that* old."

Gingerly Mandy countered, "Ruth, some people start menopause in their thirties. It doesn't mean they're old. And since neither you nor I have medical degrees, we certainly don't know all the possible ramifications of your symptoms. All we know is that . . . well, Ruth, honey, something is *wrong*. And it's not likely to get any better unless you get some help."

Ruth's jaw stiffened. "Going to Dr. Hawthorne is hard enough, and I've known him for seventeen years. I'm not about to drag myself out of town for somebody I've never even heard of."

"Then go see Dr. Hawthorne again, Ruthie. *Please*," Mandy urged her, knowing that she'd be lucky just to get Ruth to do that much. "Explain your symptoms in more detail this time. Let him know that even though Karen's behavior is improving, you're getting worse."

In the end Ruth said she'd think about it, and Mandy reluctantly backed down. But two weeks later, when she found Ruth weeping one Thursday evening for no reason whatsoever, Mandy made a decision of her own. Before she left for school the next morning, she copied down Dr. Hawthorne's number and made a point to call him during lunch.

ON FRIDAY AFTERNOON, Joe picked up Ira at two o'clock, took him to the dentist, and dropped him off at his piano lesson at three-fifteen. By three-thirty he was already back on the schoolgrounds, steaming. This was one time when he wouldn't let his ex-wife talk to the school officials for him.

"You go *where* for social studies every day?" he'd barked at Ira when his son had chirped his happy intention to ask Uncle Brady to come lecture his class. "Does your mother know about this?"

Yes, Ira had innocently informed him. Sarah knew. Gerry Cottonwood knew. Patty Richardson knew. The only one who'd been kept in the dark was Joe Henderson, who sure as *hell* had earned the right to be treated with parental respect as Ira's father!

He's rehearsed a dozen threats and admonitions for Gerry by the time he rammed his station wagon into the parking lot and all but ran up to the school office door. But the principal wasn't in, the young secretary cheerfully

informed him; he was at a meeting with the county super-
intendent of schools. Was there anybody else who could
help him?

Still fuming, Joe stormed out to Patty Richardson's
classroom. *If she doesn't know why I asked to have Ira
moved to her class she ought to!* he fumed. *I'll be damned
if I'll let String Bean Sawyer do to my precious son what
she did to me!*

With all the humiliation of his sixth-grade year thundering through his heart, Joe pounded up to Room Six-A
and plowed through the open door.

The room hadn't changed much in twenty-three years.
The same old chalkboards were in place. The bookcases
were full of records and textbooks. The desk, each one a
combination of chair, tabletop and cubbyhole, still seemed
like tiny cages to the man who'd hated them as a child.

Patty was sitting at her desk, looking fresh and doe-
eyed. *God, she's just like a kid,* Joe realized with sudden
empathy. He'd come roaring in here to chew her out, and
she hardly looked old enough to tie her own shoes!

Fortunately he had a moment to temper his anger because Patty didn't spot him at once, nor did she hear him
enter because of the rollicking version of "How the West
Was Won" played in the background from a cassette recorder about three feet from Mandy Larkin's hand. And
after a moment, Joe didn't care whether Patty Richardson had noticed him or not, because Mandy's sparkle
seemed to fill the whole room.

She was wearing a floor-length Mother Hubbard dress,
black button-up pioneer shoes, and a red calico scarf
around her head. Gushing out a stream of ideas with
barely leashed enthusiasm, she was scribbling "black-
smith" on the chalkboard under "wagon master,"
"seamstress" and "cook."

"So each child will be assigned to a specific position on the Redpoint Wagon Train," she bubbled to Patty. "I'll start with volunteers for the most prosaic positions so nobody feels like he or she is an also-ran. According to their roles, they'll act as leaders, complainers, hunters, mothers and scouts. Every day I'll create a new scenario for them to cope with—a prairie fire, an Indian attack, a dried-up water hole, a siege of cholera. They can study my original pioneer diaries and an 1846 travel guide to the Santa Fe Trail written by a cavalry officer. I'm going to be the grandma they left behind so they can write to me with all the news of their troubles on the trail." Her rush of words came to a halt as she grinned, flushed, at Patty. "Well, what do you think?"

"I think it's terrific!" Patty declared, bouncing off her chair in delight. "And that kickoff with Brady Trent's wagon is just a great idea. By the time they realize that this was your idea and not theirs they're all going to be so excited they won't care! You're a genius, Mandy."

Well hardly that, Joe countered silently. Still, listening to Mandy's creative zest, it was hard to sustain his furious indignation. This wasn't a woman who planned to torment his son. This was a teacher who clearly intended to give all the kids her best.

Mandy offered the younger woman a generous smile that spoke of her vast experience but didn't rub it in. "None of my ideas are entirely original, Patty. I've just had enough years in the classroom to gather up everybody else's ideas. You should have seen me when I first started. Nobody thought I was so brilliant then." Her eyes grew sad with the memory. "Some days I went home so depressed! I tried so hard, but I felt like I was running in place."

In spite of his own distress, Joe was touched by the re-membered sorrow in her tone. He tried to think of her as Patty's age, sweet and green, frustrated with her short-comings. It was beyond his imagination.

And yet, the fuzzy image of the younger Mandy he did conjure up lacked the sharp clarity of the warty witch of his sixth-grade memory. Not once, as her student, had it ever occurred to Joe that String Bean Sawyer went home feeling as rotten as he did, let alone that his behavior might have something to do with her despair. But, as a man, he knew that he'd probably hurt Mandy by moving Ira out of her class. And now, as he started to cool down, he real-ized that he wasn't looking forward to hurting her again.

Mandy flipped off the recorder and pulled out the tape. As she turned back to face Patty, her glance fell on Joe, and she looked so startled that he felt like a Peeping Tom as he grated out, "Hello."

Mandy blanched and swallowed hard; her knuckles whitened around the machine. Her eyes did not meet his as she said softly, "Hello, Joe." Quickly she glanced at Patty, then tugged off her calico scarf. "Thanks for let-ting me run it by you, Patty. See you tomorrow."

Mandy nodded briskly at Joe as she fled, but she didn't say anything else. *And what the hell did you expect her to say?* Joe chided himself. *Gee, it's great to see you, Joe? I can hardly wait for you to pull your son out of my social studies class because you think I'll poison his mind with a measly half hour a day?* Of course she didn't know why he'd come to see Patty. Or were her instincts good enough to guess?

"Good afternoon, Mr. Henderson," Patty Richardson greeted him, looking incredibly young and uneasy. "Can I help you?"

With Mandy's face so fresh in his mind, Joe couldn't bring himself to tell Patty why he'd come, so instead he asked how Ira was doing and learned that things were going very well. Then, inevitably, Patty asked if there was anything special on his mind.

He didn't know quite what to say to that. In fact, he didn't know quite what to say about anything when he was at Redpoint Elementary, so he decided that the smartest thing he could do for himself was get out of the place before he stuck his foot in his mouth. Again. Too quickly, he said goodbye and headed for the parking lot.

Unfortunately, in order to get there, he had to walk past Room Five-B.

The door was open, and Mandy, still in her Mother Hubbard dress—but barefoot now—was sitting in the middle of a rug in the book corner. She was flanked by open magazines and books about the West. On her right was a pile of Charlie Russell pictures; on her left lay a huge poster of a Frederick Remington bronze—the famous bronc buster with a rattler striking at the horse's hooves. She looked oddly childlike with her toes poking past her ragged hem. He wondered where she'd found the old dress.

He knew that he should just walk on past the door, head for the car and make good his escape. But for no good reason that he could fathom, Joe strolled across the room until he stood above her, looking down on the collage of pictures on the floor.

Mandy turned sharply as she heard his boots; a flash of fear darkened her pretty face. "Oh!" the word was a strangled whisper. "It's you."

He tried to smile but failed. "Is that good or bad?"

She shook her head. "I just . . . wasn't expecting anybody. It doesn't take much to startle me since I . . . well, since I've been alone."

He realized dimly that she was speaking about her husband...the quiet fear of solitary widowhood. It was odd to imagine Miss Sawyer alone and frightened, odder yet to see her scrambling to get to her feet, stumbling as she stepped on the long hem.

As Joe reached out to steady her, she took his hand. Neither the setting nor the reason for the moment's shared touch could alter the impact of her skin against his own. His upper half trembled and his lower half swelled. He longed to squeeze her fingers and pull her closer; he longed to touch her face.

But Mandy's fingers were cold and tight despite the heat of the autumn afternoon, and she pulled away from him the moment she was steady on her feet. Quickly she busied her hands as she turned away, neatening papers, stacking books, moving things here and there.

"How may I help you, Joe?" she asked quite formally. "Would you like a report on your son's work?"

Her fear was not as transparent as Patty's, but it was there in her face all the same. And there was something else in the tight set of her mouth and the small wrinkles around her eyes. Anger. The old anger he recalled so well.

"No," he said slowly. "I imagine if there were some kind of a problem with the time he spends in here for social studies, you would have let me know."

"That is correct." Each syllable was so brittle it snapped.

"He seems to be...interested in studying the West."

"I got that impression. Ira doesn't express his feelings to me very openly, but he did volunteer to ask your friend Brady to come to school with his wagon and artifacts, which I took to be a good sign."

It occurred to Joe, quite suddenly, that he didn't like the way the conversation was going. Granted, Mandy wasn't treating him like snot-nosed little Joey—she was talking to him as a teacher, giving him a parent's due respect. But nowhere in her freckled face was there a hint of the intimacy they'd shared at the wedding, or even the next day in the parking lot, when she'd made her frightened confession. She was still as brittle as she'd been at the library the last time they'd talked.

"Talk to me, Mandy," he said abruptly, taking a step onto the rug. His eyes met hers and their bodies nearly touched as he ordered, "Forget this teacher talk. Don't treat me like Ira's father. Treat me like Joe."

A red flush darted across her face. "Like Joe? You mean good old Joe, my ever-so-trusting *friend*?" Her tone was acerbic. "My dear pal who was so eager to give my new boss a vote of confidence that he pulled his son out of my room before I even had time to find the right key to the door?"

"Mandy, you know I had to do that! I couldn't let Ira get caught between us in some . . . sexual tug-of-war. I—"

"I don't know about you, Joe, but I finished my war with you long ago. You won. I left town with my tail between my legs. I only came back for my sister."

To his amazement, her eyes began to fill with tears. "When Ira was placed in my class, I didn't expect you to rejoice, Joe, but I did think you'd grown up enough to give me half a chance."

"*Grown up?* Are we back to—"

"Dammit, Joey!" she burst out, genuine tears slipping down her cheeks now. "Don't you know how much I wanted to prove to you that I could do it? That the tenderfoot teacher who you knew had matured into a capable educator who could actually do your son some *good*? Do you have any idea how much it hurt to learn that you preferred to have him fall prey to all the mistakes of another green, new teacher than entrust your precious boy to *me*?"

"Mandy, I—" He stopped, struck dumb by her tears. The last time he'd seen her cry it had thrown him off guard, made him think twice, but he'd known that those tears were for Karen. But *these* tears were not for Ira. Not really. These tears were for *him*.

Joe wanted to reach out to her, to wipe away the tears, the hurt...to feel her close beside him. But she was drying her face with the long Mother Hubbard apron, turning away from him again, picking up some pencils strewn on the floor.

"Mandy," he tried once more, his voice softer this time. "I'm sorry. I didn't do it to hurt you. I swear it. I only wanted to protect my son."

He knew by the way her back stiffened that his honest explanation had only made things worse. Still he touched her arm, held her when she tried to pull away. Desperately he lied, "If I didn't have some faith in your teaching, do you think I would have let Ira come to your class every day for social studies? Don't you think I would have rushed right down to Gerry's office and—"

"You mean, like you did today?" She whirled to face him, even angrier now. "Dammit, Joe, things are bad enough between us! Do you think it'll help anything if you lie?"

Suddenly he couldn't stand it anymore; he did what he'd wanted to do since the first instant he'd seen her today. He closed the last gap between them and cupped her face with both hands.

Her skin was soft against his callused fingers, and tinged with delicate, alluring scent. Up close her lips were naturally pink, long after her lipstick had disappeared, and the flush in her cheeks gave her face a youthful zest that not even her tears could diminish.

Joe forgot why he'd been so angry when he'd stormed into the school; he forgot why he'd come. All he knew was that his fingers were lightly stroking Mandy's cheeks, and he was about to slip them into her hair. He was a man, she was a woman, and he wanted her.

"I don't think anything will help but admitting that we want something more together, Mandy," he bluntly confessed. "Ever since this summer, we've been fighting for all the wrong reasons. Half the time I end up yelling at you because it's so damn hard to keep from taking you in my arms."

He wasn't yelling at her anymore, but he wasn't keeping a safe distance, either. He took a step closer, so close that his thighs quivered next to Mandy's and his elbows grazed her breasts. For a moment she stood there, frightened, cornered, her pulse hammering visibly in her throat. Her eyes locked on Joe's as he lowered his mouth to hers, and he willed her to give in, to stop fighting, to just let it happen.

For just the tiniest breath of a moment, he was sure that she'd surrender. He felt the relief deep in his heart, felt that joy, the throb of his body as it welcomed her embrace.

Then Mandy dropped her chin so that only her temple met his lips. She even laid one hand on his chest and pushed ever so gently...so gently that another man might have taken it for a caress.

Joe's fingers shook. Mandy still felt soft and seductive where he'd touched her, and his body longed to press closer yet. But when she whispered, "Joey, please," he could not fight her, could not put his own desperate needs before her own. Ever so reluctantly, he released her face.

Mandy took a step back as though to widen the gap between them. She crumpled a corner of her apron to her hands. She did not look at him.

Quivering with frustration and a whole new brand of shame, Joe growled, "Just can't seem to do anything right with you, can I, Miss Sawyer?"

Mandy faced him again, blinking hard, her sprinkle of freckles making her look hopelessly young. One nervous hand tugged a lock of hair behind her ear and twisted it into tiny knots. "I'm sorry," she whispered. And then, incredulous, she added, "And I'm sorry for what I said before."

Mandy could have been referring to almost anything, but Joe didn't need to ask for clarification. He knew she was referring to her parting shot the morning after the wedding, when she'd accused him of using her to exact some sort of revenge. And then she'd insisted that she had no interest in him at all.

"I am...attracted...to you, Joey," she confessed, each word a private agony of sound. "But *I don't want to be*. Nothing can ever come of it and it makes me feel...unclean. Not because there's anything wrong with you—or with me—but because you'll always be one of my kids. *Any* one of my kids, Joe. It's not because things were so rough between the two of us." She licked her lower lip. "At least I don't think that's the heart of it."

It was the most honest thing she'd ever said to him, and Joe felt compelled to respond in kind. With inordinate care he searched for some healing words out of the jumble of love and hurt in his mind. "Maybe I...acted too fast when I asked for Ira to be moved," he admitted. "Maybe the fear was just too deep for me to be rational about the situation. Maybe...subconsciously...I *was* trying to get back at you for...well, for lots of things."

She nodded, slowly, as though to honor the fact that he'd told her the truth. "Maybe now that we've...cleared the decks...we can treat each other more cordially when we...happen to meet."

Joe took her hand, laced her warm fingers and pressed their joined palms against his thigh. "I want more than that, Mandy," he confessed, his voice hoarse with desire. "You want it, too."

For a moment—for a long moment, it seemed to Joe—Mandy tolerated his possessive touch. In fact, her fingers curled around his own, tugged his hand closer. Some part of him—that very male part centered in his groin—answered her unspoken beckoning. But just as he took hope that he might yet feel free to kiss her, she released his hand and took another step toward the bookshelf. And turned her back on him.

"Joe, please do this for me," she whispered, her low tone throbbing with straitjacketed desire. "Please don't make it hard. I've told you that I want you, admitted it straight out. Isn't that enough for you?"

He stood there, staring at her richly curved hips and graceful, naked feet, aching to press himself against her long legs as he had at the wedding. He wanted to sweep aside her hair and kiss her shoulders; he wanted to close the classroom door, pull the shades and take her down on the rug.

But her stiff, unrelenting spine gave him no quarter. And no hope. Little Joey Henderson would have pressed her, taunted her, tormented her until she yielded or ran. But Joe Henderson, the man, stood his ground in silence for a long, rocky moment before he admitted hoarsely, "No, Mandy. It's not nearly enough."

Shaking, Mandy covered her face with her hands, but she did not answer. Nor did she try to stop him when he turned and left the room.

CHAPTER EIGHT

IT WAS WINDY the day that Brady Trent arrived at Redpoint Elementary driving a Conestoga wagon pulled by four energetic quarter horses. He was dressed in chaps, a rawhide jacket and a battered Stetson with a bullethole in the brim—John Wayne wouldn't have dressed the part any better. But the funny thing was, Brady didn't give Mandy the impression that he was an actor trying to look like a cowboy. He simply looked like a man doing his everyday job.

The children were delirious. Even Ira, who had seen the covered wagon and even ridden in it several times, was grinning from ear to ear as the team pulled into view.

"It's here! The covered wagon's here!" shrieked half a dozen voices. "Look at the way it wobbles! Look at the way the wind blows the sails! Look at all those reins all over the horses!"

Mandy, who'd planned to wrap up her math lesson by the time Brady's team lumbered over the last hundred yards, gave up the struggle and closed her book. "Let's go!" she called to her class. "But don't scare the horses!"

Her warnings fell on deaf ears, of course. Twenty-nine sixth-graders—Frank Raskin was absent that day—poured out of the room and charged across the playground making Indian war whoops and rifle sounds. One teacher came out and pointedly closed his classroom door, but Mandy ignored him. Anything that could get a group of twelve-year-olds this excited about history simply had to be a good idea, in her opinion. And anything that made sad-eyed Brady Trent smile so widely couldn't be all bad, either.

"'Morning', ma'am," he greeted her with a tip of his broad-brimmed hat, one boot casually braced against the running board. "I hear tell ya got some pilgrims wanna join my wagon train headin' fer Californy."

The kids hollered in approbation. Brady scowled dramatically.

"Cain't take no buncha noisy small-fry. Don'tcha got no wagon master in charge a this here group?"

The kids looked at each other, giggled and grinned. Then, in unspoken agreement, the half dozen nearest Ira pushed him forward.

"What's your name, son?" Brady asked.

Ira gave him an exasperated grimace. "You know my name, Uncle Brady."

"Never seen you before in my life," Brady countered with a "Come on and play the game, Ira" wink. "And it's Mr. Trent, *sir*, to all ya young whippersnappers."

Suddenly shy with all the attention, Ira scuffed the crabgrass and replied, "I'm Ira Henderson, Mr. Trent, *sir*. And I guess I'm in charge of this wagon train. We'd like to learn about the best trail to California."

Brady squinted in the sun, tossed out the long stem of hay he was chewing, and jumped off the wagon. Reaching under the hooded canvas, he plucked out a worn map that Mandy decided, based on its condition, must have been an original.

"Well, there's really only two ways to go, son, even if you start right after the first thaw," Brady began. The children gathered eagerly around him. "Now this here is th' Oregon trail, an' ya don't have ta cross no desert. But

we're so close to th' Santa Fe Trail here in south'n Colorado that it don't make no sense..."

For the next hour, Mandy didn't say a word, just
grinned happily as her eager students lapped up every pearl
of wisdom that dropped from Brady's lips. Not one of
them questioned Brady's expertise; nobody ever asked
"how it was back then" but simply referred to their wagon
train problems *now*. Brady shared his ideas, his artifacts
and his boundless enthusiasm for covered wagon travel. By
the time he was done, the children were ready to read every
book ever written on the subject or maybe write a few. And
Mandy was ready to climb up on the buckboard and travel
west herself.

Brady's visit was a real picker-upper, just what she
needed after her dismal morning. Ruth had been more ir-
ascible than usual, especially after she'd discovered that
Mandy had called Dr. Hawthorne behind her back the
week before. The old doctor had been sympathetic to
Mandy's concerns and clarified that Ruth had never given
him reason to probe deeply into her current condition. But
he was more than happy to call a physician friend in Grand
Junction to get his recommendation on a gynecologist for
Ruth and—should it prove necessary—a psychologist as
well.

Longing to share her concerns with somebody other
than Karen, Mandy had reported her call to Patty, who
had listened compassionately until she'd discovered a
sealed note in her office box from Susie Boswell's divorced father. By the rapt expression on her face as she'd
torn open the envelope, Mandy suspected that Susie's
academic progress was not the subject of the missive, but
she made no comment. After all, she couldn't begin to defend the bizarre feelings she had for another student's dad.

Her last encounter with Joe had shaken Mandy to her roots. If Joe had pressed her the tiniest bit more, if he'd stayed a moment longer, she doubted that she could have insisted that he keep his distance. And yet, now that she'd escaped unscathed, she was relieved and grateful that Joe had honored her decision. She knew that a future between them was impossible, and every one of Joe's sensual overtures made it worse.

If he knew about my dreams, he'd never give me peace, she realized with a swirl of desire left over from last night's erotic fantasy encounter with Joe. This time Joe had found her in the classroom in her bed—still clad in her Mother Hubbard dress. But Joe wasn't dressed at all, except for a cowboy hat and vest and a pair of leather chaps that only covered the outside of his thighs and lower legs. While he'd explored the pioneer fastenings that kept her chaste, Mandy had kissed his hungry mouth, his throat, his naked chest, his navel...and kept on mouthing his virile body all the way down.

Even now, she trembled with the remembered sensual anguish of that dream...and the last time Joe had really touched her. As time went on, Mandy's dreams were becoming more graphic, more intense, and her willpower seemed to be slipping from her grasp. But every time she felt the urge to say, "To hell with it! I'm a grown woman. An affair won't hurt me!" she'd have a sudden vision of Alan, clucking at her, shaking his head.

That's not my Mandy talking, he'd remind her. *Sex is just fine with the right man in the right place at the right time. But this time is wrong, this place is wrong, and this man will never be right for you. You don't owe me chastity forever, Mandy, but you owe me the decency of choosing a replacement of whom I would approve.*

The trouble was, sex was only part of what she wanted to share with Joe. She was also drawn to his sense of humor, his casual intelligence, his sensitivity and compassion for kids. Even though their encounters had often been stormy, Mandy knew that most of the hard words between them had been her fault. And she also knew—though she was terrified to admit it—that at any time, all she had to do was say, "Joe, I've changed my mind—I want you," and all the darkness between them would dissolve into radiant day.

With a jolt, Mandy realized that her romantic fantasies were cutting into her daytime concentration as well as haunting her nights. Brady had finished his discourse and the children were beginning to drift back to the classroom, and Mandy was still...waiting for Joe to remove his imaginary hand from under her dress.

Vigorously thrusting away the image, she took a moment to thank Brady for his time. "It was just marvelous the way you got their attention," she praised him honestly. "This whole afternoon was about a dozen times better than I expected."

He smiled, clearly pleased with her praise. "You must not have had much confidence to begin with if you thought it was *that* good."

Mandy laughed. "Oh, I expected you to be knowledgeable, Brady. I just was surprised that you had so much...well, zest for the whole subject. For a while there you actually had me believing you were a real wagon master."

"You think I'd be a good one?" he asked almost seriously.

"I think you'd be great. Of course, we'd have to push you through a time travel machine that would drop you in the 1830s for such a profession to do you much good, but—"

"That's not entirely true, Mandy," he corrected her thoughtfully as he offered the lead horse a pail of water. "There are modern-day wagon masters, you know. Folks who run wagon train tours—they're supposed to emulate the Old West. I promised Ira I'd take him with me on one someday."

Mandy shook her head as his use of the word "emulate" reminded her that he wasn't a wagon master at all but a very educated modern man. "Well, it sounds like fun, Brady, and maybe you could do it on a vacation sometime. I doubt you'd want to make a career of it."

He seemed to leave her then, even though his eyes were still trained on her face. "I could think of worse careers," he said quietly.

"Name one," Mandy challenged him.

His whole face seemed to lengthen. "Banking," he growled.

"Well . . . I guess that depends on how good you are in math."

Brady looked at her then, shook his head, offered the pail to another horse and gently scratched its ears. "Actually, Mandy," he answered morosely, "I don't think it depends on that at all."

She wanted to ask what he meant, but she had a group of noisy children lined up outside her room that she couldn't leave unsupervised. Yet, after she thanked him once more and said goodbye, she had the feeling that Brady was still stewing on the subject, because he stared fuzzily off in the distance—to the south—as he watered another horse and bent to croon softly in its ear.

"SO HOW'S MARRIED LIFE TREATING YOU, Jake?" Joe asked Brady's father when he arrived at the bank a week later to withdraw some cash. "I saw Arleen downtown yesterday. She looked fit and sassy."

Jake grinned with an almost boyish delight. "Yep, she's doing all right. Hasn't tried to leave me once. I don't think the honeymoon's over yet."

"I should hope not. We only got you married off a month ago."

"Ah, Joey, it's been closer to three. It's October now, you know."

"Yeah, I guess it is." Three months since the wedding; three months since the first time he'd felt Mandy's body pressed so intimately against his. Three months of casual hellos and goodbyes at the Slow Joe; half that time, maybe more, since Ira had started going to her social studies class.

Three damn months and I still want her, he silently cursed. *My God, I've never known a woman harder to forget!* The worst of it was that his feelings for Mandy were starting to color his reaction to other females. A week ago he'd met a very appealing woman—the visiting cousin of an old friend—and he'd been glad to take her out to dinner and show her a good time. She was so bright and easygoing—with a sense of humor that uniquely matched his own—that Joe thought she was exactly the kind of person he'd always hoped would brighten his life someday. She'd given him every indication that she wanted to get to know him better, and a few months ago, he knew he would have jumped at the chance. But now something crippled his interest, and though he'd promised to get in touch with her, he found himself in no hurry to call her back.

"Tell me, Joey... you hear much from Brady lately?" Jake asked, oblivious to Joe's private thoughts. It was a casual question, one he often heard around town. But since Joe was speaking to Brady's father, it was a telling inquiry. Joe was saddened, but not surprised.

"He checks in every couple of days, Jake. He's doing all right. Nothing new." He considered mentioning that Brady was thinking of begging his dad for a loan, but decided that Brady would have the best chance approaching Jake on his own.

Jake nodded, shrugged and scuffed one polished black shoe. "He heard from Claudia lately?"

"Just her lawyer. The final papers should be coming through any day now."

For a moment Jake said nothing, just pursed his lips. At last he asked, "Has he . . . come to grips with it yet?"

"In his head or in his heart?" Joe asked.

Jake didn't answer. Joe knew there wasn't much he could tell Brady's father that he didn't already know. Still, he said softly, "I think it's the ranch that still hurts the worst, Jake. He knows he can't get Claudia back. He's more or less accepted that. But the Rocking T—that's only a matter of money, and it's up for sale again. He wants to buy it back."

Jake threw up his hands. "Damn fool kid! Will he *never* learn?"

"No!" Joe snapped, his friend's anguish the night they'd ridden together still painfully fresh in his mind. "And why should he? Everybody told me I was crazy to want the Slow Joe, insane to think I could live out my childhood dream. But I did it, dammit! And I didn't even have a dad to help me out."

Jake flushed. "Now don't you start on me, Joey! You know why I didn't bail him out after Claudia left him!"

"I know, and I still think it was a rotten excuse, Jake. I *believe* in Brady even if I don't share his dream. If there was any way on earth I could have found the money to help him hold on to the ranch after she left, I'd have done it. Unfortunately I only owned an old railway line, not a private bank."

He didn't want to end on that note, but a teller started gesturing for Jake. Jake shook his head, placed one hand on Joe's shoulder, squeezed, then ambled off toward the teller's cage. Joe headed slowly for the door, then hurried when he spotted Mandy on the other side.

He pressed open the door, virtually forcing her to brush by him in order to walk into the bank. She glanced up, said, "Thank you," by rote before she focused on his face, then stopped so abruptly that she literally crashed into him. Joe slipped his arm around her as he let the door clang closed. Deftly he pulled her out of the line of foot traffic.

"Good afternoon," he greeted her warmly, his eyes taking in the tense lines of her face. She looked a lot more worried than she had the last time he'd seen her at school, but he couldn't tell whether his presence was the cause of her apprehension. "I've missed you, Mandy," he told her honestly. "It's been a while."

Mandy tried to look away, but her gaze kept coming back to rest on his face. She opened her mouth to speak, then closed it without a word. For a moment she just looked at him with naked longing. Then, incredibly, she whispered, "I've missed you, too, Joe."

He couldn't stifle the wild surge of hope somewhere deep in his stomach, couldn't keep his arm from tightening around her waist. A woman who didn't want him, he was certain, would simply have moved out of his grasp. But Mandy stayed.

Still, her eyes implored him to understand her thinking as she said, "You shouldn't touch me in public, Joe. If one of my kids' parents sees us, it would be hard to explain."

"I want you. You want me. We're both single," he pointed out reasonably. "What's complex about that?"

She glanced away, studied the bank. He could feel her warm breath on the crook of his arm. "Please, Joey," she said simply, as though she were asking for some simple, meaningless favor like helping her carry her groceries to the car. "Please help me with this."

Despite the sparks that hurled themselves between Mandy's body and his own, he managed to release her, reluctantly taking a step back. "So how is my son doing in social studies, Mrs. Larkin?" he asked in a slightly louder tone. Somehow he managed to keep his sarcasm veiled.

Mandy rewarded him with a grateful smile. "Very well, I'm happy to say. The children have elected him wagon master of the Redpoint Wagon Train." She went on in great detail, explaining that Ira would be in charge of finding the trail, supervising supplies and stoking morale. Joe had heard every word of it from Ira already—sometimes on two or three different days—but he wanted to hear Mandy's side of things. He was delighted to hear that his son was doing well with her... and still a bit ashamed that he'd tried so hard to keep the two of them from getting together. He listened attentively, watching the sparkle in her green eyes, until she had told him everything he could ever want to know. And reiterated how much she'd appreciated Brady's help. When she started to tell him it had been great to see him—and slung her purse strap over her shoulder as though preparing to go—he caught her elbow and asked, "How's your sister? It's been a long time since I've seen Ruth."

Joe had asked the question only to postpone Mandy's departure; he hadn't expected the simple question to trigger more than the most casual reply. But to his surprise and chagrin, Mandy's face clouded. She looked as though she might cry. "Don't get me started, Joey," she whispered. "There's nothing you can do and . . . I really have to go."

On that note she pulled away from him and Joe knew he had to leave her there, had to walk on out to his car. But the panic in her eyes when she spoke of Ruth haunted him, and he vowed to ask Karen what was wrong with her mother the very next chance he got. In many ways Mandy was quite alone in Redpoint, and Joe had no intention of letting her rejection of him as a lover keep him from standing by her as a friend.

"SO, WHAT'S NEXT?" Patty asked a few days after Brady had visited the school. Eyes aglow, she showed every sign of a young woman head over heels in love, and even though she had not mentioned any man in particular to Mandy, it was obvious that something special had happened over the weekend.

"What do you mean, 'what's next?' "

"I mean, now that Brady Trent came. We've got the wagons rolling. What do we do now? Indians?"

Mandy nodded. "I've found a local Ute—Harry Painted Hat—who's going to come talk to us. A friend of Brady's actually. And there's a fine Ute museum in Grand Junction I'm considering as a possible field trip."

Patty nodded eagerly, then tossed out, "After the Indians it's the railroad, right? Should I arrange something with Ira's dad?"

Mandy closed her eyes with the remembered pain—of both her first field trip and her last encounter with Joe—and Patty, to her surprise, noticed at once.

"You've got a thing for him, don't you?" she asked bluntly.

Mandy blanched. "What do you mean?"

"I mean, you and Joe Henderson. You think I'm stupid? That day he came to talk to me about Ira, he didn't even see me once he realized that you were in the room. Don't try to tell me that you'd never met before."

"Well, of course we've met," Mandy answered hurriedly. "My niece works for him. I've talked to him at the station once or twice."

"Right." Patty's smug tone said it all. "And I spent five hours last Saturday night explaining to Susie Boswell's daddy why she needs a little more help in math."

Mandy took advantage of Patty's mention of her weekend to redirect the conversation. "I take it you had . . . a reasonably good time with Mr. Boswell?" she asked.

Patty smiled. In fact, she grinned so radiantly that at least ten teeth showed. "I think that would be a fair assessment."

"Would it also be a fair assessment to guess that you aren't calling him Mr. Boswell anymore?"

The younger woman giggled. "It's hard to call somebody Mr. Boswell who's seen you without any clothes." Suddenly Patty blushed and covered her mouth in a terribly girlish way. "I guess I shouldn't have said that, huh?"

Mandy wasn't quite sure how to answer, so she decided to tell Patty the truth. "You can say anything you want to me, Patty, because we're friends. But I think you ought to . . . exercise some prudence where the rest of the staff is concerned. And I certainly wouldn't let your students or their parents know how you're spending your free time."

Patty sobered. Her full lips drooped in a pout. "Don't spoil it for me, Mandy. I really care for Fred. Do you think I'd sleep with just anybody?"

Mandy sighed. Quietly she sat down beside her young friend. "Honey, I'm not saying you shouldn't fall in love. Right now, he likes you and you like him and everything is hunky dory. But have you considered what might happen if you lose interest? Or he does? It could be terribly awkward."

"That won't happen," Patty declared with stubborn naïveté.

"Okay, maybe it won't. For your sake I hope it doesn't. But Susie might feel uncomfortable if the other kids tease her. Or her mother might take umbrage just because... well, not everybody has easy divorces and maybe this one wasn't her idea. Or Gerry Cottonwood—who is a sweetie, you know, but very traditional when it comes to teachers and their professional roles—might have something to say about it."

Patty looked truly depressed now. "I think you're wrong. Fred's been nothing but courteous and discreet in front of the children." She lifted her chin defiantly. "If Fred were still married, or I was, I could see your point. But I've never felt this good about a man, not *ever*, Mandy. I honestly think he might be the one for me."

Mandy patted the girl's hand. "I hope it works out for you, Patty. Really I do."

She stood to start taking down the materials on her bulletin board, dismissing the subject at hand. But suddenly Patty's high voice rang out across the room. "Is that why you won't go out with Ira's father?"

Mandy whirled sharply. "What I do with Ira's father is none of your business." The words came out with far too much force, and Patty looked as though she'd been slapped in the face. Quickly Mandy backpedalled. "I'm sorry, Patty. I didn't mean it quite like that. All I mean is... you're making me nervous talking about Joe Henderson that way in such a loud voice. Somebody could overhear and misunderstand.''

''What's there to misunderstand? He's single. So are you. If you like each other—''

''We don't.'' Her tone was rigid, but she could not meet Patty's eyes.

''Methinks thou doth protest too much,'' Patty countered.

''Come on, Patty!'' Her nosy friend was getting too close to home. ''This is just a fantasy on your part. I have no interest in Joe Henderson except as a possible field trip contact.''

''Okay, then as a field trip contact,'' Patty tossed out with a gleam in her eye. ''Are you going to call him to set up our visit to the Slow Joe or should I?''

''You do it,'' Mandy ordered her. ''I've got to call back Ruth's doctor this afternoon.''

Patty sobered. ''Things aren't any better?''

''Things couldn't be much worse. He said he would rustle up a list of recommended specialists in Grand Junction. The trouble is, I don't know if I can get her to go.''

''Well, Mandy, it's obvious from what you said before she needs a good gynecologist. What's her objection to that?''

Mandy shook her head. ''I think the gynecologist is going to be the easy part. It's the psychologist she's going to fight tooth and toenail.''

''Oh,'' said Patty.

'' 'Oh,' is right.''

''Do you really think she might be . . . well, losing it?'' Patty asked with an aborted attempt at diplomacy.

Mandy shook her head. To her surprise, she found herself fighting tears. *I wish Alan were here to help me! Just*

to give me advice. Or take things out of Ruth's hands al-
together. But there's nobody. Nobody but me.

"Can Joe help you?" Patty asked.

Mandy stared at her. Had the girl gone daft? "Help me
with what? We were talking about my sister."

"I know. It's just that . . . he strikes me as the sort of
person who's very levelheaded and dependable when the
chips are down. Have you told him about Ruth? I think he
might have some ideas to offer . . . or at least moral support."

Mandy exhaled sharply. *Oh, Joe, could you really stand
by me, help ease this confusion and despair?* she asked
herself. Then she remembered that Joe was just a grown-
up kid, a burr under her saddle, a memory of trouble and
pain. Or at least she tried to remember that. But her
memory of the Joey-child was fading, and now, when she
tried to visualize him, all she could see was the man who'd
stood in the bank last week and removed his arm from her
waist because she'd begged him to, even though the
yearning in his eyes had mirrored the anguish in her own.

"I told you, Patty," she lied without conviction. "I have
no romantic interest in Joe."

Patty harrumphed, then grabbed the small mirror that
hung on the wall by the coat closet and thrust it into Mandy's hands. "Look in there and say it again. See if you can
lie to yourself any better than you lie to me."

Mandy didn't bother to look in the mirror. Without another word she put it back on the wall.

"So?" Patty pressed.

"It can't be, Patty. Please just leave it alone."

Suddenly all the sparkle faded from Patty's eyes as tears
sprang into Mandy's. The two women stared at each other
for an honest moment before Mandy turned away.

"I'm so sorry, Mandy," Patty said with uncommon gentleness. "I didn't realize it was so involved. I knew you were attracted to Joe, but I had no idea you were already... in love with him."

"Neither did I," said Mandy.

And then she started to cry.

THE KIDS ARRIVED at the station house at nine o'clock the next Wednesday morning. To Joe's dismay, Grandpa Howard, his head engineer, had had a mild stroke the night before. Though he'd appeared fine this morning when Joe had rushed over to the hospital, both Joe and his doctor had insisted that Howard take several months off. Joe had told Wilma to start tracking down a temporary replacement at once. However, today he had no choice but to take the field trip with Mandy.

He knew it would be tricky for the two of them to spend a whole day together in front of other people, which is why he'd tried to arrange to be "too busy" to join Ira's group in the first place. Now, trapped by circumstances that neither he nor Mandy could alter, he grimaced as he set off to greet the kids.

"Good morning, everybody," Joe declared, doffing his conductor's hat to the grinning youngsters. "Anybody feel like taking a train ride today?"

Most of the kids readily admitted their delight, but one tall boy in the back stared at Joe sullenly. A few minutes later, as the other kids listened with rapt attention to Joe's summary of the Slow Joe's history, the same boy punched the nearest classmate in the shoulder, then glared at Patty when she shook her finger at him.

With a curious, shameful sense of déjà vu, Joe recognized his younger self in the child. He understood perfectly the baiting tactic, knew that the boy was going to spend the day pitting himself against the young teacher. Unconsciously he glanced at Mandy, who was watching the scene as though she understood the ramifications of the boy's opening gambit, too.

Joe looked away before she noticed his eyes were on her... before she noticed that he ached with the remembered pain. *Dammit, Mandy, we could have had something special!* he silently stormed, doubly angry because his second date with his friend's cousin had confirmed his suspicion that Mandy had gotten under his skin too deeply for him to hunger after any other woman. *Why the hell did you have to throw it all away?* She'd confessed in half a dozen ways that she wanted him, and he knew that if he'd been anybody else but Joe Henderson—and if they'd met in any other town—she'd have been his woman by now. He also knew that forgetting her would be the smart thing to do, but it seemed all but impossible when his heartbeat picked up its tempo at the sight of her and he knew—by the way she trembled at his simplest touch—that she was always shaken by his presence, too.

"I'm going to give you a tour of the station now," Joe informed the group, trying to focus on the business at hand. "We'll have plenty of time to talk about the train once we get under way." That got a cheer of approbation from everybody except the sullen boy in the back. "We're going on a four-hour trip. We'll stop at a stunning natural rock mesa around eleven for a picnic lunch before we come back."

With that he turned and ushered the group through the main station house, explaining how it was first nailed together, then rebuilt after the fire of 1866. He had originally planned to ask Mandy or Patty if there was anything special they wanted him to bring up as a seed for later discussion, but Mandy always kept a safe distance from him and Patty's hand were full. The rowdy boy, now flanked by two or three others following his lead, was leading her on a merry dance.

As Joe walked and talked, he watched the trouble in the back, watched Mandy's quiet, tight control of her own kids and her obvious frustration with Patty's inept but conscientious efforts to control her class. When they finally boarded the train, Joe waited on the ground, giving Mandy lots of space, but she turned to him just once as she passed by.

Her eyes looked ... well, not hopeful, exactly, but ... almost pleading. *For what?* Joe asked himself. *For forgiveness? For another chance? For help?*

As he listened to Patty shrilly begging the tall boy to stop jabbing Susie Boswell in the ribs, he realized what Mandy wanted him to do. As a fellow teacher, she couldn't help Patty out without totally usurping her authority over the children in her charge. But Joe, as the owner of the train, could get away with stepping in.

For a moment his gaze locked with Mandy's, locked and held. The request for help he read there faded, change to sorrow tinged with frustration. He felt the need to hold her all over again and clenched his teeth against the desire. *I can't go on like this,* he realized. *And if she's feeling even half of the agony that I am, neither can she.*

Resolutely he turned and swung on broad. "Who's the strongest boy in your class?" he called to Patty. "I need a volunteer to help me fill the tender."

Patty looked flustered and Ira looked hurt, undoubtedly because his father had not directly asked him. Joe knew he could explain the situation to his son later, but his scheme would be a waste of time if Patty didn't figure out what he had in mind before she directed him to some cooperative youngster.

Mercifully Mandy intervened with a comment just loud enough for the difficult boy to hear. "I don't think any of our boys are really strong enough for such an important job, Mr. Henderson. Don't you need a real man to help you do that?"

Mandy knew her stuff; he had to give her that. A moment later, the stormy kid stood, swaggered down the aisle and thrust his thumbs through his belt. "Don't bother with the rest of them," he arrogantly announced to Joe. "I'm the man you want."

Joe met his eyes and pretended to think it over. "Okay, if you're sure you can handle it," he finally declared.

The boy nodded smugly. "Ain't nothing' I can't handle, mister."

At this point, a very nervous-looking Patty stepped in. "Mr. Henderson, are you sure that—"

"I'm sure." Before she could botch things up, Joe asked the boy his name, led him off the train and back to the coaling shed. Behind him he could hear Mandy launching into a spiel about how it must have felt for nineteenth-century travelers to board this train or one just like it back east and head out west for parts unknown.

The instant Frank was inside the shed, Joe slammed the door behind him and prepared to play a bullying role that was quite foreign to him. Brusquely he faced the boy, his arms across his chest, and painted on his sternest "I'm the boss" expression.

"Here's the name of the game, Raskin," he declared coldly, not even bothering to explain that the tender was full and the request for help had been a ruse. "You're a screwup. You want to screw up this trip. I know because I was a screwup in sixth grade. I came on the Slow Joe and *I* screwed up the trip."

"Oh, yeah?" the boy taunted. "What did you do?"

"I locked a girl in this coaling shed and told the teacher I threw her off the train. They sent for her father, the cops, the whole works." He decided not to mention the teacher's name.

The boy chuckled. "That's good. Thanks for the tip."

"It's not a tip. It's a warning. You breathe when I tell you to for the next four hours or I'll throw *you* off the train and let you walk back."

The boy stiffened. "You don't scare me none."

"Okay, if that's the way you want it," Joe said calmly. "I'll just lock you in here right now and then I won't have to worry about it."

As he turned to leave, the Slow Joe's wonderful steam whistle blasted just a few yards from the shed, shaking the tiny building dramatically. The coal dust swam in the air, creating a murky atmosphere worthy of a haunted house at Halloween.

Joe jerked open the door, letting in a ghost of sunlight, then slipped through quickly. The door was almost closed when the boy cried out, "Hey, you can't do that! It's probably against the law or something."

Joe turned back to face him, hoping the kid wasn't quite smart enough to call his bluff. "On the Slow Joe, *I* am the law, Raskin. Case open and shut."

The boy reached out, a flailing, helpless motion that Joe caught out of the corner of his eye. He remembered it then: the anguish, the loneliness, the sense of total isolation every time he was told to sit in the corner or alone outside the class. *My God, I forced Miss Sawyer to treat me like dirt,* he realized. *I couldn't help what I did, but maybe she couldn't, either.*

He stopped and waited for the boy to plead, "Okay. I won't mess up."

Joe stood still for a moment, tried to think of the best way to make Frank Raskin toe the line without breaking his spirit. Quietly he asked, "Do I have your word?" He faced the boy. "As a man?"

The eyes dropped, but the spine straightened. "Yeah. I guess so."

"'Yes, sir, I give you my word,' is the answer I'm looking for, Raskin."

"Okay."

"Say it!" Joe's tone sharpened.

The boy's eyes flared. He took a fierce breath. "Yes, sir, I give you my word." His tone was half-apologetic, half-angry, but Joe knew he'd won the round.

When he suddenly held out his hand, the boy ducked. It was a gesture that said everything about his home life...and the reason he had major troubles in school. *Poor kid hasn't a clue what it's like to be loved,* Joe realized, grateful that abuse was one childhood disaster he'd been spared. He tried to pretend he hadn't noticed, and kept his hand open, waiting until Frank recognized the gesture for what it was. Slowly, almost wonderingly, Frank took his hand and held it limply. Joe shook it with manly approbation before he said, "You can ride up front with me if you want and I'll show you how to run this thing."

"Okay," said Frank, veiling his pleasure with care. Then he met Joe's eyes and added, "I mean, okay, sir."

Joe risked a small grin. "I think you'll do just fine, Frank."

The boy didn't smile back, but his chin came up half an inch.

The rest of the trip up was pleasant and without incident. The kids were eager to listen to most of what Joe had to say, especially when he let them join him in the cab, one at a time, to ask questions and pull the Slow Joe's ancient whistle. Frank Raskin never left Joe's side, but he saw little of Ira until lunchtime, when his son bounced up and said, "Ya gonna eat with me, Dad?"

Pleased that his twelve-year-old was still proud to be seen with him in public, Joe said, "You bet. Pick out a nice spot in the sun and I'll be right with you."

Most of the picnic tables were in the shade because it was so hot during the busy tourist days of summer. But now, in October, it was chilly, almost overcast, and a brisk wind sent the kids scuttling for their sweatshirts.

After Joe readied the train for the rest stop, he grabbed his paper-bag lunch and glanced around for his son...who had chosen to sit right next to Mandy.

The next hour was a nightmare for Joe. Although Mandy was a good four feet away from him, every time their eyes met, only the knowledge that his son was with them gave Joe the strength to keep his desire for her at bay. He could smell that floral scent she used, remember the delicate feel of her skin. He could hear the slightly breathless tone of her voice as she asked teacherly questions of her eager charges. And when one of the kids accidentally tripped over her as she stood and Joe tried to steady her, she took way too long to release his hand. If they'd been alone, he wondered, would she have pulled away?

In the end, Joe cut the lunch hour short, hoping that his stated concern for the worsening weather would serve as a believable excuse. But as David stoked the fire and Joe made a last safety check, he knew that he'd run out of excuses to keep his distance from Mandy and he desperately hoped that she'd run out of excuses, too. He'd done his damnedest to forget her, but the plain truth was that he'd failed. Jake Trent had taught him young that a wise man always admits when he's beating his head against a brick wall and knows when to start building a wall made of straw.

Abruptly Joe decided that it was time to change his strategy, time to quit letting Mandy call the shots. He'd overheard her tell Patty that she had to give a speech to the parents' organization that evening on her social studies program, and he suddenly decided that he had every right to attend. After all, he was a parent, too.

But twenty minutes later, Joe wondered if either one of them would make it back to Redpoint for the parents' meeting, let alone safely deliver two classes of kids. They'd barely begun to climb the first hill when his beloved Slow Joe began to lurch drunkenly to the left with such force that he wasn't sure he could bring it to a stop before it jumped the tracks.

CHAPTER NINE

"WHAT'S HE DOING?" Patty asked, her eyes flitting back and forth from Joe to Mandy, who was standing anxiously in the center aisle a good hour after the train had bucked to a stop under Joe's skilled hand. "Do you think we're going to get back to school in time for the kids to catch the bus?"

Mandy patted her on the arm and offered an encouraging smile. It was already quite obvious that they'd be lucky to get the kids home before dark. If Mandy was really lucky, she'd have enough time to shower and change her clothes before the parents' meeting.

The wind had picked up and the temperature had dropped considerably since they'd gaily wrapped up their picnic. A few doomsayer children were prophesying snow. Any way Mandy looked at it, things weren't going well on the Slow Joe.

From the moment she'd arrived at the station this morning, she had realized that she was skating on thin ice. On her own ground, she could keep herself together enough to hold Joe at bay. But in his world—the world of his ancient locomotive—she felt powerless. She should have spent this day remembering the terrible humiliation Joe had caused her on this very train as a child. Instead she'd spent lunch all but trembling with desire because his eyes had begged her to reconsider her insistence that there could be no future between them.

Now that she knew she loved him, it was hard to remember her litany of reasons.

"Do you think one of us should go talk to him?" Patty asked. "I mean, at the very least we ought to get a message to Mr. Cottonwood. And maybe the police."

Mandy shuddered at the very thought. The last time she'd taken a group of kids on the Slow Joe the police had been summoned, and she didn't think she—or Joe—could endure it again. But she volunteered to go talk to him about the situation, even though she knew he wasn't likely to be patient when he was upset about his beloved train.

But Joe did not grump at Mandy when she crawled over the tracks to stand behind him. He did not acknowledge her at all.

His biceps glistening with sweat despite the icy wind, he was struggling with an ugly piece of metal on the tender that clearly was not about to give even though Karen's friend David was doing his best to help him. Mandy had no idea what was wrong with the train and knew enough not to ask, but she had to fulfill her responsibilities to the children.

Gingerly she queried, "Joe, may I ask you a question?"

Without turning around, he grunted in a husbandly fashion as he picked up another tool.

"Is there a way to get in touch with your people at the station house so we can notify the school that we'll be late?" she persisted.

Joe nodded, then told David to go radio the message. A moment later, Mandy and Joe were alone outside the tender.

She could have left him then, returned to the safe indifference of the train. But as she watched Joe wrestle with his problem, she wrestled with a problem of her own. She wanted to thank him for handling Frank Raskin without pointing out that Frank was a copy of the troublemaker Joe himself had been. She wanted to tell him how worried she was about her sister and how much she needed to lean on a friend. She wanted to confess that she longed to be his lover even though she knew she never could.

Before she could make any mistakes, Joe asked in his train owner's voice, "Is there anything else you and the other teacher need to know?"

Mandy straightened and forced herself back into her professional role. "Do you have any idea how long the repairs will take? The kids are getting restless, and I think Patty's a little bit scared."

"Go back on board and tell Patty that Old Slow Joe has never been licked by a breakdown," he assured her. "Then start an impromptu lesson on pioneer travel problems...not just trains but broken wagon wheels, lame horses, Indians, snowstorms, Jesse James. Make it a game, Mandy. Keep 'em happy. And send Ira back and forth if you need a messenger, or if you want one of my employees to give a little speech on some aspect of railroad history." He gave Mandy a managerial smile and reminded her, "Whatever you do, stay calm. Everybody will take their cue from you."

A quiet warmth started to fizz through Mandy. It wasn't the sensual fire that so often thrilled her during the night when she dreamed of Joe. This was something different, something that had to do with the quiet authority of the man before her, the man she was certain would get them out of this fix. To her surprise, she admitted, "I trust you, Joe."

He looked surprised. "Do you, Mandy? In what way?"

She gestured toward the train. "I feel completely secure putting the children in your hands, Joey. I know you'll get us home safely."

He nodded in wordless acceptance of her compliment, then, very softly, he said, "I'm sorry, Mandy."

"It's not your fault, Joe," she quickly assured him. "I'm sure you keep your train in tip-top condition. These things—"

"I'm not talking about the train." He laid the wrench on the edge of the tender and turned to face her fully. "I mean Frank, Mandy. I mean . . . me."

Mandy wasn't sure what to say. Gingerly she admitted, "You handled him very well, Joe."

"I didn't handle *him* at all, Mandy. I just did what somebody should have done with *me*."

Mandy bit her lip and looked away. "I did my best, Joe. I did—"

"I'm not blaming you for anything, sweetheart," he whispered, his gentle knuckles brushing her face as sweetly as the unbidden endearment brushed her heart. "You were little Patty. A sweet child. I never got it before, Mandy. Today when I looked at her battling with Frank, I knew—" Mandy closed her eyes against the tenderness of his touch "—I knew how terribly much I hurt you two dozen years ago. I wish it weren't too late to apologize."

"Oh, Joe." Mandy breathed his name, leaned her cheek against his hand, found her fingertips tugging at the edges of his striped shirt as if to bring him closer. "We both made so many mistakes. We just didn't *know*. I was so young, and you were even younger. I think we should just . . . forget it now."

Joe's broad fingers cradled her neck and trapped her windblown red hair. "I want to forget it, Mandy. All of it. I just don't want to forget *you*."

Mandy swallowed hard. She forced herself to meet his beautiful brown eyes. "Joe, I told you, I—"

"You've told me you want me in three dozen ways. I've tried not to push you. I've tried to pretend you're just another woman. I've tried to pretend I don't care."

His thumb dropped to stroke her delicate neck, enticing Mandy with a tender brand of arousal she'd never known before. "I'm going to cannibalize this tender and use the bolt to jury-rig the sheared one below the broken shock absorber," he promised softly. "Then I'm going to get us all home. Tonight, after your meeting, I want you to stop by my house. We need some time to talk when we won't be interrupted. We need some time alone."

Mandy shook her head. Panic filled her throat. "No, Joe. We can't. We—"

"Can you tell me you don't want me, Mandy?" he asked bluntly.

His eyes demanded total honesty, and she could give him no less. She ached for him; it was written in neon letters across her anguished face. Words of denial simply would not come.

"I got through with no problem, Mr. Henderson," David suddenly called out from behind them.

Joe turned to answer the boy. As he dropped his hand from Mandy's face, she closed her eyes in relief and...was it loss?

A flush of need for Joe consumed her...not just her need for his body, but her desperate need for his heart.

It took all the strength she possessed to keep from reaching out to touch him one more time before she walked away.

HOURS LATER, as the first snowflakes of the season began to flutter down on Redpoint, the Slow Joe chugged into town at half speed. Mandy let Patty say goodbye to Joe as she loaded the kids on the bus, collected Karen and drove on home. After a brisk shower and a rushed dinner with Ruth, Mandy scrambled back into the Toyota and zipped back into town for the parent meeting. She slipped in the west door just as the meeting was about to begin. A few moments later, Gerry introduced her—introduced all of the teachers present, in fact—and the audience of concerned parents clapped. Mandy glanced around the room, smiling genially, until she spotted a familiar face in the front row.

Dear God, no, she silently prayed. *He wasn't kidding. He means to call my bluff tonight.*

Joe had taken the time to change also. His hair was still slick from the shower. A few strands caressed the button-down collar of his shirt. It was a deep shade of rust that highlighted his eyes and looked sharp with his freshly creased brown pants.

Joe did not try to hide his feelings from Mandy... nor his purpose in coming to the school. From the moment he spied her, his eyes never left her face. She tried to look over him, around him, anywhere else in the room. But he seemed to fill the big cafeteria where he'd once splattered spaghetti against the walls, and her body called out to him as urgently as did her heart.

Oh, Joe, the tiny voice of longing within her begged him. *I have to give a speech this evening. I can't think with you so near me. And when I go to the lectern you'll be almost close enough to touch....*

And he was. By the time she started to speak—an anxious half hour later—he was so close that when she went to the front of the room, her skirt brushed his knee. Mandy never looked at him directly, but she felt his eyes on her face, on her breasts... imagined his hands against her legs. It was a simple speech on the value of role-playing to teach social studies, one she'd given a dozen times in Denver, but she went blank three times and actually stuttered near the end. Mercifully she was able to leave the lectern by a different route when it was over. She made sure she did not pass Joe.

She wanted to escape after that, run from the building, but there seemed to be parents everywhere asking for her opinions and advice. In fact, she seemed to find herself talking to every parent in her class and Patty's...every parent except Joe.

When the cafeteria was nearly empty, Mandy glanced around and realized, with a start, that Joe was gone. She tried to tell herself that it didn't matter; she tried to tell herself that she was relieved. She even tried to pretend that he'd only come out of deference to Ira, and that she'd imagined that scene by the tender this afternoon.

But all the lies failed her. Joe had told her that tonight would be the night, and though every piece of logic she possessed told her that giving herself to him was not right and she should not—*would not!*—go home with him, it did not change the fact that she was crushed that Joe had not followed through on his husky promise.

Come to my place, Mandy, he'd begged her. *We need to talk alone.*

The words suddenly rang in her ears. Had he discreetly gone home to wait? Surely he didn't think she'd just *go* to him after all that had happened? After she'd told him again and again that a relationship between them could never, ever be?

As the agonizing questions of right and wrong and past and present hammered at her conscience, Mandy assured a dozen parents that their children were doing well in her class and warned one that her daughter might have a

problem. That mother kept her busy until Gerry Cottonwood asked Mandy—the last teacher still present—to lock
up when she left because he'd promised to pick up his
grandson at work. Quickly she agreed, grateful that Redpoint was the sort of place where a woman was safe alone
after dark.

When the last parent left a few moments later, Mandy
finished putting her papers and books in her briefcase,
then quickly checked the east door. She was halfway to the
west one when her heart flip-flopped—first with fear and
then with joy—as she spotted a tall man silhouetted on the
threshold.

Mandy felt a great surge of heat low in her abdomen.
She watched Joe close the door, lock it, then turn to study
her face as she slowly crossed the room to his side.

"I'm supposed to lock up," she said softly, as if to explain why she alone among the staff had stayed so late.

"Everything is locked," he answered, his eyes intimately caressing her face. "Are you also supposed to turn
out the lights before you go?"

A crushing wave of desire forced the air from Mandy's
lungs as Joe reached behind himself and flipped off the
lights. As the cafeteria slipped into total blackness, Mandy
knew that Joe was done tolerating her mixed messages,
done waiting for her to decide that he deserved her love.
He wasn't even going to wait until she agreed to go to his
house or meet him somewhere else. He was going to demand her surrender. Right here and right now.

"Joe, this isn't a good idea," she protested, laying one
hand against his chest in a gesture that she hoped would
place some distance between them.

It didn't. Joe covered her hand with his own and pressed
yet closer.

"You're right," he answered in a cougar's purr. "It would be better if we went to my place before I kissed you. Or anyplace else we can be sure we'll be alone." His voice was low, sensual...determined. His warm breath caressed her face as he spoke.

Mandy shook her head, though she knew he could not see the motion in the crazy quilt of moonlit patches dancing on the wall. "Joe, I told you I don't want this," she pleaded. "I told you it's not appropriate for us to...well, to do anything. To be alone together."

"If you don't want to be alone with me, Mandy, just walk out the door." He tugged her hand closer, separated one trembling finger from the others and slipped it into his mouth. His lips were warm, questing. The sucking sensation seemed to tug Mandy's whole body another inch in his direction. "Tell me not to touch you," he dared her, his voice as erotic as his liquid touch. "Tell me this isn't what you want."

Mandy was powerless to speak at all, let alone to demand that he release her. In this giant, vacant room where she had smelled ketchup and unwashed children's bodies just yesterday, she now smelled the faint scent of aftershave and the quiet virility of *man*. Her nostrils drank in the smell with a primal need that shocked her.

Desperately she struggled to get a hold on her feelings. "Joe—" she warned as he took one more step toward her, a step that caused his pectorals to lightly brush her breasts. "This isn't proper. What if somebody—" he took the briefcase out of her hand and set it on the ground "—should see us? What if—" he slipped both arms around her waist "—somebody should come back? What if—" He lowered his mouth a half inch from hers and she couldn't remember the end of the sentence. She couldn't remember anything at all.

"I want to kiss you, Mandy," he whispered, his warm breath laving her lips. "I want to kiss you more than I've ever wanted to kiss any woman in my life. But I won't do it if it's not what you want, too."

Mandy felt something break inside her. If he'd forced himself on her, she could have hollered at him, "Don't act like little Joey!" and pushed him away in disdain. But his short, square nails were already carving tiny circles on the small of her back as he breathed deeply—urgently—in and out, causing his rock-hard pectorals to fondle the instantly stiff tips of her breasts. His mouth was so close that all Mandy had to do was lick her lips and she'd be kissing him.

"Don't do this to me, Joe," she begged, her fingertips sliding into his thick collar-length hair. "You know I can't keep on saying no."

She closed her eyes and waited for him to make the first move. It had to be Joe's move; she *had* to be able to say that he'd forced her. But he didn't move, didn't speak, just kept taking those long, breast-fondling breaths and etching those tiny, tantalizing circles with his fingertips. His virile mouth waited millimeters from her own.

Mandy's thighs parted slightly, opening toward Joe. She felt damp and fiery, despite the dry cold. Her breasts seemed to lift and tighten; she longed to press them into his big gentle hands.

She reminded herself of every reason she'd ever had to keep Joe Henderson at a distance, every reason why a romance between them could never work out. Nervously she licked her lips.

And then, because she could not stop herself, she also licked his.

In that instant, Joe's resistance broke. His mouth claimed hers with fierce, sweet hunger, then his tongue stole past her teeth and plundered hidden pockets of sensation she'd barely known.

Mandy moaned. She felt as though she'd waited a lifetime for this kiss, ached for it, dreamed of it, longed for it with every fiber of her soul. She had known it would be wonderful, but not even her most erotic nighttime fantasies had prepared her for *this*.

As Joe's work-callused fingers first brushed back and forth across her exquisitely sensitive nipples, Mandy gripped massive chunks of his thick sandy hair, sensuously tugged and twisted. She felt as though her breasts were linked to her core of desire by a set of invisible erogenous reins. In some other life, she knew that she'd been mildly aroused when her breasts had been fondled, but the remembered sensation was a pale imitation of the volcanic need Joe's preliminary touch engendered in her now.

"Joey, Joey, *Joey!*" she gasped.

It seemed to be the message he'd been waiting for. Abruptly his hot hands abandoned her breasts, slid down her back and cupped her buttocks as he thrust his whole long body against hers with the fervency of a need too long denied. Electrified, Mandy tilted her pelvis up, up, up to meet his, rocking urgently against the rigid proof of his desire.

"Oh, Mandy!" he cried out, his warm breath fondling her sensitive ear. "You feel so good. So right."

Without thinking, Mandy slipped her fingertips under his belt and tugged on his shirt. Hungrily she kissed him. "I want you, Joe! I want you so much." She kissed him again, his tongue dancing with her own, while her woman's core desperately sought to embrace his masculinity despite the fence of clothing.

And then, abruptly, Joe left her mouth, left her hips, left her wildly palpitating warmth, which surged toward ecstasy. Still gripping her elbow with one hand, he stepped away from her, into the dark, breathing hard.

"Mandy, come home with me," he begged. "Another second of this and I won't be able to stop. As much as I want you, I know we'll be sorry later if we finish this here."

His words touched something deep inside her... something inside that seemed to break. That Joe would remember the values she lived by at a moment like this—despite his fierce arousal—told Mandy how much she'd underestimated his integrity. But the fact that he actually believed, for even a second, that she would go to his house or consider completing this ill-advised first kiss with...with... *Admit it, Mandy, he's talking about making love with you. Tonight! And you want it every bit as much as he does. Maybe even more!*

The realization shocked her. Suddenly she remembered that she was standing in the Redpoint Elementary School cafeteria—ostensibly closing up for her boss—rubbing pelvises with Joey Henderson! She didn't know how it had started...didn't know how to make it stop.

"Joe," she gasped, "I'm sorry. I didn't mean to...ask for this."

"Don't, Mandy," he warned, his voice thick with need as he pulled her close again. "Don't play with me. Don't say you don't want it. Don't blame it on me."

She shook her head, gasped for words. "I *do* want you, Joe, and I know the fault for this is mine as much as yours. But I can't do this. I can't do it here, and I can't do it at your place. Please forgive me, and—" it killed her to say it "—please leave before this gets out of hand."

Beside her cheek, she heard Joe's fist slam into the door. It missed her by a good six inches—she knew he would never strike a woman—and she felt no fear.

"Damn you, woman!" he swore softly. "I should have known you'd do this to me again."

"Joey," she begged, reaching out to touch his lips with urgent fingertips, "I didn't mean for this to happen. I'm not playing with you—please believe me. I just...can't seem to get a grip on things when you're around. I can't—"

He seized her again, kissed her and pulled her back against his brawny frame. She tried to pull away but her arms mutinied, clinging to his shoulders, dragging him closer yet.

It was a long moment later before she managed to break off the kiss, pressing her face into his chest and taking comfort there even as she begged, "Joey, help me! This isn't right for me no matter how much I want it. Please be strong for me. Please just go."

He slipped one hand into her hair, wrapped the ends around her fingers and tugged so hard it almost hurt.

"Dammit, Mandy! You're breaking me," he swore.

A sob broke from Mandy's throat...a sob of frustration, not of fear.

But at once Joe's hand opened and his grip grew light. His palm cradled her against him, offered tenderness and warmth. He took a deep breath, obviously struggling for calm. A mighty trembling seemed to overtake him, and for a moment he could not still it.

"Sweetheart," he whispered against her hair, "I can't go on like this. You're tearing me up. My heart is in shreds and my body is...going berserk. If you send me away tonight, I won't ask you again. I just can't." He kissed her temple once, very gently. Then he slowly released her—broke all body contact—and stepped away.

Mandy felt like a kitten tossed into the rain. She wanted to reach out for him and pull him back. She wanted to turn on the lights so she could see his face. Surely his eyes would tell her that he wouldn't give up, wouldn't turn away.

"I mean it, Mandy," he said darkly, his breath still coming in hard gasps. "Since July I've summoned every ounce of patience I've ever had in my life for you, but you finally have used it all up tonight."

Despite her vows, Mandy reached out for him once more, clung to his chest as his arms embraced her uncertainly. "Oh, Joe, I want you." Desire painted every syllable of her confession. "I want you so much!" She pressed her lips against the skin framed by the V-neck of his shirt. Nipped at the dark hair. "But I *can't*. Don't you understand?"

"No, I don't understand!" He grabbed her hands, pushed them from his chest. "If I were somebody's husband or you were somebody's wife—"

"But I'm somebody's *teacher*, Joe. Somebody's aunt. Somebody's mother. And you're somebody's dad!"

Abruptly Joe released her hands. He exhaled sharply, once, twice. Then he pushed open the cafeteria door, flooding her with the awesome chill of the windy night.

"You left one out, Miss Sawyer," he growled before he melted into the blackness. "I'm also somebody's fool."

CHAPTER TEN

THE DRIVE HOME was a nightmare for Mandy. At no time in her life could she recall feeling more helpless, more frustrated, more aroused. At the most unexpected moments, wild flurries of desire would seize her, almost crippling curls of sensual longing between her legs. She told herself that she was a normal, healthy woman and Alan had been gone a long time. It was natural for her to feel sexual desire now and again, wasn't it? Nothing unusual. Surely nothing to do with Joe.

But she knew it wasn't true. She knew that nobody, not even Alan, had ever inflamed her the way Joe did. And she knew that she'd left him rocked with the same desire, the same anguish, the same questions about why it seemed so imperative for her to push him away.

But you didn't push him away, Mandy, not really, she had to admit to herself. *You begged him to help you and he was strong and loving enough to do it. What would have happened if he'd continued to seduce you anyway? Could you really have managed to say no?*

The thought of making love to little Joey Henderson in the Redpoint Elementary School cafeteria filled Mandy with such shame that she could hardly bear to think about it. When Joe had first touched her, she hadn't thought about it at all; it was Joe who had realized how quickly they were rushing toward the consummation of their long-banked desires...Joe who had put on the brakes for Mandy's sake, not his own.

Joe whom she'd ordered away from her body, away from her heart.

She was still fiercely aroused and edgy by the time she got home, praying that Ruth was already in bed. But Ruth was waiting for her in the living room, hovering like a mother hen.

"How was the meeting, Mandy? Did you have to stay so late?" she chided her. "I called Joyce Williamson to see what time it was over and she said that everybody left about an hour ago."

Mandy dropped her briefcase with a clatter. "Most of the parents left then but the teachers had to stay for a while," she snapped. "Gerry asked me to close up and I got pigeonholed by a parent after everybody else left."

She didn't bother to mention who the parent was or what she'd done with him...and what she longed to do with him now! How she ached to have a sister with whom she could share her true feelings! A sister who wasn't a watchdog but a friend!

Mandy knew she had no patience this evening; if she stayed downstairs she would end up quarreling with Ruth. So she told her sister, "I've had a long day, Ruthie, so I'm going to get some shut-eye. If you'll excuse me—"

"You're not going to sit down and talk to me?" Ruth asked, eyes big and mournful. "I've been waiting for you to come home all day."

Mandy stifled a sharp retort. "I'm sorry, Ruth. Really I am. But I'm just not in the mood for company right now."

"And what kind of a mood do you think I'm in?" she asked. "Here I am, stuck in this house with an ungrateful daughter, too weary to see my friends, feeling more depressed every day—''

"Only because you won't go see another doctor!" Mandy burst out unsympathetically. "Any fool can see that you're not going to feel any better without some help, but you refuse to go to one of those specialists in Grand Junction. Sometimes I almost think you *want* to get worse so you'll have a reason for everyone to feel sorry for you!"

The words were true, but Mandy never would have said them if she hadn't been out of control. Ruth's face flamed a bright red as she stood, clutched her stomach, and leveled Mandy with a glare that would have cowed a weight lifter. "If you find it so difficult to spend time in my company," Ruth declared almost malevolently, "maybe you should consider living in some other house."

"Yes—my own!" Mandy railed at her, too angry to hold her tongue. "Why the hell do you think I came back here in the first place? Do you think I *like* living in Redpoint in my big sister's shadow?"

Ruth's eyes grew wide. "I thought you were lonely! I thought it was too hard for you to live in Alan's house all alone!"

"Are you kidding?" Mandy hollered back. "I loved my life in Denver! It was poor Karen who couldn't go on living alone with you! I couldn't leave her here with you falling apart at the seams!"

The minute the words were out, Mandy's anger was spent. She felt a deep, terrible wash of shame as she realized what she'd said. *And this is your fault, too, Joey!* she wanted to scream. But it wasn't true and it wasn't fair, and she knew she couldn't keep lying to herself. She was going crazy trying to pretend she was somebody she was not—a grown woman who was perfectly happy living under the thumb of her neurotic sister, perfectly happy without Joe Henderson, perfectly happy to go on sleeping alone.

"Ruthie," she began to apologize, but she was speaking to Ruth's back. "Ruth, please listen to me. I'm just overly tired tonight. I've had a terrible day and—"

Before she could finish, Ruth's bedroom door slammed in her face.

JOE'S STATION WAGON HIT EVERY BUMP in the road between Redpoint Elementary and the Slow Joe, and despite the long day he'd put in, he didn't bother trying to go to bed. He felt as restless as a caged animal, and he knew that he had to have some vigorous exercise—fast—before he lost his mind.

He changed into a sweat suit and started to run, even though jogging was not a regular part of his routine. He did four laps around the Slow Joe grounds before he realized that such a simple routine would not be nearly enough to assuage his needs. Ignoring the brisk wind and light snow, he took off at top speed in the direction of Brady's bunkhouse, a good ten miles away.

As his feet hit the ground, he counted *one, two . . . one, two . . . one, two. . . .* After a while it was *left, right . . . left, right . . . left, right. . . .* And then, despite his vow to think of anything but the chimerical female who had left him in such torment, he found himself breathing *Man-dy, Man-dy, Man-dy. . . .*

"Dammit!" Joe burst out when he finally recognized the silent name hammering in sync with his footsteps. "Go away! Leave me alone!"

But the specter of Mandy's passion sizzled in the air all around him, and he was suffused with the tantalizing promise of their unfulfilled love. He wondered what would happen if he changed course and jogged all the way out to

Ruth's house, banged on the door and said, "I've come for you, Mandy! To hell with what anybody else thinks! I want you and you want me, so open up!"

He had a sudden vision of Mandy slamming the door in his face, a vision so real that his nose actually hurt. It was right about then that he came to a halt, took a good look around him, and realized that he was six miles from the station and utterly exhausted. It was already midnight, and he had a long walk home.

IT WAS STILL SNOWING when Mandy reached the Slow Joe, and her watch said it was almost 2:00 a.m. *Of all the asinine things you've ever done in your life, Mandy Larkin, this takes the cake,* she told herself as she boldly rang the doorbell to Joe's private abode. *There's no doubt about it; you have completely lost your mind.*

It had taken her over an hour to placate Ruth, or at least to get her to stop crying. After that she'd spent forty-five minutes with Karen, trying to work out a plan to convince Ruth to go see a specialist in Grand Junction. It wasn't until much later, when she'd crawled in between her lonesome, icy sheets, that Mandy realized that she was pleading with her sister like a child trying to con a parent into buying a Christmas puppy...or permission for a first date.

It was then, exactly then, that she'd decided to get dressed and come to Joe's. She didn't do it just because she wanted him desperately and knew she'd been unfair to him right from the start, or even because she knew that she had used up the very last of Joe's patience. If she even waited until sunrise, he would never approach her as a lover again. She went because she felt that her very personhood—her sense of value as an adult—hinged on her freedom to take action. To take action *now*. She couldn't take

Ruth to a doctor in Grand Junction in the middle of the night, but she *could* go to Joey Henderson.

And she had never wanted to go to a man so desperately in her life.

Mandy rang the bell again, shivering, wondering if there were nights when Joe did not come home. God knew she'd left him in as ripe a state of physical frustration as any man could expect to endure. She'd never asked him if he had another woman, full-time or now and then, and suddenly she realized that she'd be absolutely devastated if she wasn't the only female in his life.

She was debating whether or not to push the bell again when the door swung open. Clad only in a pair of jeans and his huge bronze locomotive buckle, Joe squinted out into the porch light, looking wild-eyed and half-asleep.

"Mandy?" he barked. "What the hell?" He took a deep breath, closed his eyes, slumped against the door frame. "Good God, you scared me half to death. I thought something had happened to one of my kids."

Mandy flushed and glanced at her watch again. *This is insane,* she told herself again. *This is not the reaction I'd bargained on.* Suddenly she remembered all the reasons she'd said no to Joe before. But this time none of them seemed to matter.

"No, no trouble with your children, Joe," she quickly assured him. "I'm sorry if I . . . alarmed you."

Joe glared at her, then asked belatedly, "Is it Karen?"

She shook her head.

"Ruth?"

"No."

Now his eyes met hers and he sobered as he took in the possible ramifications of finding her on his front porch in the middle of the night. He didn't look angry anymore, or sleepy, but he did look remarkably stern.

"What are you doing here?" he asked.

Mandy swallowed hard and focused on his naked, hirsute chest. "If I have to explain it, then I guess it was a mistake," she whispered, feeling about half an inch tall. "I'm sorry I woke you, Joe."

He didn't answer right away. She could hear his deep, heavy breathing.

"I didn't ask you to explain it because I couldn't guess," he retorted curtly, his expression more tense than encouraging. "I just think you owe me a...statement of sorts."

"A statement? What kind of legalese is that? I show up on your porch in the middle of the night after... after...after what happened at school tonight and you need some kind of a contract to gauge my intentions?"

Joe lowered his eyes, took a step back and motioned for Mandy to enter the house. She shuddered—not just from the snowy wind—and followed him. He closed the door, then slumped on the arm of the sofa.

Mandy had never been in his house before, but she was in no mood to study the American pioneer decor. Yet the living room struck her as clean and homey. Even the model train in the corner seemed to fit right in.

"I told you it was over," Joe said quietly, his expression grim. "I told you I was done playing your games."

Mandy swallowed again and struggled to speak. She couldn't seem to find her voice. *Surely he doesn't mean it. It can't be over. It just can't.* Out loud she squawked, "Joe, I know I've been...difficult—"

"*Difficult?*" he grated. "You've been bizarre!"

Mandy closed her eyes, fought the sting of tears. "Do you want me to go?" she quaked.

Joe exhaled sharply, grabbed her hand and tugged her roughly to his side. "I want you to tell me why you're here."

His fingers were not gentle or reassuring, but at least he was touching her, pulling her close.

"Joe, you invited me over. This evening. I know you didn't mean this late, but—"

"Dammit, Mandy, that's not good enough!"

Her eyes flashed open, met his and read his anger as he bluntly dropped her hand. "Say it, damn you! Look me in the eye and say it right out loud!"

She knew then what he wanted, knew that he would be satisfied with nothing less. As much as Joe wanted to make love to her—and she was certain that he still wanted it badly—he wanted to guard his ego and win this round even more. She longed to tell him that prideful triumphs have no place in love, but she wanted him too much to take the risk. And she knew, somewhere deep within her, that she owed Joe Henderson at least one victory. This was one time she was going to have to humble herself.

She kept her eyes trained on his, met his anger, his hurt, his unquenched desire. "I want you, Joe," she whispered, unable to put much muscle into her quivering tone. "I want you to make love to me."

"Say it again," he ordered, his expression unwavering.

"Joe—"

"Like you mean it. Like you'll mean it in the morning, too."

Mandy's eyes watered hotly. She found herself blubbering. "Please, Joey. I want you so much." When he still did not respond, she slipped her arms around his neck and slowly, intimately pressed herself against him. Still he made no move to touch her. "I need to feel your arms around me," she admitted desperately. "Don't make me beg."

Though Mandy was dressed in a heavy down jacket and ski pants, she'd never felt so naked. She'd just told little Joey Henderson that she ached for him, and here she stood, clinging to his totally unresponsive body, waiting hungrily for him to return her embrace.

"Would you beg if I wouldn't give you what you wanted any other way?" he asked, one bare forearm starting to rub back and forth across the feminine chest pressed against it.

Despite her heavy clothing, Mandy felt the tiny bud peak, felt the electric jolt between her legs. "Yes," she confessed, knowing how badly he needed to hear her say it. "But it would never be the same between us, Joe. It would be sex and nothing more."

The other forearm started sliding, stiffening the other nipple, inciting Mandy with a fresh wave of desire.

"And you want more from me than sex?"

"Yes."

"And you think I want more than that from you?"

Mandy heard it then, the urgency, the pleading in his angry tone. Suddenly she realized that he didn't just want to humble her, to beg for his body. He wanted to be assured of her love.

She tossed what was left of her pride on the floor and found the words for him. "I love you, Joey Henderson." She looked right into those beautiful dark eyes as she said it. "And I think you love me, too."

For a moment Joe did not move. Those virile arms against her taut nipples ceased to move, and his expression was frozen in hopeful disbelief.

And then, without warning, he confessed hoarsely, "Damn right I do."

An instant later Joe's muscular arms closed around her, pulling her clear off her feet. His full lips found Mandy, claimed her for his own. Again and again he kissed her—with hungry, flaming, openmouthed kisses that said, "You are my woman now," and fired her with an urgency she'd never known.

He did not ask permission to unzip her jacket or unbutton her blouse, nor did he waste a second before he deftly unhooked her bra and let it fall to her waist. Urgently his big hands cupped her breasts, trapping Mandy's achingly erect nipples between hot fingers, ignoring the lacy bra as it slid down to the sofa, then to the floor.

"Is this what you wanted?" Though his voice was still gruff, Mandy was thrilled by the fiercely tender undertone of his words.

She nodded. She could not speak.

Joe kissed her again. He kissed the left corner of her mouth; he kissed the right. Then he kissed each breast with urgent possessiveness, lingering moistly at the center of each one until Mandy pressed against him and moaned.

She started to shake as Joe's hand slid under the elastic of her waistband, flush against her abdomen, then lower, lower, all the way down. His fingertips tangled themselves in her woman's hair, stopping just short of the center, the ache, the yearning that had been building to a crescendo for hours.

"Joe!" she gasped, wrapping one leg around him as she tried to press her raging seat of hunger against his probing fingers.

Joe steadied her with his free hand as his other dipped to tease the moist, hot parting of her legs. Mandy started to whimper as she collapsed against his solid chest, clung to him with all her strength.

Joe's hands never ceased to work their magic—one pulling down her ski pants as the other continued to stoke the fire between her thighs—and his lips once more sucked the tight bud crowning one full breast. A moment later his tongue whipped Mandy's other turgid nipple with a hot urgency that inflamed her.

In a blur of erotic pleasure, Mandy surrendered to Joe completely, crying out incoherent syllables of need as she pressed hot kisses into the valley of his neck.

"I couldn't stay away anymore," she confessed between kisses. "If you had any idea how many nights I've dreamed of this, how many times I promised myself to forget you—" he kissed her open mouth again, his tongue sweetly wrestling with hers "—but I couldn't, and after tonight I just didn't want to try. All I wanted—" he kissed her again, sucked on her lower lip, huskily breathed her name "—was to feel your body inside me, hear you tell me you're really mine."

With a moan that seemed to answer all her questions, Joe collapsed onto the couch behind him, gripping Mandy's waist with both hands as he crushed her lower half to his. They rocked so hard that the couch could not hold them, so Joe wrapped his thighs securely around hers as he rolled them both to the thick shag carpet below.

By now Joe was trembling as fervently as Mandy. As he unzipped his jeans, Mandy struggled with his massive buckle, wrapping ten fiery fingers around his swollen shaft as soon as she achieved her goal. His sigh was fierce as she vigorously kneaded him, eager to make up for all the times she'd left him to wrestle with his desire for her.

"Mandy, Mandy! I've waited so long for this," he confessed almost frantically, his own passion further inciting her own.

At once Mandy slid down the long, hard length of his torso and took him hotly in her mouth. While her tongue whipped him into a frenzy, Joe's fingertips skated up her thigh, slipped under the tiny elastic band he found there and delicately teased her yearning flesh before he pulled down the tiny piece of nylon still hindering his quest. As Mandy's knees parted widely to welcome his hand, Joe's magic fingers slipped inside her, inciting her to sensual madness. She pressed against him in short, urgent thrusts—ever faster, ever harder—while his deft thumb flawlessly rotated the most intimate bud of her sensual center.

A moment later—when Mandy cried out and started to shudder—she couldn't stop herself from rolling over and fiercely straddling Joe. His instrument of pleasure was monumental, rigid, already thrusting, as she briskly took him deep inside.

As one breast fell across his face, he wrapped his tongue around the pointed nipple, all the while circling the other with the palm of his free hand. Mandy cried out her hunger, screamed his name, rode him and rode him and *rode* him until his volcano of need matched her own and they both, for the briefest of moments, were sated at last.

THE MORNING AFTER Joe first made love to Mandy, he felt so extraordinarily fine that he grabbed Wilma and waltzed around the office with her a couple of times the moment he walked through the door. She grinned. When he did it again just before lunch, she laughed. Right around three when he bounced toward her, she put up both hands and said, "I'm too old for this, Joey! You better let me sit down while you tell me all about her. Whoever it is, I'm thrilled for you. It's a joy to see the way you smile."

Joe chuckled, not quite embarrassed but not willing to share all of his secrets—or rather, Mandy's secrets—with Wilma just yet.

"The lady's a little shy about public declarations, Wilma, so let's not broadcast the good news, shall we? Let's just say that I'm a happy man this morning, and I intend to get a whole lot happier from this point on."

She pressed him for details anyway, but Joe held her off. Personally he thought secrecy was ridiculous at his age, let alone Mandy's, but she had a right to her feelings and he wasn't going to push it . . . at least not yet. It was enough that she'd finally given herself to him and he was almost certain that the next time he saw her, she wouldn't try to escape from the commitment she'd made to him.

But what is that commitment, Joe? he asked himself now. *She made love to you with volcanic passion. But then she scurried off after she made you promise not to tell a soul until she could find just the right way to "break it" to Ruth.* Not wanting to tarnish the mood, Joe had tried to ignore the insult and reluctantly agreed to keep the change in their relationship under his hat for the time being. But he'd also made it clear to Mandy that if anyone near and dear to him guessed what was going on, he wouldn't lie about it.

He had also decided, five minutes after she left, that he would not contact Mandy until she called or came back to him on her own. It wasn't a matter of pride—at least he told himself it wasn't—but rather a simple matter of making sure that whatever was happening between them was two-sided and more than mutual enjoyment of sex. What he felt for Mandy was complex and worrisome and he was afraid to let himself get all tangled up in what still could well be a mirage. He wanted to believe that things were different now—that they were bonded inextricably—but he was also afraid to let himself hope.

After all, Miss Sawyer had squashed his ego too many times before.

"WELL, 'FESS UP," Patty declared after class that afternoon when she wandered into Room Five-B. Mandy was correcting a host of book reports that were all blurring together before her sleepless eyes. "Joe Henderson at last or somebody I haven't heard about?"

Mandy's jaw dropped and she flushed afresh. She'd spent a good deal of the day turning pink as she recalled the boldness with which she'd made love to Joe the night before. Alan would not have approved. He would not even have recognized her as a lover. And he would not have fulfilled her the way Joe had, either.

Alan had been a good husband—protective and kind—but in bed he had been very tame. Until last night, Mandy had not realized what she had missed for so many years. Granted, Alan had always done his best to satisfy her and had usually succeeded. But there was satisfaction, and then there was . . . well, there was *Joe*.

"Is it that obvious, Patty?" she asked, knowing it was too late to hide the truth from her perspicacious young friend. "Do you think you're the only one who knows?"

Patty grinned, delighted by Mandy's confession. "I'm probably the only one looking for the signs. Dark circles that say you got no sleep, but an X-rated smile, nonetheless. For the past few weeks you've looked like you were standing on the edge of a cliff. Today you look like you don't care anymore whether you fall off."

Mandy shook her head, too full of joy and anguish to bother trying to conceal the truth. Her time with Joe—both the wildly sensuous moments and the tender aftermath, during which time they'd shared her worries about her sister and Joe's concern for his friend—was too richly embroidered on her memory to cast aside. But the knowledge that she'd told Joe she loved him weighed heavily on her conscience, because she'd promised him that she'd tell Ruth, too. In the middle of the night, it had seemed like an easy thing to do. Now that she had to go home and face the music, she feared it was impossible.

"Oh, I already fell, Patty. No doubt about that," she had to confess. "The only question is whether I should give up hiking or admit that I enjoy the sport."

Patty's grin widened in delight. "It's Joe, isn't it?"

Mandy closed her eyes, tried to fight the rush of dizziness triggered by his name. "Please, Patty, I'm begging you. Don't tell a soul."

Suddenly Patty sobered. She even sat down cautiously in a student's chair. "You're still worried about how this looks to people, Mandy? Haven't you and Joe worked through that yet?"

"Joe has. I haven't. He's ready to tell everybody he knows that he's in love with me, but I convinced him to let me break the news to my sister first."

"So? You tell her tonight and it's over."

Mandy shuddered. "You don't know my sister. All my life she's told me what to do."

"I'd say it's time to tell her to buzz off."

Mandy shook her head. "It's not that simple. Ruth doesn't boss me around to be mean. It's her way of showing that she loves me. When I was little, I really needed her guidance, Patty. She was always so good to me, and I just hated to let her down. In a lot of ways, she's always been my mother. She relaxed a little while I was married to Alan because she picked him out, and she knew that he ... well, he made most of the decisions in our house."

As Mandy said the words, she realized that Alan had made *all* of the decisions in their house. Only in her professional life had she ever really learned to stand on her own two feet, and if they hadn't needed the money, she knew that Alan never would have let her work. No wonder she'd had such a terrible time deciding to go to Joe! She had so little experience making decisions alone.

Briefly she told Patty the old String Bean Sawyer story, which she'd deliberately kept to herself when Ira had been moved to Patty's room. While her friend was taking in this new data, Mandy continued, "Ruth will have a fit. She'll give me a lecture on the family name, Alan's memory, my impressionable niece, my sons' agony of losing their father..." She stopped as she pondered the last thought, the one that troubled her the most. How on earth would she explain to her twenty-two-year-old that she'd just made love to a man who was a mere decade or so older than he was? A man who had been a little boy when she'd first started teaching school?

"Oh, Patty, I'm in over my head on this one," Mandy admitted miserably. "I just don't know what to do."

"I don't think you've got much choice," counseled Patty. "Just bite the bullet and get it over with tonight."

It was good advice, but it turned out to be easier said than done. By the time Mandy picked up Karen and a bagful of French fries and hamburgers, it was almost six-forty-five, a good half hour later than they usually got home. Ruth, she knew, would make her feel guilty abut that, and she was already feeling guilty enough about the nighttime hours she'd surreptitiously spent with Joe.

But Ruth wasn't hovering in the living room when Mandy got home, waiting to berate her. She was huddling in her bed, sobbing uncontrollably.

"I thought you were never coming home!" she screamed, clutching her stomach with both hands. "I called Wilma and she said you left at six. Where have you been? Why didn't you call to tell me you'd be late?"

Karen pointed out that they were only thirty minutes past their normal arrival time, but that only incensed her mother further. Ruth started to rave about how grossly inconsiderate they were, larking about like two young girls while she lay in agony, abandoning the woman who'd done so much for them. After enduring a good five minutes of unwarranted abuse, Mandy said a bit curtly, "Ruth, it's not good for you to get so upset. I think you should take a tranquilizer."

To her amazement, Ruth said, "I did! In fact, I took two! One at four and another at six because I was getting frantic."

A new brand of alarm gripped Mandy's heart as her terrified eyes met Karen's, then settled back on Ruth as she sat down by the bed and took her sister's hand.

"Ruthie," she said softly, "how often do you feel like this? Not... grumpy, but panicky. When even a tranquilizer won't help."

Ruth started to cry again, but she did not pull away. "Not all the time. But... pretty often, especially when you're at work."

"What does pretty often mean. Once a week? Every day?"

She nodded, and her grip tightened on Mandy's hand.

"I'm scared, Mandy," she whispered. "There's something... really *wrong* with me!"

In that instant, Mandy felt Karen's eyes on her, felt her niece silently urge, *Do something! You're the grown-up here.*

And suddenly she realized that she was the only healthy adult in the house, and she should have done something long ago. Out of love for Ruth, Mandy hadn't pushed her sister. Out of love for Ruth, she'd have to overrule her now.

And out of love for Ruth, she'd have to postpone telling her about Joe.

"Listen to me, Ruthie," Mandy said quietly, brushing a wild lock of hair out of her sister's eyes. "This is what we're going to do. Tomorrow I'm going to call that gynecologist in Grand Junction and make an appointment for you."

"I'm not that old! I told you—"

"And the psychologist Dr. Hawthorne recommended, too."

"No! What if he says I'm crazy?"

"What if he does? Whatever's wrong, Ruth, you need a specialist's help to fix it! You're not going to get any better until you get some help. And I refuse to sit around any longer and let you get any worse!"

To Mandy's amazement, Ruth did not fight her. She folded up, in a near-fetal position, and gave in to the sobs. Looking helpless and bewildered, Karen reached out to pat her mother's shoulder, then stared at Mandy with tears in her eyes.

Mandy lay down on the bed beside her sister and wrapped her arms around her, rocking Ruth and crooning as though to a child.

"I'm going to take care of you, Ruthie. Everything is going to be all right."

Mandy was absolutely sure about the first promise. It was the second that was out of her hands.

By the time Brady showed up at the Slow Joe on Saturday afternoon, three days had passed since Joe had last kissed Mandy goodbye. He still had heard nothing from her, and it was starting to worry him. Granted, they hadn't exactly drawn up a road map about what would happen after they parted in the wee hours of dawn, but he hadn't been kidding when he'd told her he loved her, and he'd believed her—foolishly, perhaps—when she'd said that she loved him, too.

At first he'd been too jubilant to worry about technical details. But his patience was fading, and he found it hard to focus on Brady's wholly impractical ideas about how to operate one hundred measly acres of the Rocking T, all that the two of them could possibly afford.

"Land is land, you know," Brady began enthusiastically. "I was thinking that if I can't run a huge herd on such a small acreage, I might start a dairy."

Joe abandoned the cracked connecting rod he was trying to replace to glare at his friend. "What the hell do you know about the dairy business?"

"Hey, Joe, a cow's a cow! What's not to know?"

"Has it occurred to you that you'd be so far out in the boonies that the milk would probably sour before you got it to anywhere, let alone to some major distribution point?"

"That's what refrigerator trucks are for, Joe."

"Refrigerator trucks cost money."

Brady didn't answer; he just glanced away.

Joe shook his head and bent back over the rod. "Any other bright ideas?"

"Sheep. The Navajo have always done well with sheep in that country."

"The Navajo have always *starved* with sheep in that country. Besides, I thought cowmen hated sheep!"

"Well, we do as a general rule," Brady conceded. "But as long as they can live on the Rocking T, Joe—"

"Well, they probably can't, Brady. With a hundred acres or so you couldn't move them around. They'd finish off every spare blade of grass in no time, wouldn't they?"

Brady was silent. Morose. He sat down on the tracks and studied Joe. In fact, for several minutes he did nothing *but* study Joe. At last he said, "Something's happened since the last time we talked about this."

Joe's head snapped up. "What do you mean?"

"Something's happened to you. You're different."

"Different? Hell, Brady, how could I be different with you?"

"I don't know." His eyes met Joe's. "You're fighting me, Joey. You promised to help me before."

"You weren't irrational before. You said you'd come up with an intelligent plan, not a bunch of pipe dreams."

Brady shook his head. "I'm brainstorming, Joey. Sooner or later we'll hit on it. At least, we would if you were with me. But you're not. You're somewhere else."

Joe clanged down his wrench. "Dammit, Brady, I'm not anywhere else. I'm just trying to fix this damn connecting rod. Ever since Grandpa Howard's stroke I'm stuck with doing everything myself. Give me a decent plan and I'll still back you up."

Brady ignored him. "Is it Dad? Did he finally convince you he's right about the Rocking T?"

The misery in his voice caused Joe to stop what he was doing, straighten fully and stare Brady right in the eye. "Never," he said plainly.

Brady dropped his glance in a gesture of relief and shame. "I'm sorry, Joey," he murmured. "I shouldn't have asked you that."

Joe shrugged, determined not to make an issue of his friend's brief lapse of faith. Fortunately Brady didn't pursue the subject. But after another few moments of silence, he prodded, "Are you having trouble with Sarah?"

Joe shook his head.

"One of the kids?"

He turned back to the driver, knowing what his friend would ask him next. "No," he insisted. "Everything's fine. I thought we were brainstorming."

He was relieved when Brady didn't answer; for a moment he actually concentrated on his work. Then Brady said wonderingly, "I'll be damned. You sly dog, you! You slept with her, didn't you?"

The wrench slid out of Joe's hand and clanged against his boot. He stifled an oath and picked it up savagely. *I knew this would happen,* he cursed to himself. *I told Mandy I could only guard her secret if I didn't have to lie to somebody I love. Why the hell does she want us to keep this to ourselves?*

As calmly as he dared, he said out loud, "I'm in love with her, Brady. I think she kind of likes the idea but she doesn't want anybody else to know." He turned to face his buddy squarely. "At least not yet. You understand?"

Brady's eyes met Joe's. Slowly he nodded. "I get the picture. The *whole* picture. The question is, do you?"

"What the hell does that mean?"

"It means you've been had, old buddy." His tone was raw with sympathy. "I'm surprised you let yourself get sucked in like that. Personally I don't think you ought to have a thing to do with her if she's still ashamed to have her name linked with yours."

"I didn't say she was ashamed."

"Hell, you didn't have to! If she wants it kept under wraps, Joe, she can't be all that proud, can she?"

Joe closed his eyes. *Damn you, Brady, for putting my worse fears into words.* "Her sister's been ill," he snapped. "She wanted to break it to her slowly."

"Slowly? Hell, Joe, Mandy's been here since July. And as I recall, things were getting hot between the two of you about ten minutes after she arrived."

"Brady—"

"The first time I made love to Claudia I was ready to put a diamond on her left hand and give her my last name," Brady continued, undaunted. "She didn't even mention me to her folks for months." He scowled. "Get my drift?"

"I get it," Joe snapped. "And I don't like it a bit. Just because Mandy's sister hasn't been well and—"

"Oh, hell, Joey, Ruth's health doesn't have a damn thing to do with it and neither do you! It's little Joey Henderson who's keeping String Bean Sawyer mum. Do you think she'll ever be brave enough to tell another living soul that she actually slept with *him*?"

Joe tried desperately to come up with a convincing answer, but each hopeful syllable dried on his tongue.

CHAPTER ELEVEN

On Monday afternoon, Joe spotted Mandy heading for the office. She looked crisp and cool in a brightly flowered sundress, but her steps were hesitant and his stomach flip-flopped in anticipation and dread. Still, he held his ground in the lobby, watched her slip inside, spot him, smile uncertainly and glide in his direction.

"Hi," she greeted him, her expression warm but guarded. "How have you been."

Joe shrugged. "Can't complain. Business is all right. Kids have been well." *And you've been keeping your distance,* he could have added. Instead he tacked on, "How 'bout yourself?"

Mandy nodded. "I'm ... fine, Joe. I'm ... here to pick up Karen."

He glanced at his watch. It was only three twenty-five; school had just gotten out. If Karen was working today—and he couldn't recall offhand whether or not she was—she couldn't have been on duty for more than fifteen minutes yet.

"When did she say she'd be through?" he asked, wondering if Karen was playing games with her schedule again.

But it was Mandy, he realized a moment later, who was using Karen's schedule to plan a daytime rendezvous.

"She said she'd be done at six. I didn't see any point in driving home when I had to come back so soon."

We have almost three hours, her eyes boldly told him now. *You're the boss at the Slow Joe. If you can spare the time. . . .*

A crazy surge of hope and joy swept through his head, followed by a spasm of need in the lower part of his body. He realized then that he'd put his feelings on hold over the weekend, not daring to hope, not risking the pain of waiting, wondering. . . .

He smiled. Mandy smiled back. His smile grew wider. Her smile grew so broad her teeth showed. Clean white teeth. Teeth that had nipped him in greedy passion, teeth that were shielded by those soft warm lips she'd so fiercely aroused him with. . . .

"Joey?" It was Wilma, standing in the open office doorway. "That young man is here for an interview. Randy Miller. I told him to go on into your office and wait."

Joe tried to stifle his dismay. *Engineer interviews today,* he remembered with an inner grown. *How many did I schedule?*

"Is there anybody coming after him?" he asked Wilma, his eyes never leaving Mandy's face.

"Just one, Joe. That elderly fellow from Utah. I rescheduled another interview for tomorrow and two people have canceled out."

Joe nodded, trying to look interested. "Tell Miller I'll be right there," he instructed Wilma. When she was out of earshot, he told Mandy, "Give me an hour. You can make some hot chocolate and rev up a fire if you want to get warm."

"I thought maybe you could get me warm," Mandy replied. Both dimples shaped her saucy smile.

Joe grinned. It was the first time since the day they'd met that Mandy had openly flirted with him.

"I'll do my best, ma'am. The Slow Joe is a full-service operation."

Mandy laughed. It was a joyful, heartwarming sound. "I think I'll start undressing now so I'll be good and chilly by the time you get there," she teased him. "How does that sound?"

Joe stifled a growl deep in his throat, managing to turn away before the need to touch her overpowered him. Somehow he got through his two interviews—and actually decided that the second man was a potential employee—before telling Wilma that he was not to be disturbed.

When he galloped up to the house, he found Mandy lying on the plush den carpet before a roaring fire. She was wearing nothing but an afghan that was draped loosely over her torso, shielding part of one breast and the curve of one hip. She smiled up at him provocatively while his breathing grew jerky and his erection firm.

"Next time I guess I should make an appointment," she suggested, her eyes shining with desire.

"No need," Joe promised, shucking his boots and tugging off the rest of his clothes. "From now on I'll hold this time slot open for you."

She stood then, and let the afghan fall. Joe went to her, spanned her rib cage with warm, searching hands and kissed her neck.

"I wasn't sure you'd come back," he confessed.

Mandy didn't answer; she just lifted her lips to his.

Joe's hands slid over her breasts, his palms flat as he rubbed her nipples in big, slow circles. At once he felt her body yield to him, felt her quiver under his loving touch.

"I can't stay away from you, Joe," Mandy admitted with a throaty growl as her warm fingers slipped down his chest, tugging on renegade strands of hair. "I want something only you can give me."

He kissed her earlobe, drew it into his mouth and sucked on it for a moment before his tongue tickled the inner shell of her ear. "What is that, Mandy? What do you need?"

"I need to get warmed up," she reminded him playfully.

But Joe wanted more from her than sensual repartee. "What else?" he demanded softly.

He felt her tense, then quiver. Her nose pressed against his neck and her flaming tongue slid across his collarbone. The soft curves of her body melted against him in complete and undeniable surrender.

"I need your body," she confessed.

"Is that all?"

"I need your heart."

The thumb and forefinger of each hand closed around her nipples, tapping and twisting as she whimpered in a way that told Joe he was doing it just right. He wanted to arouse her unbearably, but never cause her any pain.

"And who do you have to trade for my body and my heart?" He pressed one thigh between her legs, keenly aware of her hot fingers now massaging the base of his spine. "What do I get out of this gift of my soul?"

Against his chest, he felt Mandy's throat constrict, felt her swallow hard. "Do you love me, Joey?"

"Very much."

"Then I'm yours."

He stopped his ministrations for just a moment to celebrate her confession, then tugged the tiniest bit harder on her nipples as she squirmed in delight. "Even in public?"

"Yes." She kissed him quickly. "But not quite yet."

"Soon?" he persisted. "We can let everybody know?"

"Everybody," she promised. But a moment later she told him that they'd have to wait until after Ruth's appointment with the gynecologist in Grand Junction next month.

"But you'll tell her after that?" Joe was determined to wait for a promise, but at that moment Mandy dropped to her knees and took him in her mouth. In an instant, speech was beyond him, and by the time he realized she'd never answered his question, it was six-fifteen and she was gone.

EVERY DAY FOR THE NEXT FEW WEEKS, Mandy scrambled to wrap up things in her classroom and gallop to Joe's place the instant she was allowed to leave the school grounds. And every day she found Joe waiting with hot chocolate and a cozy fire, eager to warm her body inside and out.

In some ways Mandy felt like a teenager in love for the first time. Part of it was the urgency of those brief, stolen hours arranged by secret rendezvous. Part of it was the sheer force of her physical desire for Joe and the compelling emotional bond they'd forged despite their early resistance to each other. And part of it was the knowledge that when she finally told Ruth the truth about their affair, something magical about it would have to end.

She knew that Ruth would spoil things. There was no way that her disapproval could not color the way Mandy felt about Joe. And even though she thought she had the strength to pick out her own lover, she still hated the idea of her big sister clucking at her poor judgment, hounding her for her capricious feelings and reminding her that her beloved late husband deserved better than to see her fall so low.

She couldn't share her fears with Joe; she couldn't bear to get him riled up again. She knew he was tense about her delay in telling Ruth, and every explanation she offered only seemed to exacerbate the problem. So for a flurry of delirious weekday afternoons—and one Saturday when Mandy stopped by for half an hour on her way back from running an errand for Ruth in town—she devoted herself to making love, not solving problems. Every time they bonded, Mandy wanted Joe more. And every time he said, "I love you, Mandy," she read the depth of his feelings in his caring eyes and knew that he deserved more than her secret approbation, knew that in time, he would *demand* more.

She was relieved when she finally took Ruth to Grand Junction, but too nervous to do more than flip through a magazine while she waited in Dr. Olson's plush lobby downtown. When a nurse asked her to join the doctor, Mandy was so rattled that she accidentally dropped her open purse on the ground and had to spend a minute reassembling the contents.

She found Ruth sitting in an overstuffed chair in the doctor's office, fully clothed but terribly pale. The doctor, a tall, balding man with a reassuring smile, sat behind a huge oak desk littered with pictures of youngsters Mandy assumed were his grandchildren.

"I think your sister has endometriosis," he explained after the standard pleasantries were out of the way. "It's a condition in which uterine tissue moves out into the abdominal cavity and attaches itself to various other organs. Unlike standard uterine lining, however, the menstrual blood does not empty each month, so the tissue becomes swollen and engorged, increasing in size and discomfort with each cycle. The pain is generally greater when the patient is ovulating or menstruating, as is the hormonal imbalance."

"Hormonal imbalance?" Mandy echoed, trying to take in his diagnosis.

"Emotional sensitivity. Excessive edginess or depression is quite common, as is considerable fatigue."

Abruptly Ruth began to cry. "I'm not losing my mind?" she whispered. "There's really something physically wrong with me?"

Mandy took her hand, battling her own tears. She had wondered—oh, yes, she had wondered!—if Ruth was falling apart at the seams. Her condition sounded terrible, but at least she wasn't losing a grip on her sanity!

Without commenting on Ruth's tears, the doctor said, "Fortunately, this disease is entirely treatable. In a few months our girl should be as good as new."

Ruth started to sob. Mandy took her in her arms, felt the hot tears against her cheek and silently offered a prayer of gratitude that Ruth's situation was not beyond repair.

Dr. Olson gave them a moment, then continued matter-of-factly, "Sometimes this condition can be cured or at least controlled with drugs, but unfortunately this is a very advanced case. I'm afraid Ruth has gone without proper treatment for so long that the only remedy now is surgery."

"Surgery?" Ruth yelped with a shudder. "You want to cut me up?"

The doctor sighed at her characterization of his craft. "Not necessarily. Nowadays we have a minor procedure called a laparoscopy, which involves a form of microsurgery on an outpatient basis. Essentially we just make a small slit at the navel, insert a long tube and sear the pockets of endometriosis that we find. If the adhesions are quite extensive, we'll need to open the abdominal cavity and scrape out all the infected tissue. Frankly I think that's more likely in this case, but we might get lucky."

When Ruth lapsed into another spasm of weeping, the doctor gave Mandy an understanding look and quietly left the room. "I'll call you with the details later," he said on the way out. With a jolt, Mandy realized that he was talking to her as though Ruth were the younger sister, Ruth the child.

I've taken over, she realized with a shock. *I'm in charge of the family now.*

On the heels of that discovery came the realization that everything in the life of their tiny family would have to be put on hold until Ruth's surgery came to pass. *Everything.*

Even Joe would have to wait.

THE DAY AFTER RUTH'S APPOINTMENT, Joe kept close to the office, waiting for a call or impromptu visit from Mandy. But Karen, who worked that afternoon, got a ride home with a friend, and the phone remained silent. It wasn't until the following morning, right around lunch, that Wilma came into his office grinning like a Cheshire cat.

"I have a message for you," she sang out, her eyes atwinkle.

He eyed her warily. He wasn't in the mood for games or secretarial questioning. He just wanted to hear from Mandy. "And what might that be?"

She sashayed toward him, almost wiggling her hips in delight.

"I have a message for you from Karen's aunt. Only—" her grin widened "—she didn't say she was Karen's aunt. She said, 'This is Mandy. Please tell Joe I won't be able to see him till Friday because I have to take Ruth back to Grand Junction for more tests.'"

Joe wasn't sure whether he was relieved or still miffed. At least she'd called, but she certainly wasn't in any great hurry to see him. He wanted only one message from Mandy, no matter when she had time to drop by. *I told my sister, Joe. Now I'll tell the whole world I'm yours.*

"Is that all she said?"

Wilma twittered and smiled. "No, it's not. Do you want to hear the rest?"

Joe scowled. "Do you want to keep working at the Slow Joe?"

At that she sobered. "Oh, Joey, you know I wouldn't tease you if it weren't good news! Do you think I'm blind? Do you really think I never noticed how often you disappear after Mandy shows up in the afternoon?"

He shrugged. "Wilma, I would proudly have told you the first moment we got together. I never intended to keep any secrets from you. Mandy's the one who's got this fixation about privacy. I've just been trying to honor her feelings."

Wilma patted his shoulder maternally. "Well, you don't need to sneak around anymore. Her last words were—and I quote—'Give Joe my love and tell him I still feel the way I did the last time we said goodbye.'" She hugged herself. "What I'd give to eavesdrop on those sweet nothings out in the parking lot!"

Joe leaned back in his swivel chair, his hands swinging behind his head in an unconscious gesture of triumph and relief. *Forget the parking lot, Wilma,* he hollered joyfully in silence. *The last time I said goodbye to Mandy I was still nude in bed. She leaned over to kiss me and I circled her nipples with my palms until she begged me to stop so she could calm down enough to drive home. So I did stop... just long enough to slide my hands ever so slowly*

all the way down to the union of her thighs. About the time
my thumbs came together at the very center...

Suddenly the hot rush of the memory vanished when
Wilma gave him a conspiratorial wink and promised him
she could be trusted with the lovers' secret.

"But it's not a secret anymore," he protested.

Wilma shook her head. "Oh, yes, Joe, it is. Mandy told
me in 'strictest confidence.' Those were her very words."

THE DAY MANDY CALLED WILMA, she promised Ruth
she'd rush right home after school got out, but she had to
make a quick run to the grocery store first. She considered taking a moment to drop by Joe's, but she knew that
he was going to need a lot more from her than a half hour
of razzle-dazzle hugs and kisses. This time he would want
answers, and she didn't think he'd let himself be dis-
tracted until he got some.

She had promised him that she'd tell Ruth about him
right after her first trip to Grand Junction, and she'd truly
intended to do exactly that. But Mandy had expected Dr.
Olson to give Ruth a prescription, not an appointment for
surgery! Ruth had been clinging to her even before the
news. Now, with Ruth agonizing over every possible sur-
gical problem, how could she casually toss out, "By the
way, Ruthie, I've been having a clandestine affair with one
of my former students so don't be surprised if I don't come
home tonight?"

Yet she knew that Joe was waiting... expecting imme-
diate proof that she did not intend to keep their affair under wraps any longer. Mandy's delay in making it public—
a whole month now—was already making him chafe, and
she couldn't say that she blamed him. Sharing the news
with Wilma had been the only bone she could throw to
him. She desperately hoped it would be enough.

It wasn't. She knew she was in trouble the minute she glanced up from the frozen-food aisle with a package of broccoli in her hand and found Joe leaning against the pizza door. He was scowling.

"If it isn't *my woman*," he said darkly, his arms crossed as he glared at her. "See her throw her arms around me. See me joyfully welcome her home."

Mandy dropped the broccoli into her basket. "Hi, Joey," she said as tenderly as she dared. "I've missed you this week."

"So I heard. That little piece of information came right before the news that you welshed out on me again."

Mandy's chin came up. "I told Wilma. Doesn't that count for anything?"

"Wilma already knew." He shook his head. "Karen knows, too. I can see it in her eyes. And Brady knows. He saw it in *my* eyes."

Mandy sucked her lower lip. "Patty figured it out right away," she confessed.

"Uh-huh. The whole damn town has probably figured it out by now. You know what's really funny? You're afraid that everybody is going to talk about you if they know you're in love with me. What's going to fuel their gossip is the fact that you've tried so hard to keep things under wraps. It gives people the feeling that you've got something to hide." He leaned forward, his expression grim. "It sure gives me that feeling."

Mandy flushed. "Joe, we've been over all of this—"

"I think you should kiss me hello," he interrupted. "I haven't touched you in three days."

"Oh, Joey," she whispered, feeling something inside of her melting, "you don't know how much I wish I could."

"It's not illegal," he said quietly. "Come here."

Mandy shook her head. "Somebody might—"

He stepped toward her and took her face in his hands. "Kiss me hello, Mandy," he said simply, his tone a cross between a plea and a command. "Nobody's watching. Nobody's here."

Mandy wanted to kiss him right, but all she could think of was that somebody might see her—see Miss Sawyer kissing little Joey—and she couldn't relax enough to look him in the eye. Knowing she couldn't just ignore his plea, she kissed him quickly and tried to pull away, but Joe pulled her back and claimed her lips with his. Or tried to, at any rate, before Susie Boswell's father suddenly rounded the corner of the aisle. Mandy jerked away from Joe so sharply that she jammed into the other man's cart and found herself apologizing profusely before he even had time to say hello.

But Patty's lover was all smiles—for Mandy and for Joe, who greeted him with a terse, "'Evening, Fred," before he sharply turned to go.

"Joe?" Mandy surprised herself by calling after him. When he stopped and turned around, his eyes dark, his lips thin and rigid, she tossed out clumsily, "Are we, er, done here?"

Before her, the face of the man she loved turned into the visage of a stranger, and answered, "It sure looks that way to me."

AFTER MANDY SNUBBED HIM in the grocery store, Joe was too restless to go home, so he dropped by Sarah's to ask his kids if they wanted to go out for hamburgers. They'd eaten already, but were more than happy to join him for some ice cream and an evening playing Monopoly, so he bundled them up, paid for four banana splits, and took them back to his house so he could spend the evening playing a game he heartily disliked. He was in a lousy mood and didn' expect to be good company, but he didn't feel like being alone. Besides, he'd hardly seen the kids since the first time he'd slept with Mandy—afternoons were their regular time with him, too—and he was feeling a little bit guilty. He was also having trouble answering their straightforward questions about how he was spending his time these days, and his answers were growing increasingly clumsy.

Joe found Mandy waiting on his front porch. Mandy pale and trembling. He was too angry with her to feel sympathetic, let along try to guard her secret any longer. Besides, at the moment he wasn't sure there was any secret left to keep. Brady was right. The plain, horrid truth was that Mandy was ashamed of him.

"Good evening, Ira," she said, doing a fair job of masking her shock at seeing the kids. She smiled at the girls, then said, "Hello, Joe."

He nodded with all the indifference he could muster. "What's up?"

Ira dug at the welcome mat with one toe. Sally whispered, "What did you *do*, Ira?" and Lynne gave a nervous laugh.

Mandy, looking almost paralyzed with despair, didn't seem to realize that all the kids thought she'd come to see Joe because Ira was in trouble. In fact, she seemed totally overwhelmed by their presence as Joe ushered her into the house.

He was too angry to care how Mandy felt at the moment, but not angry enough to let the backlash hurt his son. "Ira's not in trouble, is he?" he asked directly. "That's not why you've come?"

Mandy stared at him as though he were crazy. *Surely you know why I've come,* her eyes pleaded. But then she glanced at Ira, saw his stricken face, and soothingly touched the boy's arm. "Oh, Ira, honey, I'm sorry. I didn't mean to frighten you. You're doing very well in school and I didn't come here to report any misbehavior. I just needed to see your dad about something . . . personal.''

Ira's head snapped up. "You mean it, Mrs. Larkin? I'm not in trouble?" His relief took life and all but floated around the living room.

"I mean it." She gave him a teacherly smile of approbation that Joe had never received once during his year in her class. "You're doing excellent work and I'm very proud of you."

Ira sighed dramatically as he turned to Joe. "I told you I wouldn't let you down, Dad. I promised you I wouldn't mess up with her."

Joe nodded and reached out to shake his son's hand. "I know, Ira. I never doubted you for a minute."

Ira gave him an appealing grin, which, for some reason, reminded Joe of that sweet toothless smile he'd had five years ago. The boy gripped his hand, then, as though he didn't want to press his luck before he declared, "We'll all go play in the den."

"But I want—" started Sally.

Ira glared at his little sister and grabbed her shoulder. "We're *going* to play in the *den*," he ordered her, tossing Lynne a brotherly look that said, "Follow me." With a last curious glance at Mandy, Lynne skipped after her brother down the hall.

An hour ago Joe had been eager to spend some time with Mandy, but now he wasn't sure he wanted her in his house. He had too many conflicting feelings waging war in his soul. He'd thought she was done pushing him away the night she'd first surrendered to him. Now, quite belatedly, he realized that even her surrender had been a game.

"Can we . . . talk, Joe?" she pleaded now, those green eyes begging for some hint of reassurance.

He shrugged uncomfortably, wishing that his native courtesy wouldn't prevent him from telling her to get lost. "Have a seat," he suggested, his tone neither warm nor cold as he perched on the edge of his favorite recliner. "What do you want to talk about?"

Mandy hovered by the couch for a moment, then crossed the room to stand uneasily by his side. One soft, feminine hand reached out to touch his face. He remembered the texture of her skin, remembered the scent of her each time he'd kissed her mouth. "I love you, Joe," she told him earnestly. "I love you very much."

Coolly he met her pleading gaze. "Do you now? Do you even know what those words mean?"

"Joe—"

"To tell you the truth, I think your 'affection' for me is only skin-deep, Mandy," he told her bluntly. "You like the way I make you feel in bed, but other than that, you're ashamed of me." He glowered at her and pushed her hand away from his face. "You almost make me ashamed of myself. I feel like some damn gigolo."

"Joey, you're a wonderful lover, but it's more than that. It's—"

"I'm a family man, Mandy. I want to be a good model for my children. I've never feigned love for a woman just to get her into bed, and I never expected a woman to do it to me."

This time Mandy didn't answer, but her lovely eyes started to cloud with tears. Still, Joe pressed on. This time he would not be swayed by her sorrow. He had to cope with his own heartache.

"I've got all the kids I need, Mandy, but I wouldn't mind a loving wife. There was a time when I thought that you and I might be slowly heading in that direction." His tone hardened. He faced her coldly. "But we're not. In fact, our relationship hasn't moved at *all* since the first night you showed up here and begged me to take you to bed. I'm still begging for you to tell Ruth you love me, and you're still begging for sex.''

Mandy's face flamed. ''You don't really believe that's all I want from you, do you, Joe?''

She reached for his hand, clenched it, but Joe pulled away from her grasp. Slowly his eyes met hers.

''To tell you the truth, Mandy, I think you want somebody to fill in the gaps of your lonely life until you move back to Denver. If you ever marry again, it'll only be to a man who meets with your sister's approval. Maybe I'm a little more to you than a fun bedmate, but I don't think I mean anywhere near to you what you mean to me.'' The confession cost him, and he had to look away. ''I don't want to be your plaything, Mandy. I have a lot more respect for myself than you do.''

''Joe—'' she started again, but he raised one hand to silence her.

''I understand you've got a problem. All you can think about is Ruth. She's scared, upset, heading for surgery. It's not a good time to burden her.'' He shook his head. ''I don't have a problem with your concern for your sister, Mandy. My problem is that I don't appreciate being viewed as bad news. I've had plenty of time to think about this, and I honestly believe that if you were happy about our time together—deeply contented and proud to be my woman—you could make Ruth happy about it, too. Hell, as traditional as she is, she ought to be relieved and delighted that you're no longer mourning Alan.''

For a long moment she did not answer, did not move. He could feel her body near his arm, sense the strain in her. She stood so still that he could feel her quiver, hear her swallow back a sob.

"Joey," she finally whispered. "If one of your kids was injured, would you expect me to stand by you?"

"I don't expect anything from you, Mandy," was his sharp reply.

She didn't contradict him. "But would you *want* me to?"

"If you're trying to find out if my kids come first, of course they do. Especially if one of them is hurt."

"Ruth is hurt. Ruth is hurting. She's almost crazy with this hormonal imbalance and she's absolutely terrified to have surgery. She's always had a thing about doctors."

Reluctantly Joe met her eyes. "She's an adult," he pointed out.

"Not right now. She's as delicate as a baby." She licked her lips. "And she's my sister, Joe."

Joe glanced away, feeling like a heel. Why did she always do this to him? Twist things around so it looked as though *he* were in the wrong?

"I'm in the middle of a family crisis, Joe. I need your support, not your insecurities and accusations." She touched his shoulder, and this time he did not pull away. "Please believe that I love you, Joey. But I love my sister, too, and she's just a basket case right now. Please don't ask me to choose between you."

Joe could have pointed out that she'd already chosen, in her way, but he told himself that if he were the one who was facing surgery, Mandy might have decided to passionately stand by *him*. Quietly he asked her, "*Are* you ashamed of loving me, Mandy?"

She touched his chin, made him face her. "Absolutely not."

"Are you over all your reservations? All the reasons that you told me in the beginning that we could never have a future together?"

Still she met his eyes. "I threw them all away the night I first came to you. They belong in the past."

"And you're certain, in your heart, that the only reason you're asking me to keep our love a secret is that you don't want to upset Ruth? You're sure that if she weren't facing surgery, you'd tell her? And you'll tell her as soon as she's on the road to recovery?"

It seemed to Joe that Mandy hesitated for an instant before she replied, "I'll tell her, Joe. I swear it."

Joe wanted desperately to believe her. Slowly he touched her hand, the one he'd pushed away, then enfolded her in his arms as he pulled her down to share the roomy recliner.

She came willingly, but there was a tension in her body he had not felt in her since the first time she'd come to him in the night. He kissed her, kissed her gently, and it helped make things better, but it couldn't completely erase the doubts in his heart.

As Joe quietly dried her tears, Mandy dropped her head against his shoulder. "I'll tell her as soon as she's over this, Joe," she vowed again. "As soon as the doctor says she's well."

Joe didn't answer. He'd heard the promises before. He held Mandy silently, his arms loosely draped, until he heard her beg, "Are we okay, Joey?"

He kissed the top of her head and tried to sound loving even though he felt broken and jagged inside. "I love you, Mandy," he assured her. That much was the truth. It was the line he tacked on after it—"Sure, everything is okay between us"—that was a lie.

CHAPTER TWELVE

THE NIGHT BEFORE RUTH'S SURGERY, Mandy sat by her sister's bedside in the hospital, listening to old stories of her life that she'd heard a hundred times before. Karen was spending the night with Sandra, and Mandy had taken a room in a nearby hotel. Joe had offered to join her there— for moral support if nothing else—but even though the chances of detection were awfully slim, she just didn't feel right about deceiving Ruth at such a sensitive moment.

Still, she felt terrible about turning Joe away. Their relationship was so precarious right now! He had truly frightened her that night she'd broken off their kiss in the grocery store. Granted, by the end of the evening he'd apologized for his hard words and assured her that everything was okay. But now there was a strain between them that had not been there before. Even in bed she could feel him holding back. His hands were still gentle, but stiff somehow, and his beautiful eyes often watched her with more pain than desire. Mandy tried to think of a way to break through the plastic curtain, but she knew that until she could say, "I told her, Joe," even bringing up the subject could only push him farther away. At the moment he was still reaching out to her, but Mandy was terrified that she might yet lose him.

Poor Patty had lost her lover the week before and was still teary-eyed every day. Just as Mandy had predicted, the other teacher's encounters with Susie's father were now awkward and strained. Once Mandy had worried greatly about how she'd relate to Joe as Ira's father after he'd been her lover, but now—when the reality of losing him seemed so frightening—she found that her professional role in the scheme of things was the least of her concerns.

While Mandy grappled with her secret fear, Ruth babbled on for an hour in an obvious effort to conceal her own terror. Finally, when a nurse dropped by to say that in a few minutes Mandy would have to go, Ruth took her younger sister's hand.

"Thank you, Mandy," she whispered with uncharacteristic humility. "Thank you for taking care of me."

Mandy squeezed Ruth's fingers. "It won't really be so bad," she lied, eager to reassure her frightened sister. "Maybe they'll only have to do the laparoscopy. And even if they have to do the bigger surgery, the important thing is that you're going to be *well*, Ruthie. No more hysterics and no more pain."

Ruth nodded, hopeful but not quite convinced. "You were right to make me go to Dr. Olson. Do you know that that's the first time you've ever disobeyed me?"

Mandy stiffened at Ruth's use of the word "disobey"—it made her feel like a child. "Well, it's been a long time since you gave me orders, Ruthie."

Ruth chuckled. "Orders, advice, same difference. It's been a burden sometimes, Mandy."

"What do you mean?"

She licked her lips. "Well, I *could* have been wrong, you know. About some really important things."

"Such as?" Mandy was intrigued by her admission and curious as to the depth of soul-searching likely to come about tonight.

"Well, I think your career was a pretty important decision. But you've been very happy as a teacher, except for that first terrible year with Joey Henderson."

Mandy read her sister's eyes, looking for some clue to a deeper meaning, but she couldn't detect any proof that Ruth knew about her relationship with Joe. "I don't recall your making that decision for me, Ruth. I wanted to be a teacher right from the start."

"You wanted to be a teacher because I steered you in that direction! From the time you were little I encouraged you to gather up dolls and stuffed animals and then neighborhood kids and teach them whatever you'd just read in some book. I got you your first job as a teacher's aide, remember? I called your counselors at high school and college to make sure they steered you right. *And* I got you your first teaching job in Redpoint. That was a mixed blessing, I know, but not because *I* made a mistake. It wasn't my fault or yours, either, that that horrible child was dumped in your class."

"Joey wasn't a horrible child," Mandy insisted. "He was a very unhappy youngster acting out his frustrations any way he could."

"He was a brat."

Mandy wanted to deny it, but her honesty forbade her. Hadn't she used the same term to describe Joe to Karen just a few months ago? Instead she declared, "I appreciated your advice, of course, but I think I would have gone into teaching no matter what."

Ruth shook her head. "Mandy, you've never stood up to me about anything before this doctor thing. If I'd been wildly opposed to your chosen career, I would have convinced you to do something else. Just as I would have convinced you not to marry some totally unsuitable husband."

For one terrible moment, Mandy thought she was re-ferring to Joe. Granted, they'd never seriously discussed marriage, but the subject had cropped up more than once. Alone with Joe, it seemed like an idea born in heaven, but here by her sister's bedside, it seemed to Mandy like an uphill fight.

As Mandy pondered her sister's words, she realized that in Ruth's eyes, the only real lover she'd ever had was Alan. She had never seriously acknowledged the boy Mandy had been dating at the time Ruth introduced her to Alan . . . a boy Mandy had truly cared for before Ruth had virtually run him off.

"I was happy with Alan," Mandy answered defen-sively, feeling the need to assert herself. "And I'm glad that you liked him as a brother-in-law. But that doesn't mean that I wouldn't have married somebody you didn't like as well if I'd thought he was the one for me."

Ruth chuckled. "Not a chance. That's one reason I'm glad you stayed in Redpoint, Mandy. When I'm well I'll be able to start looking for a suitable second husband for you. I don't think you'll ever marry again if I don't pick some-body out."

Mandy knew she was supposed to take Ruth's com-ment as a joke, but the line echoed Joe's accusations so painfully that she could not bring herself to laugh.

MANDY CALLED JOE TWICE the day of Ruth's surgery—once to tell him how hard it was to wait alone and once to say that it was finally over and everything seemed to be all right. Ruth had required major surgery rather than the la-paroscopy, but the doctor was pleased because he was cer-tain he'd removed all traces of the painful adhesions. Joe hated himself for his selfishness, but he was sorry Ruth had required the more extensive surgery partly because it meant she'd need longer to recuperate, which meant he'd have to wait even longer for Mandy to tell her the news.

Still, the next few weeks were not too hard for Joe. Although Mandy could not come see him in person, she called him every day, which she had not done before. Sometimes she'd tell him everything that had happened in the hospital, and sometimes she asked him to talk about something else to keep her mind off of it. Those were the calls when he'd bring her up-to-date on the station, or the kids, or his plans to secure a loan to help Brady buy back the Rocking T as soon as he came up with a workable plan. When he'd first promised to grubstake his buddy, he'd only had to worry about his children and himself. But now, in the back of Joe's mind, he wondered if he should consult Mandy before he applied for the loan. It was possible—wasn't it?—that their finances would be mingled by the time Brady's dreams came true.

Mandy had dreams that Joe knew might involve him, too. By the first of the year she would be a grandmother for the first time. Joe enjoyed babies, but he'd never expected to be a grandfather while his oldest child was still in grade school! Still, Mandy was tickled pink about the baby, and he felt so close to her that her grandchild already felt like his own.

Sometimes Joe would be working in the office or already asleep in bed when she'd call.

"Joey?" Mandy would say, sounding utterly fatigued and more than a little frightened.

"I'm here, sweetheart," he'd assure her warmly. "How'd the day go?"

And she'd tell him about the latest go-round with the medication, the forced breathing, the agonizing trips they made Ruth take around the nurses' station three times a day to build up her strength. She'd talk about Karen, about Ruth's tears and weakness and mood swings, and then, after she'd poured it all out, she'd say, "Oh, Joey, I wish I could see you. I need you so much."

"I'm as close as the phone, Mandy," he'd promised her. "Anytime you want me closer, just call and I'll drop everything."

"Oh, Joey," she'd sigh. "You're so good to me."

And so it went, day after day, for almost three weeks as Ruth battled predictable soreness, an unexpected infection and her own recalcitrance to the doctors and nurses. She demanded Mandy's presence at all possible times, and Mandy, to Joe's dismay, did everything her sister asked.

He missed seeing her lovely face, missed holding her in his arms. He missed those passionate afternoons in his bed that he'd disparaged, and he was sorry for the harsh words he'd meted out the night he'd kissed her in the grocery store. Still, Joe did not regret the change in his relationship with Mandy during Ruth's long recovery. Limited to soul-searching phone calls, it got a chance to develop in a way it could not during the early days when they'd always had to watch the clock, too aroused to waste time talking. But Ruth's surgery had inadvertently brought them together in a completely different fashion, melded their hearts as completely as those steamy afternoons had joined their bodies.

One night Mandy called and said wearily, "I'm too tired to talk, Joey. Besides, there's nothing new to say. I just wanted to be with you for a while. It's the highlight of my day."

A month ago, he might have thought she was kidding, or deliberately cajoling him into thinking he mattered to her in a way that he knew he did not. But now, despite her fatigue, he caught the thread of tenderness in her voice, a message of love that was louder, somehow, than the words

"I love you" she'd once so urgently begged him to believe.

"It's the heart of my day, too, Mandy," he confessed, no longer afraid that she'd use the knowledge against him. "In fact," he tacked on guilelessly, "you're the heart of my life."

She was quiet for a moment, which was a good thing because Joe himself needed a moment to digest the words.

"Surely you don't mean that I'm more important to you than your beloved locomotive," she teased him. But there was little humor in her voice. Her tone was full of awe.

"I think," he said quietly, "that you just might elbow out the Slow Joe." He didn't mention the kids. They weren't part of the debate. His love for them lived in a different part of his heart. Mandy's space was all her own.

"Joey," she said softly, "the last time I was at your house and I told you I loved you, you said I didn't mean it. But I—" She stopped then, stopped and drew a great breath. "You know now, don't you? I mean, you still don't think I'm just . . . using you for a playmate?"

He shook his head, then realized that she couldn't see him. "I know, honey. I know."

And he did know. Not because she'd told him, not because he'd bulldozed her into begging him not to give her up. In fact, he couldn't pinpoint exactly when he'd realized that things had changed between them, gone from power plays and passion to honest, everyday love.

During the long, loving silence that surged through the telephone line, Joe did not feel the need to speak. And when he finally did, it was with no sense of challenge, no desire to force Mandy to make promises that would make her squirm. He simply wanted to speak the truth.

"Mandy," he said gently, "do you think we ought to get married? I think we could make it work."

When she didn't answer right away, a tiny marble of fear started to roll around in his stomach. But before it worked up much speed, she replied, "I kind of like the idea."

He chuckled uncertainly. "You like it a little or you like it a lot?"

Her laughter was as nervous as his own. "I like it a lot, Joe. I like it too much. I'm so tired and burned out that I don't think I'm quite rational at the moment. How about if we wait and see how it sounds in the morning?"

He grinned. "Fair enough. I'm not trying to pressure you into anything, Mandy. I know you've got enough on your mind. It's just an idea you can chew on in your spare time."

"I'll do that, Joey." She paused for a moment. Then, before she hung up, she said softly, "Thank you. And I do...truly love you."

He closed his eyes, felt her tenderness wash over him. "I love you, too."

Joe went to sleep with a curious sense of well-being, wrapped in a net of confidence that his future with Mandy was finally assured. It was not until around 4:00 a.m. that he was shaken by a nightmare.

Mandy, with long gray hair and granny glasses, was standing at the altar of the Pioneer Community Church, holding his hand and pleading with octogenarian, wheelchair-ridden Ruth, "But I'm only picking up Karen after work! Surely you don't think I'd ever *marry* little Joey Henderson! Ruthie, darling, don't be absurd...."

And tuxedo-clad Joe, losing a grip on her hand, slowly melted from a proud, virile man to a boy about Ira's size, dressed in a dirty orange T-shirt and raggedy jeans. Mandy turned her back on him as mud clots appeared on his clothes. While she continued her litany of excuses to Ruth,

Joe kept shrinking, hunched and ashamed, as he listened to the communal laughter of the townsfolk in the church.

MANDY HAD BEEN WITH RUTH every spare moment for three weeks when Karen said to her one evening as she was cleaning up the kitchen, "I can stay with Mom, you know, if you want to go anywhere."

Mandy eyed her closely, congratulating herself on having lifted Karen's grounding bit by bit as the family's needs required it. Karen had made adjustments of her own in the past few weeks, and her quiet support of her mother had provided the base for the first tentative steps toward healing the breach that had long separated the two of them.

Now Karen looked her aunt straight in the eye. "I thought you might like to see Slow Joe."

Mandy blanched, licked her lips, and tried to hold her niece's steady gaze. "Yes, I would," she answered quietly, trying to conceal her discomfort. Not once had she mentioned her relationship with Joe to Karen, though she'd often wondered if Karen really had figured it out. "It just hasn't seemed appropriate lately."

She was referring to her need to stay near Ruth, but Karen answered smartly, "I can't imagine you ever thought it was appropriate. If you had, you wouldn't have tried so hard to keep it a secret."

Mandy thrust her hands deep into the soapy water. "I'm single and so is Joe, Karen. There's nothing... unsavory... about our friendship."

"Friendship? Is that what you call sneaking into his house from the time school gets out till I leave work at six? You expect me to believe that all you do is talk and play with his model trains?"

Mandy turned on the hot water without thinking and almost scalded her hand. "What I do with Joe Henderson is really none of your business, Karen."

"Right. But what I did with George Masters was *your* business, right?"

"That's different," Mandy snapped, hating herself for falling back on the oldest line in the book.

"How is it different? Aren't you the one who told me that no man was worth lying to your family for? That no man worth his salt would see you on the sly?"

The accusation stung, and Mandy had trouble thinking up a quick answer. "I'm not sixteen years old, Karen. I'm a mature woman and I've been married before."

"I know you're not a kid, Aunt Mandy. What I don't get is, why are you acting like one?"

Mandy felt hot and oddly confused by the question. Still, she struggled to give it a dignified answer. "Karen, you know how your mother is about...lots of things. And lately she's been so distraught that I simply didn't think it was appropriate to upset her."

Karen shook her head. "That might be part of it, Aunt Mandy, but I think the bottom line is that you're as scared of her as I am. I've got a crush on a wonderful boy—David, you know, who works for Joe?—and I really want to go out with him. Go out with him *right*. I don't want to sneak around in the bushes this time. But I know that if I ask Mom for permission to date him, she'll come up with some reason why I can't. She'll find something wrong with him! So I haven't let him know how much I really like him, because as soon as he does ask me out I'll have to make a decision." Her eyes glistened. "Oh, Aunt Mandy, I want to do the right thing for Mom and for David and for me! But I just don't think that's possible!"

I want to do the right thing for Ruth and Joe and me, also, Mandy ached to tell her. *But I don't think it's possible, either.*

So far, Joe had been incredibly patient. But Mandy knew that he'd force her to prove her loyalty very soon.

"WHAT ARE YOU DOING for Thanksgiving?" Brady asked when Joe met him at Peggy's Diner on Friday night. "I've got an idea you just won't believe!"

Joe hated to dampen his enthusiasm, but whatever Brady had in mind couldn't beat the holiday plan he'd been hatching. Since Ruth was obviously not up to having a Thanksgiving meal in her home, even if Mandy took care of it, he'd decided to invite Mandy, Ruth and Karen to his house—and even Mandy's kids if they planned to join her for the day—and show them all he knew how to cook. When his stepsister, Connie, had briefly joined the family in his teens, she'd insisted on making him do everything fifty-fifty. At the time he'd resented it, but now, in hindsight, he was glad he'd learned the rudiments of running a house.

Trying to conceal his excitement, he said casually, "I'm planning to prepare a feast at my house this year, Brady, and I'm expecting to set a place for you." It wasn't an afterthought; Brady was family, and if he wasn't comfortable going to his dad's, there was always room for him at Joe's. As often as not he spent his holidays at the Slow Joe anyway.

But this time Brady shook his head. "Thanks, old pal, but I'm not going to be in town on Thanksgiving. I have what you might call a . . . business trip in mind."

"A business trip?" Joe asked, eyebrows arched. "What is it, a cattle drive or a rodeo?"

"Close," Brady replied with a grin. "I'm going on a wagon train ride."

Joe gagged on his coffee. "You're doing *what*?"

"You heard me. You know it's something I've wanted to do for a long time. I promised Ira I'd take him someday."

"I know that. And I can see why a cowboy like you might enjoy such an event. I can even see why Ira would. What I can't see is why you call a wagon train ride a 'business trip.'" He grimaced. "Tell me you're not thinking what I think you're thinking."

Brady's glorious smile began to fade. "Don't, Joey. Don't rob me of all hope again."

Joe steepled his fingers and stared at his friend. "Brady, I want to help you. I'm trying my damnedest to help you. But you're going off the deep end!"

"No, I'm not!"

"Brady!"

"I mean it, Joey!" He grabbed Joe's forearm. "Listen to me for a minute. I've thought this out. Really and truly. I've got it all on paper, too."

To Joe's surprise, Brady produced a folder full of neatly hand printed data—start-up estimates, ongoing expenses, required equipment—the whole nine yards.

"A hundred acres is enough for a ranch headquarters base," Brady insisted. "If I can lease the surrounding area for part of the year, I'll have enough land to keep the tourists happy. I'll come collect them in a van at the Slow Joe. With any luck at all they'll ride the train first and spend a night or two at the hotel before they take off for civilization. We can advertise together. We might even get Harold to chip in, too."

Harold Dobson ran the historic Redpoint Hotel sandwiched between the Slow Joe and the church. He was always eager to drum up business based on nostalgia for the "good old days," and Joe had no doubt that he'd support Brady's heroic notion. But Harold wasn't going to put up any cash for this venture. He wasn't going to risk his shirt for a buddy's dream.

Joe skimmed the pages Brady waved before him, then slowly glanced back up at his friend. "What kind of profit do these wagon trips make?" he questioned seriously.

"I've made some calls. The figures are all on the last page," Brady answered quickly. He straightened, looked Joe in the eye, and said, "I know I went off half cocked before, Joey, but only because I was so desperate. After the last time we talked, I realized that I was selling you short. I had to come up with something that would be financially viable for both of us. I've worked out a dozen ideas since then. None of them sounded good enough to present to you." He laid both hands on the table for emphasis. "But this one did. I honestly think this could work for me, Joe. I think it could work for you."

Apprehension flooded Joe's stomach. When he'd promised to help Brady get the ranch back, in essence he'd taken the risk of losing the Slow Joe. Between the two, he'd rather sacrifice the train than his best friend, but it would be a terrible choice to make. "I take it you'll be able to find out a lot more during this Thanksgiving trip?"

Brady nodded. "It's the last trip of the year because it's getting so cold. But I didn't want to wait until spring. I'm scared to death that somebody else will try to buy my land, Joe. I've got to find a way to make this work."

Joe wasn't sure what to say. "Are you sure it's still for sale?"

"Yes. I called this morning. If we can come up with a down payment for the hundred acres around my house, I think he'll go into escrow."

"It's not as if I can just write you a check for that kind of money, Brady. Even if—" he ruffled the assembled pages "—I decide this is a smart thing to do, I'll have to convince somebody to give me a loan. And that won't be easy since all my accounts are at Trent."

Brady bit his lower lip. "Dad might give you the money, Joey, even though he won't help me."

Joe shook his head. "It's the same thing. The most we can hope for is that he won't try to nix my credit when somebody gives him a call. I think our best shot is John Carleton at Redpoint Savings. Our boys have played ball together for years." He pondered the situation for a moment and then asked, "Do you think I should ask your dad for a reference ahead of time or just let my application go through regular channels?"

Brady thought a moment. "Just let it be. Off the cuff, he'll give you a hearty recommendation. If he has time to think about it, he might try to block me."

Joe agreed. Still, he felt a profound sadness that he, almost a son to Jake Trent, and Jake's real flesh and blood had to map out a surreptitious strategy to get a loan from the man who had a whole thriving bank at his disposal.

But he knew it was only one of Brady's many heartaches. His divorce from Claudia would be final any day.

"Have you received your papers yet?" he asked, hoping to have some solid financial figures on that front before he got in any deeper.

Brady shook his head. "Not officially, but my lawyer's told me what to expect."

And I expect Mandy to tell Ruth about us any day, Joe reminded himself. He and Brady had survived many changes. Joe had been getting a divorce about the time Brady had gotten married; now Brady was ending his marriage while Joe was about to start a second one. He didn't think it was the right time to bring up the subject, but Brady seemed to read his mind.

"How are things going with Mandy?" he asked after Joe promised to study Brady's plans and contact John Carleton if it seemed viable. "Am I still supposed to be keeping everything hush-hush?"

Embarrassed, Joe nodded. "Just for a few more days. Ruth's recovery hasn't been as rapid as we'd hoped for, but—"

"Who the hell are you kidding?" Brady barked. "Dammit, Joey, I was stupid enough to marry a woman who treated me like something that crawled out from under a rock, but I should hope to God that after watching the hell she'd put me through, *you* would have more sense."

Joe stiffened and gritted his teeth. "I don't think it's fair of you to compare Mandy to Claudia. Mandy's problems with me have nothing to do with . . . well, with the sort of problems the two of you had. She just had to get over this teacher thing. So did I. But now we're—"

"Hell, Joe, you're not over it and neither is she! If she weren't ashamed of you, she'd have told her sister up-front that she was in love with you and she wouldn't give a damn what anybody in Redpoint had to say. And if you weren't still acting like a little boy trying to please his teacher, you'd tell her outright that if she's not willing to shout her love for you from the rooftops, she can damn well sneak in and out of somebody else's bed while she's stuck in this one-horse town!"

If Brady had brass-knuckled Joe in the gut, he could not have hurt him any more deeply. It was a one-two punch for which he had no defense, no answer. The pain of Brady's entirely too accurate perception was even greater because it was the first time in twenty years that Joe didn't feel he could count on support from his best friend. And yet he knew—in spite of his great anger—that Brady had spoken out only because he wanted to protect him.

Joe sat perfectly still, struggling for words to defend his love for Mandy, struggling for lies to defend her secret love of him.

None came.

It was Brady, after dinner and a dessert that was unaccountably tasteless, who said apologetically, "Maybe you're right, Joe. Maybe she just needs a little more time."

But Joe suddenly realized that he had no more time left to give.

MANDY DROPPED BY JOE'S PLACE on Tuesday afternoon after school, knowing that she wouldn't see him again until after Thanksgiving. She'd tried to come by several times in the past week—now that Ruth was well enough to be left alone—but each time she'd called Joe to set something up, he'd already had other plans. She'd actually begun to wonder if he were trying to avoid her by the time they'd been able to mutually agree on a day and time.

She knocked on the door and entered when he called, "Come in!" But he made no effort to welcome her when she found him in the living room playing with his model train.

"Hi, Joey," she greeted him eagerly, slipping both arms around his neck as she gave him a kiss designed to make up for the long weeks they'd been apart. *How I've missed you!* she confessed with her eyes. *How I've longed to hold you, to love you, to....*

But Joe returned her kiss with cool brevity, then turned back to the small steam engine he was coupling to a long yellow reefer. "Hello," he said calmly. "How have you been?"

Something inside Mandy curled up, cried out, wanted to run and hide. Every instinct she possessed told her she was in terrible trouble.

"I've been . . . busy. Tired. Eager to see you."

He nodded almost nonchalantly, then attached a tiny tanker to the reefer car. "Yes, I noticed how eager you were to spend your four-day holiday with me. I also noticed how delighted you were to give me this chance to meet your boys."

Mandy watched his back, formidable in the turtleneck. She wanted to reach out and touch him, beg him to look at her, but she knew that in his current mood, it would do no good.

"My boys are meeting me in Denver, Joe, not Redpoint. I told you that." She'd told him on the phone one night last week. And he'd said—what had he said? Nothing that she could remember. Nothing crucial at all.

"Your kids are 'coming home' was your exact phrase, I believe. Funny. I could have sworn you'd moved to Redpoint."

"Joe, it's the house they grew up in. It wouldn't be the same if they came here!"

"It won't be the same house they grew up in *there*. You don't live there anymore, and their father is dead." At last he turned to look at her. "Or are you all expecting to find him there?"

Mandy took a step closer, laid a hand on Joe's arm. "Is that what's wrong, Joe? Are you jealous of Alan? Surely you don't—"

He shook his head, then shook her hand off of his arm. "Alan is the least of my problems. At least he's dead. You've used every member of your family who's alive as an excuse to keep from getting close to me."

"*Close* to you? Joey, how could we get any closer? Last week you asked me to *marry* you, for Pete's sake. And I said—"

"You said what you always say. 'I love you, but...' You haven't mentioned it since, and you deliberately side-stepped a perfectly natural opportunity to introduce me to the rest of your family." His eyes darkened. "It never even occurred to you that I might expect you to want to spend the day with me, did it? It never even occurred to you that I could go with you to Denver or you could bring your family here." Pain rippled across his virile, ragged features. "I was planning to cook for your whole clan, Mandy. I'm really that big of a chump."

Mandy fought a quiet rush of tears. "Oh, Joe, you're not a chump! That's the sweetest thing a man has ever offered to do for me. If it were any other time—"

"It's not any other time, Mandy, and there's not going to *be* any other time. You found an excuse to shut me out on Thanksgiving and it's just a matter of time until you come up with one for Christmas and Easter and the Fourth of July. We've got the roles reversed here, but I think I recognize the pattern. If you were a married businessman seducing your secretary on the side, everybody would say, 'How can she be so naive as to believe he'll ever leave his wife for her?'" He glared at Mandy, then turned back to his train. "But I've been that naive, Mandy. I actually thought I was more to you than a convenient source of afternoon delight. You had me buffaloed into believing that I was going to be the center of your life."

For a moment Mandy didn't answer. She knew her next words were crucial, and she didn't dare make a mistake. Fear stilled her tongue.

Joe flipped the switch that turned on the tracks, and watched the train go around. Mandy watched, too—waiting, her breath held painfully—as the little cars whizzed by once, twice, three times before he spoke again.

"From the moment we met as adults, I've been trying to make things easy for you, Mandy. Partly because it's my way and partly because I wanted so much to prove to you that that troublesome little hellion is gone." He reversed the engine. "But Brady pointed out rather astutely last week that I'm still acting like your student. 'Look at me, Miss Sawyer,' 'I'll try to be good, Miss Sawyer,' 'I really am a nice boy, Miss Sawyer.'"

He stopped the train and turned to face her once more. "Little Joey would have done anything to get you to like him, Mandy. But this man—this man who loves you despite the fact that you've treated him like dirt—" he lifted both hands to gently squeeze Mandy's shoulders as his dark gaze met hers "—will not bend another millimeter or *he will break*."

Mandy's eyes closed against the pain. Fear all but strangled her. *Don't leave me, Joey,* her heart begged him. *Just give me a little more time.*

If Joe felt her trembling, he gave no sign. "I want no more promises, no more excuses, no more lies," he ordered firmly. "You go to Denver. You do what you have to do. When you come back, give me a call. Say yes or say no. If you say yes—yes, you told them all, yes, you'll marry me, yes, you're proud as punch to let the whole world know it—then we'll celebrate for a week and get married in a month and spend the rest of our lives loving each other." One thumb dipped lightly over her lips in a gesture that could not conceal how desperately Joe still hoped that scenario would come to pass. Then, very slowly, he dropped his hands from her body, leaving her flesh and her heart icy cold.

Slowly he slipped both hands into his pockets, as though he were afraid he could not keep from touching her. Still, his tone was firm as he decreed, "Otherwise, as of Monday night my door is closed to you, Mandy, and—" he took a deep breath that seemed to underline his final words "—I'm going to start dating again."

CHAPTER THIRTEEN

BY THE THIRD NIGHT of the wagon train trip, Joe's back felt as though it had shattered into tiny shards and his bottom was a mass of bruises. Most of the other greenhorns had pampered themselves with pillows inside the wagons—one of which had padded benches—but Brady, naturally, refused to ride anywhere but on the back of his horse. And, as fate would have it, he'd brought along a spare mount for Joe.

Joe had nothing against horses—in fact he liked to ride every now and again—for an hour or so. But it was beyond his imagination how Brady could consider eight straight hours of being jostled and bumped as fun, especially when he did this every day for a living!

"Look, Joey, it's like you and trains," his friend explained. "You spend all day working on a steam engine, and what do you do as soon as you go home? Rev up your model N gauge. This is the same thing."

"My N gauge doesn't break my back or bruise my bottom," he pointed out disagreeably. "And it doesn't fill its belly full of air every time I try to tighten the cinch."

His pleas fell on deaf ears. Brady was in his glory, charging ahead, circling behind, giving directions and advice to every tenderfoot on the wagon train. One of the trip leaders had broken his ankle on the second day and had been helicoptered out. Brady had instantly volunteered to take his place—without pay—and since it was obvious that

Brady knew more about horses and wagons than half o
the staff, Ragweed Willie, a burly old guy in his sixties, had
urged the owner to take him on. After that, Brady was a
happy as a clam, but Joe was positively morose.

By the third night—when autumn suddenly vanished in
Wyoming and winter decidedly arrived—he was cold
cramped, miserable and thoroughly sorry that he'd le
Brady talk him into this adventure.

It wasn't the only thing he was sorry about. He was sorry
that Sarah had nixed his last-minute plan to bring Ira along
on the grounds that she and Bill had already made ar
rangements to take "the whole family" over to Topeka to
see her parents. To Joe's chagrin, Sarah had even berated
him for "acting like a weekend father who only wants the
kids when he doesn't have anything else to do." He wa
stunned to realize how rarely he'd picked up the kids after
school since he'd started seeing Mandy. He wasn't ever
spending as many weekends with them. With a jolt he re
alized that his priorities had become somewhat whopper
jawed by his total absorption in Mandy. Mandy who loved
him so much that she hadn't even considered inviting him
to have Thanksgiving in her home.

Home. Funny word. To him it meant Redpoint; to
Mandy it meant Denver...the house she'd shared with her
husband. It should have meant the same thing to both o
them—anyplace where they could always be together.

After an hour of tears and apologies, she'd promised
Joe that all the waiting would be over when she came back
from Thanksgiving with Ruth, Karen and her children
and he tried to believe it was true. But as far as Joe wa
concerned, the only thing that had changed since the be
ginning was that he'd frightened her enough to consider
the possibility of losing him. And he didn't want Mand
to make their love public because she was afraid. H

wanted her to do it because she was proud to be his woman.

If she wasn't proud enough by the time he got back to Redpoint, he knew there was only one thing he could do.

IT WAS NOT YET DAWN on Thanksgiving Day when Mandy woke, stretched once or twice, and noticed that Alan was not sleeping by her side. It was an odd sensation. At Ruth's, the only man who filled her mind as she lay in bed was Joe, but here in the house where she and Alan had raised their children, it still seemed odd that she should sleep alone.

And yet, as she lay quite still in the predawn light and tried to focus on her feelings, she realized that it was not Alan who seemed so far away today but Joe. And it wasn't the distance between Redpoint and Denver that troubled her. It was the distance he'd put between them at his house on Tuesday night.

I love you, Joey, she said to herself, then flushed as if she'd said the words out loud. Yet the curious sense of disloyalty she'd experienced the last time she'd slept in this bed was somehow reversed. How could she share Alan's bed now that she belonged to Joe?

Alan could not have satisfied her now. In bed or out of it. She had changed—because of his death and Joe's life. She wasn't Alan Larkin's widow any longer, but a young woman eager to become Joe Henderson's wife.

Well, eager, but also... well, a little bit chagrined. She had to face Alan here—or at least Alan's ghost—and though she knew that between the two men Joe would win any contest for her affection, the man who'd guided her outlook on the world for twenty years still had a powerful grip on her self-esteem.

Mandy sat up, pulling on a robe as though to shield her own nakedness, as she formally announced to the empty room, "You've been gone a long time, Alan. It's not as though anyone could ever replace you. It's just that I'm lonely, and he's good to me."

She had a sudden vision of Alan giving a dramatic sigh of disapproval. *Good to you? Isn't this that little monster you groaned about so many times? The one who destroyed your first year of teaching and made you doubt your abilities, your integrity and your faith in yourself?*

Mandy shook her head, as though to clear the memory, and hurried into the bathroom to splash cold water on her face. It didn't do any good. Alan's imaginary voice was replaced by Ruth's. *Joey Henderson?* she could hear her sister bark. *Have you lost your mind?*

But he's different now, Ruthie. He's everything I've ever needed. . . .

Mandy brushed her teeth fiercely, as though each stroke could scrub away her apprehension. But she knew her sister too well, and she knew the words that sprang into her imagination were the softest of the accusations that she would have to face. Ruth would point out the very strikes against Joe that a few months ago, Mandy had been claiming herself.

On top of that, she had to tell her children. Vince was driving in this morning; Kevin and his pregnant wife were coming in on a 2:00 p.m. flight. Mandy had not tried to explain to Joe why she couldn't just show up at the airport with a new man in tow; she had only told him that she'd find a way to share the news with everyone some time in the next few days.

Don't bother to make me any more promises, he'd answered sharply. *Just tell me the truth when you get home.*

Deep in her heart, she knew that Joe didn't believe she'd do it; he didn't believe she loved him at all. But he'd terrified her on Tuesday night. The instant he'd mentioned dating, her choices had become extraordinarily clear. If she didn't find the courage to face her family, she would surely lose Joe.

She would no longer be whole.

Mandy pushed away the dark vision of the abyss her life would be without him. He loved her; he still wanted her to be his wife. Over and over again she told herself that everything would be all right. The moment he heard her say, "I told them, Joey! I told them all. Go ahead and set the wedding date!" he'd crush her to his chest and all this heartache would evaporate.

Mandy had promised Joe she'd face the music, and she would. But today was a family day, and time for happy memories with the children who were her living link to Alan. There'd be time enough to break the news about Joe to them tomorrow. And if tomorrow got jammed, there was always Friday.

It was almost four on Monday afternoon when Joe came back from a Slow Joe run and spotted the white Toyota in the parking lot. He bolted off the train with the minimum of required checks, then glanced in his office to make sure Mandy wasn't there.

"She's waiting for you at the house," Wilma announced dramatically. "She's only been here about fifteen minutes."

Joe thanked her and jogged across the back lot, not bothering to explain his hurry to the few hapless visitors who scurried to get out of his path. He was covered with soot, but that didn't stop Mandy from throwing herself in his arms the minute he walked in the door. It was a dream come true...coming home from work, finding Mandy waiting for him.

Acting more like a wife than a lover.

"Are you really going to marry me?" he asked as he clutched her tightly.

"Yes, yes, yes!"

"Right away?" he prodded.

"Yes, yes, yes!"

"Did you—"

He couldn't finish the question because Mandy was kissing him, kissing him with her warm lips and searching tongue, and her thighs were pressing against his as though they had not made love for years.

An instant later he found himself sliding his hands over her breasts, relishing her instant whimper, nuzzling the lobes of her ears. "I want you so much, Mandy," he whispered, "but I'm so dirty. I shouldn't touch you this way...."

"Then let's go get you cleaned up," she suggested in her most sultry tone. "I've already got a hot bath waiting."

He pulled back to study her face—round, girlish, full of darling freckles. And the waiting, the wondering, the hurt suddenly seemed like a faint memory. She finally belonged to him now.

"Are you kidding?" he asked.

"No, I'm not kidding! When Wilma said you were running the train today I knew you'd be a mess when you came in. What good is a wife who can't anticipate her husband's needs?"

"I love the way you say that word. *Wife*, Mandy. What did Ruth say when—"

She silenced him with another kiss, a kiss that started with a hot meeting of her lips and his but ended when her tongue stole past his teeth and commandeered the softest reaches of his mouth. He knew then that it was going to be one of those afternoons when Mandy felt her woman's power, wanted to lead him, control him, tease him, make him beg...and then give him absolutely everything he wanted.

And to think I was afraid I'd never be able to hold her again. I was so sure she lacked the courage to own up to her love for me.

He let Mandy lead him to the bathroom, let her strip off his dirty clothes with tantalizing intimacy. She ordered him to get into the tub and wait while she undressed herself. But she didn't do it quickly, and she made sure that he watched while she teasingly opened her blouse, button by button, then freed her full breasts from her bra before she offered each one for his tongue's thorough, wet inspection. Ever so slowly she peeled off her panty hose and underthings, then pulled up her silky blue skirt and dangled her toes in the tub. She perched on the edge, wearing nothing but the skirt hunched around her bare hips. With the arch of her right foot she rubbed Joe's calf...then his knee...then his thigh.

"Mandy," he pleaded, "it's cold out there. Don't you think you ought to come in and get warm?"

She leaned over casually and traced the same path with her fingertips. She rested her hand on his thigh only an inch or two from the meeting of his legs.

"I think I'd be chillier if I got undressed. Don't you think so, Joe?" She suggested, grinning wickedly.

Joe rolled over on his side and pressed his rigidness against her teasing hand. Then he grabbed her ankle and drew circles around it with his thumb. "I think I might pull you in with that skirt on. I doubt that it's keeping you very warm."

She laughed and splashed some water on his chest, abandoning his throbbing stem. "I dare you to get me to take it off before you pull me in," she challenged him.

He grinned and sat up in the tub. He was so aroused that his organ stood up on its own, pleading for Mandy's fingers, which swooped down his thighs again, lightly stroking while he groaned. "I'll take your bet. Loser has to say 'You're the greatest lover who ever lived.'"

"You're on."

"No holds barred?"

Her hands closed greedily around his urgency. "None."

For a moment he just celebrated the majestic feel of her hot, soapy fingers, kneading him with almost unbearable joy. He knew she was feeling her power, rejoicing in his need of her, and he also knew he couldn't hold out for very long.

He placed both hands between her knees and slid his palms up her inner thighs as far as they would go. She licked her lips and let her knees fall open; she tugged on him harder and he groaned. "Take off your skirt," he whispered, but Mandy ignored his command.

Joe knelt in the tub, pressing himself urgently into her hands and parting her knees with his elbows as his fingertips closed around a tiny clump of intimate hair and gently seized.

She cried out hungrily and leaned over to kiss him with eager lips. He slid a finger inside her, and she began to shake.

"Take off your skirt," he said again.

Mandy shook her head and smiled at him, moving now in rising rhythm against his warm hand. "I'll just come in." She started to lower herself into the tub, on top of him, but Joe held her on the side.

"Going for the gold, are you?" she teased, a bit breathless now.

"A bet is a bet. My honor is at stake." He was quivering now, and he knew he wouldn't last much longer. Any minute Mandy would lean down and take him in her mouth, and he'd pull her into the tub, bet or no bet.

Instead he pushed her silky skirt out of the way and thrust his head into her lap.

She whimpered as his tongue laved her soft folds of trembling flesh, tapped at the tiny bud of desire. She dropped her erotic hold on his body and gripped his shoulders, her frenzy rising as she rocked against his mouth.

"Joey!" she cried out in vibrant, sensual delight. His tongue probed more deeply, darting inside her, and the next time she said his name it was almost a scream.

"Take off your skirt," he ordered, his lips erotically brushing her sensitive woman's core as he spoke.

She did.

Or at least she tried. She was shaking so badly that Joe didn't have the heart to make her wait. As soon as Mandy started to pull the fabric above her waist—the instant she gave in—he gripped her hips and gave her everything she wanted with his tongue.

She clung to his hair and cried out his name—again and again—then clung to his neck while the spasm of pleasure spiraled to a frenzied peak and gradually subsided. For a moment she just slumped against his shoulders, spent, content to cradle him in the afterglow.

While Joe lingered unbearably on the edge himself.

Then Mandy bent down to kiss him—on his neck, his shoulders, his face—and she lowered her hands to embrace his fierce erection once more. Now it was Joe's turn to tremble, to lose control while he trusted his urgent need to her.

She didn't make him wait long before she moved off the edge of the tub, beckoning him with her hands to follow her as she stretched out on the thick bath mat.

Mandy put her arms around Joe and pulled him down, wrapping her ankles around his as she welcomed him inside her. Her warm hands slid over his backside and pressed him closer, relishing his thundering pleasure. And when he reached the precipice, his blood pounding in his ears, he heard her whisper, "You *are* the greatest lover who ever lived."

And in that moment, he believed her.

It was not until later, when he realized she'd deliberately deceived him about their impending marriage, that he wondered if she'd lied about that, too.

BY THE TIME JOE DRIED HER OFF and carried her protectively to his bed, Mandy was feeling acutely guilty about what she'd done. She knew she'd let Joe believe that she'd told her family everything, and she had intended to do exactly that. And she did want to marry him. Desperately. How could she explain that the right moment had never come?

Vince had started to reminisce about Alan the moment he walked into the house, admitting privately to his mother that he was having a terrible time in medical school and longed for his dad's advice. Kevin, soon to be a father himself, had repeatedly lamented that his dad hadn't lived long enough to know his granddaughter or grandson. His new bride—on poor terms with her own family—had begged Mandy to come spend a week with her after the baby was born. She'd said yes, of course, wondering how she could explain that by Christmas she might be married

o a "grandpa" who was only a few years older than the
baby's dad.

Worse yet, Ruth had regaled the boys with stories of
Mandy's first year as a teacher with "this perfectly horrible child," then pointed out the irony of Karen's employer being the very same person. How could Mandy have
darted in at a moment like that and said, "By the way, I'm
planning to marry him"?

But she knew that Joe would brook no excuses, honor
no explanations now. He was past such logic. This afternoon Mandy had told him she loved him in the only way
he was sure he would still understand. Was it really so
wrong?

While she guiltily luxuriated in the warmth of the electric blanket that Joe had turned on for her, he zipped out
to the kitchen to make them some hot chocolate. When he
returned, still naked, he sat down beside Mandy and gently
took her hand.

"I can't begin to tell you how hard these past few days
have been for me, sweetheart," he confessed, every syllable laden with tenderness. "I was so sure I'd end up sleeping alone tonight. So sure I'd have to accept the fact that
it was over. So sure I'd have to—" the hurt still haunted his
ow tone "—let you go. I'm not sure I could have done it.
I'm damn glad you didn't put me to the test."

Mandy laid one hand on his cheek and caressed his
stubble gently. "I'll never let you slip away from me, Joey.
I'm going to stay right beside you for the rest of my life."

He leaned over and kissed her as though to seal the bar-
gain. It was a gentle kiss, a husbandly forever-kiss, quite
different from the wildly passionate kisses they'd shared
on the bathroom floor, and Mandy wished more than
anything that she could have savored it with a clean heart.
But she knew it was just a matter of time before Joe asked

a question she could not answer, before she told him that
he was going to sleep alone tonight after all.

"So, what did Ruth say when you told her?" Joe asked
when he finally released her. His eyes were still warm and
gentle, a bit glazed from their wrestling match in the tub.
"Was it really so awful?"

Mandy tried to meet his loving gaze, tried to bluff her
way through a reply. But no words came to her, and try
though she did, she could not look him in the eye.

"Joey, I want to marry you," she repeated staunchly.
There didn't seem to be anything else to say.

Joe must have heard the hesitation in her voice—or
maybe the guilt—because he didn't answer her, and the
fingers stroking her neck suddenly ceased to move. There
was a long, tense silence, before he said, "You didn't tell
her." It was not a question. "You didn't tell your boys."

Mandy's eyes flashed up at his as she desperately sought
forgiveness. "I tried, Joey, honestly I tried. It was just
impossible. But when we go back for Christmas—"

"Get out."

The words were so low, the tone so dark, that Mandy
couldn't believe she was hearing Joe correctly. The man
who had so lovingly called her "sweetheart" just moments ago would never have said such a thing! She wedged
herself a little more tightly under the blanket, but Joe, incredibly, pulled the mug of hot chocolate out of her hand
and tugged the blanket off her naked body.

"I said, get out of my house!" he roared.

"Joe, I'm not even dressed!" It was a stupid thing to
say, but the logical part of Mandy's brain suddenly
jammed.

"I don't give a damn," he yelled at her. "I don't care if
you get picked up for indecent exposure or freeze to death
in the snow!" His voice cracked on the last word; his pain

had colored every syllable of fury. "How could you do this, Mandy?" he demanded. "Do you really think I'm some little puppet to dance in your hand?"

Mandy sat up, pulled the blanket back around her body and reached out to grip his arm. "Joe, I won't leave this house while you're screaming at me. I'm going to be your wife. We have to learn to settle our—"

"Like hell you are! I'm no longer interested in linking my life to yours, lady! You go find another patsy. This fish is getting off the hook!"

"Joe, I love you! You still love me and you know it. Now we're going to talk this out!"

He pulled the blanket off her again. "There is nothing to talk out! Nothing left to say! I gave you an ultimatum and you made up your mind. Now *get out*!"

Suddenly Mandy started to cry. She covered her face with her hands and sat there, shattered, while Joe roughly started to dress himself. She did not try to touch him, or reason with him, or beg for more time. She couldn't move, couldn't think, couldn't do anything but cry.

She heard Joe stomp down the hallway, listened to him rev up the model train in the living room. *At least he hasn't left the house,* she told herself as she waited in the bed, sobbing, desperately struggling for self-control. *If I wait long enough, surely he'll come back*. She knew what Joe was like when he flew off the handle. Sooner or later he was sure to cool down. He'd never had this good a reason to be livid with her before, but Mandy still had to believe that his love would overrule his fury. Little Joey would have tossed her out, but Joe Henderson would be willing to talk things out.

Ten minutes passed before she finally heard him coming. Prostrate with dread, Mandy stiffened, her gaze fixed on the foot of the bed.

Joe walked in quietly, sat down on a chair near the door and studied the shag carpet without a word. For several minutes, in fact, he did not speak. Nor did he look at Mandy.

At last he said softly, "I guess I'm supposed to apologize for screaming at you. And I guess that—deep down— that's not really the way I want to end it."

Mandy took a deep breath. *This* was her Joey. She could reason with this man.

But then he continued in the same low, ragged tone, "But I do want to end it, Mandy. I meant what I said. I don't want to see you anymore."

Mandy suddenly felt gravely ill. It took all of her strength to speak. Quivering from the inside out she pleaded, "Please don't leave me, Joey. Please give me another chance."

Joe rubbed his forehead. She could see he was in pain. But he did not waiver.

"What's the point, Mandy?" he asked hopelessly, his gaze now resting on her face. "You'll never own up to loving me."

"I will, Joe," she vowed. "I won't wait until Christmas. I'll take you to Ruth's tonight if that's what it takes. Just—"

"No." The single syllable spoke volumes abut despair. "It's too late for that now."

"Joe, just because I didn't tell her in Denver doesn't mean—"

"It's more than that, Mandy. It's even more than—" he gestured toward the still-sopping bathroom rug "—the way you tricked me today. It's the whole thing, right from the beginning. I just don't *trust* you anymore."

Mandy swallowed hard. She started to cry again. A raging fear was whipping her heart like a prairie wind on the roof of a soddy. She hadn't felt such panic since the moment Alan had died.

"What can I do?" she begged him. "Tell me how to make it up to you, Joe"

Sadly he shook his head. "I don't think you can, Mandy. You've just got too much to explain."

Desperately hoping that he would listen to an explanation anyway, Mandy blubbered, "I didn't mean to mislead you today, Joe. I just wanted to celebrate our engagement before I told you that . . . I wasn't quite done telling everyone."

"Mandy," he snapped, "you haven't even *started* telling anyone!"

"That's not true. I told Wilma. And Karen and Patty know."

"They guessed. All three of them. You really didn't have much choice."

And I don't have much choice now, she realized with stark urgency. *If I want him, I'll have to beg.* And she did want him. Desperately. Not the way she'd wanted him the first time she'd come to this house in the middle of the night; not the way she'd wanted him when his head was between her legs and he'd licked her until she had screamed. She wanted something more from Joe Henderson, something that would last her for life. She wanted it more than she had ever wanted anything from a man before.

Mandy moved out of the covers, crossed the chilly room and knelt at his feet. Still naked, she edged between his knees as closely as she dared, then put both hands on his rugged, anguished face. "Please, Joe. I'm begging you," she whispered. Every ounce of her love for him throbbed in her desperate tone. "Tell me what you want and I'll do it."

Joe's beautiful brown eyes studied hers for an endless moment while he pondered the agony of her words. Then, as if relenting, he ever so tenderly touched her cheek. Mandy's heart began to jab wildly at her ribs when Joe cautiously brushed his lips across her forehead in a touching tribute that could have been either a hello or a goodbye.

Then he said softly, "I want you to get dressed, Mandy. I want you to go home." For a moment he pressed his face against hers. His fingertips grazed her hair. Then his voice broke as he decreed, "I don't want you to come to see me anymore."

Gently he pulled Mandy's hands off his face as he stood and left the room.

This time she knew he would not return.

CHAPTER FOURTEEN

IN THE NEXT FEW DAYS, Joe almost called Mandy a dozen times, but he couldn't think of anything to say. He wanted to tell her he was sorry he'd lost his temper and ordered her out of his house; he wanted to tell her that those precious few minutes in the tub, when he'd truly believed she was going to marry him, had been the sweetest they'd ever shared. But she'd stolen them from him, stolen all the sweet moments from their future, and he couldn't think of anything she could do that might make up for that. There really was nothing left to say.

On Thursday, John Carleton called with the news that Joe's "business expansion" loan had been approved. He was too miserable to feel like celebrating, but he did manage to sound properly grateful. *At least Brady will have cause to rejoice,* he told himself. *That's a lot better than both of us feeling down.*

He drove out to Brady's bunkhouse in the afternoon, though he'd planned to go see the kids that day. He'd been too depressed to visit them earlier, but he hadn't even talked to them on the phone since Thanksgiving and he was getting eager for the sound of their sweet voices. He was aching for the sound of Mandy's voice, too.

"Brady's not back yet," one of the other cowboys told him when he knocked at the door. "If you mount up you can find him mending fence on the north range."

It was freezing cold and snowfall was imminent, but Joe saddled up a horse anyway. Despite his leather gloves, his hands got so cold he had trouble with the reins, and the speed at which the mare lollygagged along made it clear that *she* could certainly think of better things to do. Still, he survived the hour-long ride, spotted Brady in the distance, waved his conductor's hat and gave a high thumb's-up, which he hoped his pal could read even from a distance.

Brady did. He let out such a cowboy hoot 'n' holler that Joe's startled mare crowhopped to the side in alarm. A moment later Brady came barreling down the low slope, hollering, "Joey, old buddy, old pal! You did it! You saved my life! I'm going home! Joey, Joey!" When he reached Joe he pounded him on the back, leaped off his gelding, did a clumsy cartwheel, then leaped on again. He rode in wild little circles that made Joe chuckle, and the chuckles helped him feel like a human being again. It was a good fifteen minutes before Brady calmed down enough to ask for the details and figure out that Joe had signed away his life savings and very probably the nest egg he'd hoped to use for the kids' education someday. Still, his joy was beyond rational thought, and Joe did everything he could to let Brady rejoice in his perfect day.

It wasn't until they'd written up some more papers, reviewed Brady's list of supplies and picked up the Santa costume Brady had agreed to wear for the annual Slow Joe staff Christmas party that his friend, sacked out in front of Joe's fire, said quietly, "So things are not going well with Mandy, I take it," as though Joe had told him everything.

Joe poked the fire, pulled off his boots and sat pensively on the rug. "It's over," he confessed.

"She broke it off?"

"Nope. I did."

Brady raised his eyebrows. "I though you wanted to marry her."

"Can't marry a woman who's ashamed to tell a soul she loves you," he admitted darkly. He laughed without mirth. "You sure hit the nail on the head on that one, Brady. I can't believe I was such a chump for so long. 'Just give me a little more time, Joey,' she said. A thousand times she said it! God, you don't know how many excuses that woman had! Always some incredibly good reason that only an insensitive boor would fail to understand—" He broke off and hung his head in his hands.

For a while Brady said nothing, just leaned back in his chair and crossed one long, skinny leg over the opposing knee. At last he said, "How did she take it? Was she sorry or relieved?"

Joe closed his eyes, trying to shut out the memory of Mandy on her knees, begging him for another chance. "She said she wanted to marry me, but she hadn't told a soul."

Brady leaned forward, his elbows on his widespread knees, and said the very thing still whipping around in Joe's own mind. "Joey, maybe now that she's...well, really had a chance to see what her life is like without you...maybe she's ready to make a greater sacrifice."

Joe shook his head. "It doesn't matter anymore, Brady. It's just too late."

"Are you sure, Joe? Are you sure that winning this round is more important to you than a life with the woman you love?"

Joe's head shot up. "What the hell does that mean? You're the one who told me all along she was just playing with me! I should think you'd be thrilled that I finally saw the light."

Brady's eyes grew sad. "When I see you hurting this bad, old buddy, it's kind of hard for me to be thrilled about much of anything." After a moment of fraternal silence, he said softly, "If I thought I could have saved my marriage by eating a little crow, I would have done it, Joe."

And Joe answered softly, "I would have, too, Brady. But I don't have any marriage to save."

THE NEXT FEW DAYS were sheer hell for Mandy. Every time she answered the phone or opened a letter or checked her office box, she hoped to hear from Joe. For half an hour every day she had to look at Ira's sweet young face and try not to notice how much he looked like his dad. Each evening she had to go home and act as though she were happy, though her resentment toward her sister stuck in her throat.

She had hoped that, over time, the anguish would start to recede. After all, the pain of Alan's death had. But she'd always known that there was nothing she could do to bring Alan back; she hadn't banished him from her life with her own hand.

Yet Mandy had nobody but herself to blame for losing Joe. She could find no last-minute remedies, no magic cures. No way to make up for her own stupidity and cowardice.

Oh, she could have gone to him again, humiliated herself further. And if she'd left while he was still in anger, she might have found the courage to do it. But their last parting had been so gentle, and so sad, that there was no way she could pretend he'd changed his mind at some point down the road.

No way to pretend it wasn't truly over.

IT WAS LATE THURSDAY NIGHT, well after ten, when Joe's phone began to ring. It was right about the time that Mandy used to call when Ruth was recovering from surgery, and he wondered, for just a moment, what he would say if he heard her voice on the other end.

His hand trembled as he picked up the phone. "Hello?" he greeted the caller darkly.

"Sorry to call so late, Joe, but we have a problem," his ex-wife declared. "Ira's been moping around here all week and I finally got him to tell me what's wrong. I knew he was upset that he didn't get to go on that wagon train trip, but when Brady came by and told him all about it I thought he'd cheer up. But he just keep getting worse and worse." She took a deep breath, not waiting for Joe to answer. "He thinks you don't love him as much as you used to, Joe. He thinks you're drifting away. I told him that it was my fault he couldn't go to Wyoming with you, but he says that you've hardly bothered with him lately anyway, and when you do, you're grumpy and withdrawn. He's afraid you'll end up like the divorced fathers of so many of his friends. In the beginning you saw the kids almost every day. Pretty soon he thinks you'll give up weekends, too, and just see them on holidays."

Joe was in shock. He'd been so sure that his caller would be Mandy that he'd focused all of his energies into deciding how to greet her, how to tell her *God, yes, I miss you, too* or simply *It's just too late, honey, let it be.* Instead Sarah was dumping a completely different problem in his lap, a problem he could blame on no one but himself.

"If I thought you just didn't care anymore, Joey, I'd try to help him accept the situation," she continued evenly. "But I think you just let this slip by you because you're so involved with that woman. And—"

"My God," he finally burst out, "does everybody know about her?"

Sarah snorted. "For Pete's sake, Joe, I was married to you for fifteen years. I know when you're in love! And since you usually avoid school functions like the plague and then suddenly developed a keen interest in your son's social studies class, I—"

"Never mind," he cut her off. "That's all over now. What's important is that somehow I let her get in the way of my time with Ira. Is he still awake?"

"Maybe. You want me to get him on the phone?"

Joe thought for a moment, then said softly, "No. I'll come over. I think he needs his daddy to tuck him in tonight, don't you?"

Sarah agreed. Ten minutes later Joe slipped in through the front door, apologized to Bill for showing up at such a late hour, then disappeared into Ira's room.

He sat by his boy's bed, watched the peaceful rise and fall of his young chest. Quietly he took Ira's hand. In the darkness Ira turned over, opened his eyes and stared at Joe. "Dad?" he asked. "Is that you?"

"Of course it's me. Do you think I'd let you go even one night thinking I'd stopped loving you? Why didn't you tell me you were feeling pushed aside?"

For a moment he thought Ira was going to throw himself in his arms as he had when he was young, but at twelve, all he did was clench Joe's hand tightly. "I was scared, Dad. You've just been so different lately."

"Different how?"

Ira shrugged. "I don't know. You stopped coming by so much, and when you did, you were always so...well, so short with us. It was like you didn't want to talk much. You stopped telling us about your day. Even Sally noticed it."

Damn you, Mandy! he cursed silently. *The busyness is my fault, but you're responsible for this communication snafu.* Now, no longer willing to let Mandy's concerns interfere with his obligation to his son, he said softly, "You're right, Ira, and I'm very sorry. I had a secret I was afraid I'd accidentally share, a secret I had no business keeping from you."

Ira sat up, intrigued now. "What was you secret?"

Joe met his son's eyes. "I was in love."

"With a *girl*?" Ira asked in disbelief.

"A grown woman, to be precise. Your mother's remarried, Ira. Do you think I should always live alone?"

The boy shook his head. "I just . . . I mean, you never said anything. I never saw you with anybody. And why wouldn't you tell us good news?" Suddenly he seemed to whiten in the dark. "Is she...married to somebody else?"

"Absolutely not."

"So why did you keep it a secret?"

"Because it was very important to my friend. She felt that the news would upset someone very special to her, so I tried to be patient." Then he added quietly, "But I told her right from the start that if you ever asked me about it, I wouldn't lie to you."

Ira grinned as he released Joe's hand. He looked sleepy and enormously relieved.

"Because she wanted to keep it under wraps, I couldn't go out with her at night. I saw her in the afternoons, Ira, when I should have been with you. I'm sorry. I didn't mean to neglect you. I love you more than ever, son. And I really wanted to take you with me to Wyoming. I just couldn't change your mother's mind about that."

The boy nodded, placated and sufficiently inspired by Joe's comment to ask, "Is it true that Uncle Brady might be starting up a real wagon train on his old ranch? When he was here the other day he said I might be able to spend the summer helping out."

Joe managed to smile. "It's true. In fact, since you last talked to Brady we got the go-ahead from the bank. I imagine he'll schedule the first wagon train ride for next summer, and if it's okay with your mother, you can be his right-hand man."

"All right!" This time Ira did lean forward to give his dad a hug, and Joe clenched him tightly, feeling a wash of relief and keen paternal love.

"You mom's going to drop off the three of you for the Slow Joe Christmas party tomorrow night," he told his son. "And then we can spend the weekend doing anything you want. Okay?"

"Okay, Dad," Ira agreed, slipping back under the covers as Joe reached out to ruffle his hair.

Feeling enormously better, Joe said good-night and headed toward the door. Just as he opened it, Ira's young voice reached him again.

"Daddy?"

"Mmm?"

"Who was she? Your girlfriend?"

It seemed to Joe that half the town knew about his relationship with Mandy, but still he was reluctant to violate her confidence, to reveal the secret she'd prized so highly. And yet he could not, would not, lie to his son.

Suddenly it struck him that this must be how Mandy felt—torn between family and lover, desperately wanting to do what was right for both when it seemed that the right thing was the opposite for each. He had a sudden vision of her standing by Ruth's bedside, trying to shield her from pain by not telling her about Joe just as he now stood by Ira's, tying to shield Ira from pain by telling him the truth.

It was not an easy row to hoe.

"Ira," he said quietly, "it's over between us now, so it probably doesn't matter anymore. But would you . . . just let me not answer that question, please?"

For a moment Ira was so quiet that Joe was afraid that by honoring his promise to Mandy, he'd really hurt his son. But then the boy said softly, "You must still love her an awful lot, Dad."

Joe closed his eyes against the pain before he answered, "Good night, son."

BY THE TIME SCHOOL GOT OUT on Friday, Mandy thought she was going to lose her mind. The children were getting into the holiday spirit and the teachers were starting to come to school dressed in green and red. Even Patty was starting to bounce back from her depression since her new twenty-five-year-old landlord had found it necessary to check on some potential "repair" in her apartment every night this week. Mandy was the only one who couldn't seem to joke about the mistletoe in the office.

The laceration of her heart had not yet scabbed over, and a dozen times each day she had trouble controlling her tears. Patty had urged her to go back to see Joe one more time—after she told Ruth that she was going to marry him. What he needed, Patty assured her, was not another promise, but a fait accompli.

Mandy knew she was right, or would have been, a month ago. But by now it was too late to do anything, even if she'd found the courage to face Joe again.

She was so eager to escape from the seasonal cheer of the school that she almost bypassed the office on her way to her car, but duty forced her to stop by and check her box. There was a new sample math book, a copy of the last school board meeting's minutes and a couple of quickly

scribbled notes from the secretary. The first was so exciting that Mandy forgot everything but the news.

"I'm a grandma!" she burst out to the handful of people in the office. "I've got a baby grandson who weighs
five pounds, six ounces and is named Alan Paul!"

For a few minutes Mandy was swamped with a plethora
of good wishes from her friends. Quickly she tried to figure out how she could leave Ruth with Karen while she
went to help out Kevin and his wife with the slightly pre-
mature baby; she tried to think of a substitute teacher for
her class. But she hadn't gotten past the most rudimen-
tary plans when the secretary said, "Mandy, you dropped
your other note. It's from a parent who called about an
hour ago."

At the moment, Mandy was not very interested in parental concerns, but out of duty she glanced quickly at the
message. When she caught the word "Ira," she read the
missive again. It was a short note with few facts and no
elaboration, but it shook Mandy's world off its axis.

"Ira's dad called to say you could make the announcement tonight if you're still interested."

Mandy gasped and crumpled the note against her chest.
"Is that all he said?" she asked the secretary.

The young woman nodded. "I asked him what meeting
he was talking about and if he was sure it was tonight, but
he said you'd understand." She thought a minute, then
tacked on, "Actually what he said was, 'If she doesn't
understand, then it's too late anyway.'" She glanced at the
ringing phone, then said before she picked up the re-
ceiver, "Do you have any idea what that means?"

It means I'm getting married, Mandy's heart answered
with a wave of joyful confusion. But nobody was paying
attention to her by then, so she didn't say it out loud.

MANDY CONSIDERED DRIVING straight to the Slow Joe, but she realized that Joe had not fully relented yet. He'd given her another ultimatum—a miraculous second chance. But he would not accept any more promises, or any secret plans. He was going to make her tell the whole world all in one dash.

Of course, it couldn't have been a worse time to tell her family. She had to call Kevin about her precious new grandbaby, and it would diminish the moment, somehow, to toss out the news that she was getting married at the same time! And how could she go rushing off to Atlanta with everything so shaky with Joe? And Karen had confided just that morning that she intended to confront her mother this evening so she could go to the staff party with David, so Ruth would be at her worst by the time Mandy got home.

Don't even think about the problems, Mandy told herself. *Focus only on the joy of your life with Joe.*

And there really wasn't a debate on that subject anymore. The past few days had nearly broken Mandy. Nothing that Ruth or Kevin or Vince could say to her could possibly hurt any more than believing that she had lost Joe.

I've got a second chance. That's all that matters, she told herself as she hurried home.

It wasn't that simple, of course. The moment Mandy walked into the house she could hear Ruth browbeating Karen. But to her surprise and secret pride, her favorite niece was standing tall.

"No, Mother, you're not listening," she said firmly, tugging on the hem of her below-the-knee skirt. "I have *not* been sneaking out to meet him. We work together on Wednesdays and Saturdays. That's all."

"It sounds like a lot of time to me," Ruth said grumpily. "If I find out you've been cutting classes and telling Mr. Henderson you're sick again—"

"Mother, for once in your life will you *listen* to me?" Karen's voice hovered on the edge of despair, but this time she did not lose control. "I'm telling you that I don't *want* to sneak around. I don't *want* to do this wrong. But I don't want you to forbid me to see David, either, and I'm afraid you will because you always hate everybody I'm interested in!"

"That's hardly true, Karen," Ruth denied. "Just because you pick sleazy fellows who—"

"David's not sleazy," Mandy offered bravely, still standing by the living-room door. "He's worked for Joe Henderson for two years, and I've talked to him a number of times myself. The day the Slow Joe broke down, Joe counted on David as his right-hand man. I think this time Karen's made an excellent choice. I'm delighted she's caught such a nice boy's eye."

Karen turned to gaze at Mandy with wondering, grateful eyes, then straightened proudly. "David knows all about George," she told her mother. "He used to watch me leave with him before I knew David was alive. He told me he won't ever see me on the sly like that, and he wants to ask you if he can take me to the party in the right way so you won't just throw him out." Karen licked her lips. "I told him that I don't know how he can do that, because I honestly don't know what it would take for you to give a guy a chance. If you don't like David, you'll never like any boy I want to date."

"He's squeaky clean," Mandy added. "And I think his father is a deacon in the church."

Ruth glared at her. "I don't think there's any cause for you girls to gang up on me," she declared, as though

Mandy were also sixteen. "I did just fine picking out your husband, Mandy, and I'll do just as well by Karen."

"I'm not picking out a husband!" Karen wailed. "I just want David to be my date for the party!"

"And you're not picking out another husband for me, either," Mandy countered, her desire for Joe's love giving her a new brand of strength, "because I've already picked him out myself."

The room grew suddenly still. Mandy's words seemed to bounce around in the air. She hadn't meant to make her announcement so bluntly, hadn't known those words would rush out of her mouth. But suddenly she realized that in Ruth's eyes, she and Karen were practically in the same boat, and until she changed the cycle, she was always going to be Ruth's little sister. And Ruth's little sister could never be Joe Henderson's wife.

Ruth positively glowered. "I presume you're jesting, Mandy. You're thinking of Robert Redford or Tom Selleck or—"

I'm going to marry Joe. She tried to say the words, knew they were the only words that would ever set her free. But they wouldn't come, not with Ruth staring at her like that, and she glanced at the toes of her shoes.

"I told David I'd call him back by six at the latest," Karen persisted, ignoring the byplay between her aunt and her mother. "Now this party is really important to me, Mom, and I've been as good as gold for six months. If you don't reward me when I'm good, what's the point? I don't mean that I've been good just to get something, Mom. I've really been happier this way. But since I have been playing by your rulebook and David is exactly the sort of guy you'd pick out for me, can I go?"

Ruth glanced at Karen briefly, but Mandy knew from the expression on her face that her sister had already dismissed Karen's situation from her mind. Mandy's comment was far more crucial. Ruth clearly understood that Mandy was not joking; she understood that the two of them had come to some critical turn in the road.

"I guess you can go if you're home by midnight, Karen," Ruth said quietly. "Assuming that Mandy will be able to stay with me tonight. I've had a very rough day and I can't be left alone."

Karen, jubilant in her reprieve, threw her arms around her mother, then clung to Mandy in sheer delight. "Oh, you don't mind missing the party, do you? I'm sure Slow Joe will understand."

But this was one time that Mandy knew Joe would *not* understand. If her car broke down, if she had an attack of appendicitis, if she got snowed in until spring, he still would not understand! There was no way that he would accept a simple "Ruth needed me" as an excuse for her absence this evening...or even "My son's wife just had a baby so I have to fly to Atlanta." She *had* to go to the party this evening, and she *had* to publicly declare her love for Joe. No ifs, ands or buts. No excuses, no apologies, no alternative plans...even if she had to crawl to the Slow Joe on her hands and knees through the snow.

Mandy wasn't sure if it was that frightening vision or Ruth's obvious power play that finally gave courage to her tongue. She looked at Karen—it was easier that way—and said, "Of course you can go, Karen, but would you ask David if he can give me a ride, too? I'll be spending the night at Joe's, so there's no point in my driving. He can bring the station wagon over tomorrow and help me load up my things."

Karen's eyes grew big.

Ruth gasped.

Mandy continued bravely, "Joe and I are going to announce our engagement this evening. It's absolutely imperative that I attend this party, Ruth."

Karen nodded and quickly filled in the jagged pieces of stunned silence that permeated the room. "Of course you can ride with us, Aunt Mandy. I'm sure David won't mind. I'll call him right now and then you can use the phone to find somebody to stay with Mother."

"Great minds think alike," Mandy quipped, trying to keep things light. "That's just what I had in mind."

Karen quickly escaped, but Mandy could not run away so easily. Somehow she had to face her sister, meet those smoldering, furious eyes.

"Him?" Ruth finally thundered when she gathered herself up enough to speak. "You're actually thinking of marrying *him*? Has Alan's death caused you to lose your mind?"

Mandy's anger made her straighten. "I know this is a shock to you, Ruth, but I didn't want to burden you with my problems while you were under the weather. I've actually been heading in this direction for quite some time."

"Ha! And you think I didn't know it? Did you really think I had no friends in this town who would notice how many days your car sat in the train's parking lot when that Henderson boy was not around? Did you think nobody would see you staying late after school meetings while you lurked about with him in the dark? Did you think you could make out in the supermarket unseen?"

Mandy felt a rush of nausea. *My God, I nearly lost him trying to keep it from her, and she knew everything all along!* And then she remembered the comments Ruth made about Joe at various crucial junctures, the stories she'd told about him at Thanksgiving when the boys had come home. Suddenly Mandy wondered if the whole horrible scenario had truly been coincidental.

"How dare you *humiliate* me like that?" Ruth demanded melodramatically. "And lie to me about it? If you were Karen's age I'd turn you over me knee!"

"Well, I'm not Karen's age and I'm not your baby sister anymore, Ruth. In case you haven't noticed, *I've* been running your house for the past six months. *I'm* the one in charge."

"I've been ill! Does that give you the right to have an affair with a nasty boy who's caused us all nothing but grief? Is that all the homage you can pay to Alan's memory?"

Mandy crossed the room, fueled now by anger, by dignity, by the power of her love for Joe.

"My fiancé's childhood troubles with his teacher have nothing to do with Joe Henderson and me. We are adults who live in the present. He gives me nothing but joy, Ruth. We buried the old hatchet in July. Since then the only thing we've ever fought about is *you*."

As she said the words they made her angry. Ruth had cost her hours and hours of happy times with Joe, had almost cost her his love. Now she knew Ruth would start it all again. She snide comment about Alan was just the beginning.

"I'm only thinking of you, Mandy! Can't you understand that?" Ruth implored her. "He's got a nasty disposition, a little boy's job—"

"Stop it!" Mandy yelled at her. *"I won't listen to you!"*

Ruth did stop, stunned, as Mandy faced her down, waited for Ruth to drop her glance and look away.

Raw power surged through Mandy's veins. She took one more step closer.

"Now you listen to me, for once! I don't care what happened in the past. I don't care what you think about my marriage to Alan or my difficult first year in this town. I'm living in Redpoint in the here and now, and Joe Henderson is the heart of my current life. I adore him. I crave him as a lover and I lean on him as a friend. He is there for me whenever I need him—he always puts my needs first. If you want to stay close to me, you will accept him as my husband, and you will never try to interfere with my marriage again."

The silence was awesome, eerie. Frightening. Ruth said nothing, did not fight back. She did not look at Mandy, did not make insinuations or desperate pleas. She stared at a seam in the sofa while Mandy drew a deep breath.

Mandy was relieved when Karen darted back into the room, calling out, "David says we can take you, Aunt Mandy. You want me to ask Arleen Trent or Joyce Williamson to stay with Mom?"

Mandy studied Ruth and asked in a low tone, "Do you have a preference, Ruth?"

Ruth did not reply.

MANDY THOUGHT SHE WAS CALM when she arrived at the Slow Joe an hour later with Karen and David, who were sweetly holding hands. She was clad in her slinkiest holiday satin, but the cold alone could not account for her trembling fingers. She had an eerie feeling as she surveyed the somehow surrealistic scene before her: a huge fir tree was draped with ornaments and a swirl of red and green streamers; Santa was tall and bowlegged, as skinny as a rail except for his pillow paunch; and the man she loved, oblivious to her presence, was rubbing elbows with an attractive blonde in her thirties who looked as though she'd

spent a lifetime by his side. Joe's youngest daughter, Sally
clung eagerly to her hand.

It was the last sight that nearly caused Mandy to gag o
a knife thrust of fear. Was she too late? Had Joe expecte
her to call him at once after all? Had she misunderstoo
the message altogether?

"I'd say Merry Christmas," Santa suddenly quippe
from her left, "but by the look on your face, I'd guess thi
holiday isn't going to be a very happy one for you."

Mandy licked her lips and turned to stare vaguely a
Brady. She longed to ask him who the blonde was and th
role she played in Joe's life. He would know, but sh
wasn't sure he would tell her. She was pretty sure tha
Brady liked her, but to him, Joe would always come first

"Who is she, Brady?" she asked anyway, irrationall
terrified of what she might discover. "Has Joe . . . know
her very long?"

Through the fake white mustache, Mandy could see h
wide, surprising grin. "Long enough, I reckon. When w
are all seniors in high school, her dad married his mom
just before she died. Joe's loved Connie like a sister eve
since. She always comes up from Albuquerque to help hir
with the Christmas party."

Mandy closed her eyes, battled the wave of relief an
leftover fear. She was losing her mind, losing her conf
dence. Joe would not have sent for her if he hadn't bee
sure. In spite of everything, he must still want Mandy a
desperately as she wanted him.

Suddenly Brady took hold of her arm. His expressio
sobered. "I'm not quite sure why you're here tonight," h
told her gruffly, "but you've put my pal through hel
Mandy, and if you're ready to make things right, yo
damn well better do it now before you change your mind.

Bravely Mandy met his tense eyes and tried to still her quaking pulse. "It's too late to change my mind, Brady," she proclaimed with all the strength she could muster. "I already told Ruth and my boys." She didn't add that Vince had been so furious he'd hung up on her, and Kevin, delirious over the birth of his son, had told her at least three times that he didn't understand what her engagement had to do with postponing her trip to Atlanta at such a momentous time in his life.

Brady looked shocked but incredibly delighted. "You did? Really?"

Mandy nodded.

To her enormous relief, Brady gave her a spontaneous hug. "Way to go, Mandy! Merry Christmas! Welcome to the clan!"

She hugged him back, feeling a moment's relief before the main door swung open and her sister stalked into the Slow Joe lobby.

The pathetic poor-me Ruth that Mandy had left at home had vanished. This one was the old Ruth, the big sister of her childhood, strong and crushing and determined to make Mandy do what was right. A bewildered Arleen Trent, whom Mandy had summoned as nurse of the evening before she'd left the house, trailed reticently in her wake.

I won't let you do this to yourself or to your family, would be the way Mandy knew Ruth would start her lecture. *I got rid of that silly boy you loved before you got married and I was right. I picked out Alan and I was right. I'm telling you that Joe Henderson is not the man for you and you know I'm right this time, too!*

But Mandy didn't give Ruth a chance to harangue her. Instead she scanned the merry crowd for Joe. She hadn't seen him in four terrible days and the sight of his lush

sandy hair and miserable brown eyes was almost more tha[n]
she could bear. He looked vigorous and handsome in hi[s]
blue suit and tie, but distant, like a stranger.

When he saw her, Joe froze. Surprise zigzagged acros[s]
his beloved face, but not one drop of hope colored hi[s]
rugged features. He stood perfectly still as he stared a[t]
Mandy from across the room.

Joe had steeled himself for her. She could see it in hi[s]
eyes. He had not expected her to come to the party... an[d]
he certainly did not expect her to make an announceme[nt]
that would bury forever all the hard words between the[m.]
Only desperation had forced him to take another chan[ce]
on her love for him.

Mandy knew he needed a public statement that wa[s]
dramatic, sensual and absolutely unmistakable, and h[e]
needed it *now.* Before he had time to turn away.

She didn't have a moment to lose.

Panic clogged Mandy's throat as she grabbed th[e]
mistletoe from Brady, tossed him her coat and bolte[d]
across the room. In her backless emerald dress an[d]
matching heels she ran so fast that she slipped on the snow[-]
dampened floor, causing several people to say "Who[a]
there!" and "Are you all right?" before she all but sli[d]
into Joe. He caught her as he would a football tossed in hi[s]
direction, with no intimacy, no pleasure, and no warmt[h.]

As Mandy met Joe's uncertain eyes, she tried to fill h[er]
own with all of her love for him. Then, with a boldne[ss]
that astounded even her, she lifted the mistletoe above h[er]
head and sang out, "Merry Christmas, darling!" in a su[l-]
try voice that, for all its trembling, could be heard by a[l-]
most everyone in the suddenly silent room.

And then she kissed him. She threw away the mistlet[oe]
so she could grip his neck and slide her fingers sensuous[ly]
into his hair. She pressed her scantily-clad body again[st]

his, craving his long, lean warmth, waiting for his arms to close around her. Waiting, waiting, *waiting!* ... until they finally did.

It was a slow, cautious embrace, one that gave Mandy little hope ... but more hope than none at all. She felt his arms tighten, knew his resistance had begun to ebb. Slowly his fingers splayed across her naked back, beginning to melt away the week's dark chill.

Aggressively her tongue sought his, heedless of the gasps of surprise from the surrounding partygoers. She had to tell the whole world that she wasn't merely offering an ex-student good wishes of the season. She had to declare, with words and without, that Joe Henderson was her lover in every sense of the word and she was damn proud of it.

But she wasn't quite done with her demonstration. Joe had given her one last chance to let the world know that she loved him, and she couldn't risk leaving him with the tiniest hint of doubt. There was one last boil to lance.

Still draped around Joe's neck, Mandy took a half step back when the kiss finally ended. "Hey everybody, I have an announcement!" she bravely hollered, her eyes never leaving Joe's even when Ruth gasped. "The first minute we can get a wedding license, String Bean Sawyer is going to be little Joey Henderson's wife!"

Somewhere in the background, Mandy heard a rush of applause. Vaguely she realized that Brady was raising his paper cup of punch in a toast and most of Joe's staff members were enthusiastically following suit. The celebration was punctured by the slam of a door, but Mandy did not turn away from Joe to look around. In her heart, she knew that Ruth would not march out of the lobby now, no matter how great her concern and anger. Her sister loved her. She would never publicly mar this moment of Mandy's happiness.

But a moment later, Mandy forgot about Ruth, forgot about the ghost of Alan, even forgot about her boys, because suddenly every ounce of her consciousness belonged to Joe. The mahogany eyes that had greeted her so warily just moments ago now suddenly filled with newborn trust. The arms that had cradled her with reticence now tightened with confidence and tenderness.

Trembling, Joe touched her cheek with one strong hand. "Oh, Mandy," he whispered, as though they suddenly were all alone. "I never thought you could find a way to make everything all right. I stopped even daring to hope for it."

That was the moment when the last of Mandy's fear fled. There was a breath of joy in his voice that she'd never heard before, joy that swallowed the hurt of the past and bandaged it with hope for the future. Healed all their old wounds with love.

In a tangle of happiness and relief, Mandy suddenly fell apart; all the week's banked tears came pouring out as she collapsed against Joe, sobbing. She told him about her agony, about the baby, about her terror when she'd first spied Connie by the punch. And he told her about Ira and his own grief and the loan he'd taken out to help Brady buy the Rocking T.

Then, before she could even ask him, he promised to fly to Atlanta with her at the crack of dawn.

For the next ten minutes Joe cradled Mandy, right there in the middle of the Slow Joe Loco lobby, while he crooned sweet healing words to her until her tears were dry. After his loving touch had filled her heart with calm, he cupped her face with both gentle hands and brushed her lips with his just once, in a different sort of kiss than the public one they'd shared under the mistletoe. This one wasn't for her sister or his kids or the Redpoint gossips. This one was just for the two of them. This one said, "I will love you forever." It said, "Welcome home."

By the time it was over, Mandy had forgotten that she'd ever known Joe Henderson before he was a man.

From *New York Times* Bestselling author
Penny Jordan, a compelling novel of ruthless passion
that will mesmerize readers everywhere!

PennyJordan

Silver

Real power, true power came from
Rothwell. And Charles vowed to have it,
the earldom and all that went with it.

Silver vowed to destroy Charles, just as surely and
uncaringly as he had destroyed her father; just as he had
intended to destroy her. She needed him to want her . . .
to desire her . . . until he'd do anything to have her.

But first she needed a tutor: a man who wanted no one.
He would help her bait the trap.

Played out on a glittering international stage,
Silver's story leads her from the luxurious comfort of
British aristocracy into the depths of adventure,
passion and danger.

AVAILABLE IN OCTOBER!

HARLEQUIN

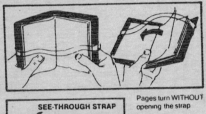

PASSPORT TO ROMANCE VACATION SWEEPSTAKES

OFFICIAL RULES

SWEEPSTAKES RULES AND REGULATIONS. NO PURCHASE NECESSARY.

HOW TO ENTER:

1. To enter, complete this official entry form and return with your invoice in the envelope provided, or print your name, address, telephone number and age on a plain piece of paper and mail to: Passport to Romance, P.O. Box #1397, Buffalo, N.Y. 14269-1397. No mechanically reproduced entries accepted.
2. All entries must be received by the Contest Closing Date, midnight, December 31, 1990 to be eligible.
3. Prizes: There will be ten (10) Grand Prizes awarded, each consisting of a choice of a trip for two people to: i) London, England (approximate retail value $5,050 U.S.); ii) England, Wales and Scotland (approximate retail value $6,400 U.S.); iii) Caribbean Cruise (approximate retail value $7,300 U.S.); iv) Hawaii (approximate retail value $ 9,550 U.S.); v) Greek Island Cruise in the Mediterranean (approximate retail value $12,250 U.S.); vi) France (approximate retail value $7,300 U.S.).
4. Any winner may choose to receive any trip or a cash alternative prize of $5,000.00 U.S. in lieu of the trip.
5. Odds of winning depend on number of entries received.
6. A random draw will be made by Nielsen Promotion Services, an independent judging organization on January 29, 1991, in Buffalo, N.Y., at 11:30 a.m. from all eligible entries received on or before the Contest Closing Date. Any Canadian entrants who are selected must correctly answer a time-limited, mathematical skill-testing question in order to win. Quebec residents may submit any litigation respecting the conduct and awarding of a prize in this contest to the Régie des loteries et courses du Quebec.
7. Full contest rules may be obtained by sending a stamped, self-addressed envelope to: "Passport to Romance Rules Request", P.O. Box 9998, Saint John, New Brunswick, E2L 4N4.
8. Payment of taxes other than air and hotel taxes is the sole responsibility of the winner.
9. Void where prohibited by law.

PASSPORT TO ROMANCE VACATION SWEEPSTAKES

OFFICIAL RULES

SWEEPSTAKES RULES AND REGULATIONS. NO PURCHASE NECESSARY.

HOW TO ENTER:

1. To enter, complete this official entry form and return with your invoice in the envelope provided, or print your name, address, telephone number and age on a plain piece of paper and mail to: Passport to Romance, P.O. Box #1397, Buffalo, N.Y. 14269-1397. No mechanically reproduced entries accepted.
2. All entries must be received by the Contest Closing Date, midnight, December 31, 1990 to be eligible.
3. Prizes: There will be ten (10) Grand Prizes awarded, each consisting of a choice of a trip for two people to: i) London, England (approximate retail value $5,050 U.S.); ii) England, Wales and Scotland (approximate retail value $6,400 U.S.); iii) Caribbean Cruise (approximate retail value $7,300 U.S.); iv) Hawaii (approximate retail value $ 9,550 U.S.); v) Greek Island Cruise in the Mediterranean (approximate retail value $12,250 U.S.); vi) France (approximate retail value $7,300 U.S.).
4. Any winner may choose to receive any trip or a cash alternative prize of $5,000.00 U.S. in lieu of the trip.
5. Odds of winning depend on number of entries received.
6. A random draw will be made by Nielsen Promotion Services, an independent judging organization on January 29, 1991, in Buffalo, N.Y., at 11:30 a.m. from all eligible entries received on or before the Contest Closing Date. Any Canadian entrants who are selected must correctly answer a time-limited, mathematical skill-testing question in order to win. Quebec residents may submit any litigation respecting the conduct and awarding of a prize in this contest to the Régie des loteries et courses du Quebec.
7. Full contest rules may be obtained by sending a stamped, self-addressed envelope to: "Passport to Romance Rules Request", P.O. Box 9998, Saint John, New Brunswick, E2L 4N4.
8. Payment of taxes other than air and hotel taxes is the sole responsibility of the winner.
9. Void where prohibited by law.

G MO Eric Hill

PASSPORT
WIN
1 of 10 Vacations
SEE INSIDE
TO ROMANCE

VACATION SWEEPSTAKES

MONTH 1 ENTRY

Official Entry Form

Yes, enter me in the drawing for one of ten Vacations-for-Two! If I'm a winner, I'll get my choice of any of the six different destinations being offered — and I won't have to decide until after I'm notified!

Return entries with invoice in envelope provided along with Daily Travel Allowance Voucher. Each book in your shipment has two entry forms — and the more you enter, the better your chance of winning!

Name

Address   Apt.

City   State/Prov.   Zip/Postal Code

Daytime phone number _____
                          Area Code

☐ I am enclosing a Daily Travel
   Allowance Voucher in the amount of $_____ Write in amount
                                        revealed beneath scratch-off

CPS-ONE